# Doctor Omega:
# The Labyrinth
# of Mentacron

# IN THE SAME SERIES

Arnould Galopin. *Doctor Omega*
Jean-Marc & Randy Lofficier (eds.). *Doctor Omega and the Shadowmen (Volume 1)*
Jean-Marc & Randy Lofficier (eds.). *Doctor Omega and the Shadowmen (Volume 2)*
Brian Gallagher: *Doctor Omega: His First Adventure*

# Doctor Omega: The Labyrinth of Mentacron

by
**Ben Spurling**

based on the character created by
Arnould Galopin

A Black Coat Press Book

ISBN 978-1-64932-413-9. First Printing: October 2025. Published by Black Coat Press, an imprint of Hollywood Comics.com, LLC, 18321 Ventura Blvd. Suite 915, Tarzana, CA 91356. All rights reserved. Except for review purposes, no part of this book may be reproduced or transmitted in any form or by any means, electronic or mechanical, including photocopying, recording or by any information storage and retrieval system, without permission in writing from the publisher. The stories and characters depicted in this anthology are entirely fictional. Printed in the United States of America.

# TABLE OF CONTENTS

*Illustration by J.-M. Breton for the 1906 edition*

## *Introduction*

The character of Doctor Omega was created by Arnould Galopin in his eponymous novel, *Le Docteur Oméga*, first published in France in 1906.

Galopin (1865-1934) is mostly forgotten today; those who remember him are most likely to do so for his juvenile serials, such as *Le Tour du Monde de Deux Gosses* [Around The World With Two Kids] (1908) and *Un Aviateur de 15 Ans* [A 15-Year-Old Aviator] (1926).

He was also the author of one of the first French Holmesian pastiches, teaming up an aging Sherlock Holmes and a young Harry Dickson against Jack the Ripper in *L'Homme au Complet Gris* [The Man In Grey] (1910).[1]

Galopin was never a major genre author, nor was he a ground-breaker like H. G. Wells or Jules Verne, but he was an old pro who knew how to spin a yarn and follow a trend. *Le Docteur Oméga*, clearly inspired by Wells, was successful and almost immediately reissued in a series of magazines in 1908, then reprinted in book form in 1949. Black Coat Press published an English-language adaptation in 2003 in two editions, one with copies of the original illustrations, the other without.[2]

That adaptation included some minor revisions to the original text, which fell into two categories. The first was some light editing, done to rewrite a number of xen-

[1] Black Coat Press, ISBN 978-1-61227-484-3.
[2] Black Coat Press, ISBNs 978-1-0-9740711-1-4 and 978-0-9740711-0-7.

ophobic passages—something, sadly, all too common at the time—and to smooth over a few particularly clumsy plot points or contradictions. The second were more cosmetic in nature and intended to pay homage, through revised "technobabble," name-dropping and visual imagery, not only to *Doctor Who*, but also to other French classics, such as Arsène Lupin and Madeline.

With *Le Docteur Oméga*, Galopin intended to combine elements from *War of the Worlds* (first published in France in 1900) and *First Men in the Moon* (first published in France in 1901). "Stellite" is nothing more than "Cavorite" under a different name, and the *Cosmos* is not that different from Cavor's spherical ship. Its shell shape and multi-terrain capabilities were obviously borrowed from Jules Verne.

Galopin's description of Mars is laudably imaginative, but conceptually not very different from what Wells and other French writers had previously imagined. Amongst those were Achille Eyraud, who described the exploration of Venus in *Voyage à Venus* [Voyage to Venus] (1865)[3] and Georges Le Faure & Henry de Graffigny, who depicted a journey through the Solar System in *Les Aventures Extraordinaires d'un Savant Russe* [The Extraordinary Adventures of a Russian Scientist Across the Solar System] (1889).[4]

What was, however, unique, was the character of Doctor Omega himself. All of his predecessors were eccentrically brilliant scientists, but they were grounded in the real world. Not so Omega—an unlikely surname to

[3] Black Coat Press, ISBN 978-1-61227-005-0.
[4] Black Coat Press, ISBNs 978-1-935543-81-8 and 978-1-935543-82-5.

begin with—who remains shrouded in mystery, his background and origins purposefully kept obscure. Why?

One cannot accuse Galopin of lacking in imagination. And from a commercial standpoint, making his main hero a cipher was surely not a good idea. How could a writer as commercially-minded as Galopin make such a beginner's mistake? When Galopin rewrote the novel as a juvenile serial, he had another chance to explain who Omega was, and where he came from, but once again, he chose not to do so.

Another puzzling decision is the *deus ex machina* intervention of the equally mysterious Professor Helvetius at the end of the novel. Helvetius is described as "British," but Galopin tells us nothing about him, certainly not how he could have independently duplicated the secret of manufacturing stellite, enabling him to build a second spacecraft in such a short time. Of all the possible ways of rescuing the characters and returning them to Earth at the end of the novel, this was certainly the clumsiest and the least convincing—unless one simply assumes that there is more to the story of Omega and Helvetius than the author is telling us...

Galopin ended *Le Docteur Oméga* with the promise of further space journeys, but despite this, he never wrote a sequel. So we are left with no clues as to why he chose to make Doctor Omega a mystery, and the unlimited potential of his hero (as *Doctor Who* later amply demonstrated) remained sadly untapped. Another French ground-breaking oddity which ended up forgotten!

*Le Docteur Oméga* was followed by three more colorful Martian novels, which we heartily recommend: Henri Gayar's *Les Aventures Merveilleuses de Serge Myrandhal sur la Planète Mars* [The Marvelous Adventures of Serge Myrandhal on Mars] (1908),[5] Gustave Le Rouge's *Le Prisonnier de la Planète Mars* [The Vampires of Mars] (1908)[6] and Jean de La Hire's *Le Mystère des XV* [The Nyctalope on Mars] (1911).[7]

Despite a number of superficial and mostly cosmetic resemblance, I do not believe for a minute that the creators of *Doctor Who* had ever heard of *Le Docteur Oméga* which, even in France, had been virtually forgotten by the early 1960s. If there is a connection between the two, it is to be found in the writings of Carl Jung, not science fiction.

However, the archetypal nature of Doctor Omega helps explain why he, like Jean de La Hire's Nyctalope or Norbert Sevestre's Sâr Dubnotal, has become one of the favorite French characters used by the contributors to our anthology *Tales of the Shadowmen*, devoted to paying homage to often forgotten heroes and villains of French popular fiction.

Finally, the Companions featured in this volume, Rollie DuBay and Cassandra Troy, first appeared in a short story entitled *Doctor Omega and the Producers* written by the undersigned and published in *Doctor Omega and the Shadowmen* (Vol. 1). It is reprinted at the end of this volume for those who may not have read it before.

Now, enjoy!

Jean-Marc & Randy Lofficier

---

[5] Black Coat Press, ISBN 978-1-61227-265-8.

[6] Black Coat Press, ISBN 978-1-934543-30-6.

[7] Black Coat Press, ISBN 978-1-934543-46-7.

# DOCTOR OMEGA: THE LABYRINTH OF MENTACRON

## CHAPTER I

Roland DuBay had the thick look of a rather dim child who had just been informed he was adopted and that his surrogate parents were only now realizing the mistake of their acquisition. He was a tall, thin, curly-headed brunet, with a pronounced brow, a lantern jaw, and gaunt cheeks, all of which gave one the false impression he was a simpleton. He was prone to stooping and calculatingly informal dress, a clamorous sign of which was his fluttering ascot.

The older man next to him was also tall and thin, but not to Roland's degree; he had a thick wash of white hair combed back smoothly over his scalp, with an erect forelock of silver hair just above his brow that bobbed and weaved at the slightest provocation; his eyes were impish and intelligent, his nose a bit too prevalent; his thin-lipped mouth seemed to naturally purse with annoyance, whether he was annoyed or not.

The older man abruptly slid the door shut, startling Roland, and quickly pressed the baryonic key against the spot where a handle would normally be; the key was the size of a pack of cards, completely smooth on all sides, and put off a faint, brief clicking sound a few seconds later when the older man brushed his finger down its unblemished length. The older man turned to face his guest and snapped, "Roland, what did I tell you about poking around the *Cosmos* without me?!"

Roland DuBay was taken aback as a flash ran through his mind. *That's a brittle side of Doctor Omega I haven't seen, at least not in the brief time I've known him. These Famous Foreign Actors are so temperamental and controlling!*[8]

Catching himself, the Doctor softened slightly and gently patted Roland's arm, offering a forced, but reassuring, smile. "Oh, I do apologize, Rollie," he chuckled, "but several of these doors lead to – well – things you're not equipped to deal with just yet, since you're new to the *Cosmos*. And to this rather odd lifestyle." Doctor Omega could see the bewilderment in Rollie's face. He absentmindedly smoothed his long, black frock coat, chuckled in a diffusive way again, and continued. "You see, the *Cosmos* is not an ordinary ship."

"You can say that again; the doors just slide open by themselves," Rollie said defensively. Wagging his finger, he continued. "And you're no ordinary actor – or doctor, or whatever you call yourself! I figured that out when I first met you." He raised his chin a bit and said confidently, "A trained actor's eye for detail, you know. Little gets past me."

Doctor Omega coughed tactfully, causing his rebellious forelock to bob slightly. "Yes, well...."

"Do you know how many movies I've been in, Doctor?" Just as the Doctor was about to answer in the negative, Rollie continued, already lost in his false reveries. "Of course you do; it's silly to ask."

---

[8] See *Doctor Omega and the Producers* at the end of this volume.

"Yes. Why ask?" Doctor Omega looked whimsically at Rollie and recalled 'the trained actor's' most recent catastrophic role as an Electroman in the failed movie about the Doctor's own life, and said, "Anyway, it's just that I've recently renovated the *Cosmos*, and the modifications have, shall we say, *expanded* the capabilities of the ship to rather astronomical proportions. As a result, a few of the doors within the ship are designed to – eh – open onto larger accommodations than normal, so to speak. The renovations aren't complete yet, so I would like to keep it all under wraps until the reveal."

Rollie shook his head as if he were in-the-know. *You're on your way, Rollie old boy. With an elaborate set like this, the budget for the movie has got to be at least a cool mil*! "Right. Got it."

"Stop being delicate, Doctor," the tall red-head said.

Cassandra Troy was just exiting one of the other rooms in this section of the ship as she faced both men. Rollie noticed that she still hadn't changed out of that skimpy leather outfit he had first seen her in a few months ago. *These method actors. Sheesh.* And he still wasn't quite sure how she fit into this sequel. She wasn't even in the first movie; he recalled the Doctor had said something about her being from the year 586, and she had worked for the Terran Hegemony, or something like that, but Rollie simply assumed the Doctor was being the eccentric "Foreign Actor" again and that the Terran Hedgehog was just some hip, new casting agency he'd never heard of. There were tons of them around, coming and going, making a big splash with the next new face, then disappearing when that new face had a series of flops.

Cassandra smiled slyly at the Doctor then turned her attention to Rollie and continued mischievously.

"The Doctor is from another pla –"

The Doctor coughed loudly, abruptly cutting her off. "Oh, my, look at the time! Perhaps we should all head back to the bridge and check our progress."

Rollie said energetically, "Yeah. Good idea. Maybe the scripts are ready, and we can do some walk-throughs."

Doctor Omega gave Cassandra a side glance and said to no one in particular, "By all means. Let's do that," as he sheepishly shooed them into the gravcap at the center of the large first floor entryway.

Along with endowing a couple of the rooms at the base of the ship with extra-dimensional capabilities, Doctor Omega had replaced the spiral staircase which had originally occupied the middle of the ship with what he called the gravcap, an antigravity elevator which allowed for frictionless travel between the ship's three sections. Even with these rather astonishing modifications, the *Cosmos* still retained its original thirteen meter length and three meter diameter, as well as its terrifically antiquated cannon-shell shape, a feature which the Doctor insisted upon, and which those few who knew him presumed was actually for reasons of nostalgia rather than for the claims of practicality he so strenuously asserted.

When Doctor Omega first tried to explain to Cassandra how the rooms worked while not affecting the proportions of the ship, all of which was due to the natural dimension-morphing capabilities of the stellite sheets the ship was covered in, working in conjunction with the kirbyon drive, even she didn't quite get it, despite being from a far more technologically advanced time than Rollie, a time after the collapse of the third space-faring human civilization.

14

As for Rollie, his disinterest in anything which didn't advance his acting career, combined with his considerable lack of mettle, had convinced the Doctor that it was probably wise to expose Rollie as slowly as possible to all of this new, outlandish reality; first, though, he had to ease his companion into the realization that they weren't making a movie after all but were, in fact, currently light years from Earth and heading toward the Vega system at a rapid pace; they were headed there due to a disquieting energy emission the Doctor had recently picked up.

Doctor Omega laughed to himself as the gravcap effortlessly worked against the ship's built-in gravity inducer and smoothly glided them to the bridge. *Rollie's shock will be quite amusing. I hope he doesn't have a heart condition. Oh, well; I have a spare.*

Once on the bridge, the Doctor left the others behind and jaunted over to a console and read the gauges connected to the heart of the *Cosmos*, the temporal rotor and vector generator; he rubbed his hands in a satisfied fashion and smiled cheerfully at the others. "Everything seems to be progressing famously!"

The bridge, like the rest of the ship, was curiously out-of-date, with odd knick-knacks of every shape and size occupying most of the space not taken up by the systems which regulated the ship. The walls were covered in intricately patterned, deep-red wall paper and fusty, old paintings, one of which took pride of place; it was a disturbingly realistic depiction of Medusa painted onto a shield and was the first thing one saw when entering from the gravcap. It somehow felt alive and as if it were hinting at a darker, elemental force that was just out of touch in the surrounding environment, adding a whisper of unease to the otherwise cozy surroundings.

The chairs behind the console were genteel and over-stuffed, apparently Victorian, matching the amenable, if dated, décor of the rest of the ship. Cassandra took a seat at the console and began reviewing the indicators.

Rollie looked around and said, "Great; imaginative set I guess, but where is everyone, anyway?"

Doctor Omega sauntered back to him and placed his hand on Rollie's shoulder. "My dear Rollie, I have something to tell you."

"Oh, no. I'm being replaced. Listen, the Electroman short circuit in the other movie wasn't my fault! The director wouldn't let me take a bathroom break!"

"No, no, you're not being replaced. Quite the contrary."

*Hot potatoes*! *I'm getting a bigger role*!

Cassandra focused more intensely on the console controls as the Doctor continued delicately. "You see, Rollie, I think your talents are so great they can't be contained within any movie, or any story for that matter."

Rollie whispered, "Really," as his chest swelled slightly and he looked off at some invisible destiny which he instinctively knew had awaited him since birth.

The Doctor spoke with exaggerated earnestness as he followed Rollie's misty stare. "Yes." The Doctor waved his hand at the opposite wall as if it were the doorway to infinity rather than the regular wall it was. "Out there, Rollie, your future is calling you, your future beckons. Something bigger waits for you out there." Then he leaned in and matched Rollie's whisper. "Something *wonderful*."

Rollie's eyes began to water.

Then, the Doctor broke off and said bluntly, "That's why we're not making a movie."

Rollie blinked for a moment, shook his head, and spluttered back to reality. He asked weakly, "Wait, we're not?"

"No." The Doctor tried to be as gentle as possible, but finally just said it. "There never was a movie. And this isn't a film set." He spread out his hands and proudly looked about the room. "This, this beauty is a trans-chronospacial schooner," the Doctor said with a broad smile.

Rollie just stared.

The Doctor deflated slightly. He had worked quite hard on coming up with that descriptor and felt a bit perturbed when no one found it impressive. The Doctor fidgeted for a second, then deflected Rollie's attention to the holovid display floating in front of the control panel where Cassandra was intensely fixated on a particular gauge.

"You see, Rollie, we're actually in space. The holovid there is a virtual window on the environment outside the *Cosmos*." The Doctor flicked his hand at the holovid image. "The area of space you see is known as the Vega system. An unusual energy emission which hasn't been seen for quite some time was picked up again just a few weeks ago, and we're going to investigate."

Cassandra looked over her shoulder at the two men. "The radiation is still low, but it's getting stronger the closer we get to the system."

Rollie tensed. "Space? Radiation? What kind of a joke is this?"

"My dear Rollie, it's exactly what I said it is; we're traveling through space, and we're headed to the Vega system because of the radiation emission; the radiation is harmless, although it may indicate a fourth dimensional breach; it's more a residual pulse than anything else." The Doctor stared into infinity and said, "What bothers me is the last time there was a hyperspace jump in the Vega system, another acquaintance of mine had a run-in with a rather nasty lot."

Rollie snapped the Doctor back to the present. "Nasty lot?"

"Oh, some vulgar reptilians from the Orion Delta. If they had succeeded in the Vega system, they could have easily conquered your planet."

Startled, Rollie said, "Wait a minute. '*Your* planet'! Where, exactly, are you from, anyway?"

Trying to distract Rollie, Doctor Omega coughed and said, "Well, we have more important things to worry about right now. Those pesky *Bouffons* tried to take over a whole planet in the Vega system a while back, but – uh – another acquaintance of mine dealt with them conclusively, or so it is believed." He mumbled thoughtfully, "We shall see."

Frustrated, Rollie said, "Listen doctor, I understand you Foreign Actors can be odd, but you're taking this whole thing too far. I'm an intuitive actor, I don't do The Method."

Cassandra smirked, then stood up and made her way around the console, tracing Rollie's chin with a kittenish finger as she passed by him, then said, "Here, maybe this will help." Once on the other side of the console, she raised her palms shoulder-high and gave a gentle nudge to the free-floating holovid, causing it to smoothly coast toward Rollie. He closed his eyes and winced as it effortlessly passed over him and warped to the shape of his head and shoulders; to his astonishment, when he opened his eyes, he was on the "outside" of the *Cosmos*, wrapped in a translucent photon-wave skin with the whole of the Vega system projected before him as a 3D light field. It gave him the woozy feeling of dropping into eternal emptiness without actually moving. He tee-tered, then fell back out of the photon skin, and plopped on the floor of the *Cosmos* like a sack of potatoes. He spluttered for a moment before Doctor Omega came to help him up.

Steadying Rollie, the Doctor asked with a playful smile, "Are you alright, my dear fellow?"

"I. You. But."

"Do you believe me now?"

Stunned, Rollie nodded, then sobered up, realizing the magnitude of his situation. "But how?"

The Doctor placed a reassuring hand on his shoulder. "It's quite simple really – well, for some of us," he said as he winked at Cassandra. He continued. "It's a modified holographic technology based on my own theory of discrete packages of sub-quantum particles called kirbyons. Only the most informed scientists know of them. They're related to mesons in some of their behavior and to baryons in some other ways, but are unlike either in several ways. Does that clarify things?"

"No, not at all! How is any of this possible?!"

"Most of the technology on the *Cosmos* is built on this exotic branch of kirbyon physics I've developed, the applied form of which is the kirbyon drive. Without it, we could still travel through space-time fairly easily, but not *as* easily, and certain other things wouldn't be possible, like the holovid. Makes sense now?"

Rollie said, "Again, no. But it'll have to do I guess," then he conjured up a wife back on Earth. "Wait, what about Melissa?"

The Doctor stopped his woolgathering for a moment. "Melissa?"

"Yes, my wife. And my son. What about them?"

Fazed, the Doctor thought for a moment, then said with labored optimism, "Well, young man, you'll have a rousing story to tell them when you get back."

"Yes, this all ought to go over quite well with the divorce judge."

At that moment, Cassandra swayed slightly, and before the other two could respond, she slumped to the floor, unconscious.

Startled, Rollie and the Doctor rushed to Cassandra's side; kneeling beside her, Rollie held up her head while the Doctor patted her hand. Rollie looked frantically at the Doctor and asked, "What happened?"

The Doctor snapped back viciously, "How am I supposed to know? Stop asking foolish questions and help get her to a chair."

Cradling her shoulders, they moved her over to the console chair she had been sitting in only minutes before. The Doctor gently tapped her cheek as Rollie stood by, bewildered as to what to do. Feeling he needed to take action regardless of his lack of medical expertise, Rollie sheepishly offered assistance, fully expecting another tongue lashing from the Doctor. He grasped at the only thing he was familiar with. "Would you like some water? To splash on her face? You know, to wake her up?" *It worked in that episode of* Emergency On Call *I was in.*

Surprising him, Doctor Omega's brittle demeanor melted away as he quietly said, "Yes. Yes, that would be good." He gestured and said, almost apologetically, "Over there, on the other side of the gravcap."

Rollie, with a new sense of purpose, dashed to the other side of the room and found an antiquated tap on the wall; there, on a shelf above the tap, he found a cup and filled it with water, then hurried back to the other two. The Doctor took the cup and flicked the water onto Cassandra's face. Nothing happened; once he repeated the process a second time, she began to come to. After a few moments, she regained her orientation and had enough strength to sit upright yet still had to rely on the arm of the chair for support.

Doctor Omega said in an overly cheerful way, "Well, there we go; the old tried and true methods still work!" Sounding like a relieved father consoling his child after a knee scrape, he continued. "You're coming round, my dear girl; you'll be just fine!" He rested a kindly hand on her shoulder more to comfort himself than her.

Leaning toward Cassandra, Rollie asked, "What happened? Do you remember anything?"

Cassandra shook her head and tried to speak but found it too difficult.

Rollie pressed on. "How do you feel? Can you stand?" He began to lift her arm in order to help her up, but before he could, the Doctor offered her water; she took the cup with shaking hands and had a few gulps before handing it back to him.

The Doctor said, "Perhaps we should get her back to her room."

Rollie responded with false confidence. "Exactly what I was thinking."

They gently lifted her, each taking a side, and staggered her over to the gravcap, lurching and careening along the way. Finally, they got her down to her room and placed her in bed, then left her to sleep.

Out near the gravcap, the two men stopped, deep in thought. Still distraught, Rollie said, "It just came out of nowhere. She was fine then, *poof*, she was out. I don't get it."

The Doctor was silent for a moment, allowing Rollie to state the obvious, before he said conclusively, "DST."

"What?"

"DST, my dear fellow. It's clear as Valir crystal."

Exasperated, Rollie said, "Doctor, please...."

"Yes. Right. Forgive me. DST stands for Deep Space Trance. It's a phenomenon similar to, but not identical with, nitrogen narcosis, better known as rapture of the deep. How DST differs is in its cause; it's not a result of gas absorption at pressure as is nitrogen narcosis, but instead is the result of a polarization within the brain's posterior parietal cortex – the area of the brain responsible for dimensional awareness, and occurs immediately after the earliest space and temporal shift exposure. Some beings it affects, and others it doesn't." He brought his index finger to his chin and mumbled, "Although, why it would strike her now, so late in her travels, I have no idea. And there should be accompanying hallucinations. Strange."

Rollie responded ironically, "I'll say."

Surprised, the Doctor looked at him, a moment passed, then both men broke out laughing.

What seemed like hours later, Cassandra woke to find herself on Oneiros, the Dreamer's Planet; she was lying deep in the planet's lush, blue grass, her head resting felicitously against the knotted, blood-red root of a darthano tree, the shade of which washed over her and caused the light from Oneiros' triple suns to draw flame and dance a melodic, drowsy dance. She intently watched the turquoise clouds above as they lazily sailed across the velvety, pink sky, forever merging and dissolving, merging and dissolving, melting into nothingness only to return again and again as wisps of chiffon froth. As with everyone who visited, she felt safe here, and cocooned. And, as with everyone who visited, her mind was devoid of concern. Which was the point of coming here to begin with.

*Leave your cares behind for a while; vacation on Oneiros and let your personally-appointed Dream Ambassador handle your responsibilities for the duration of your visit! No fuss, no muss, no more gloomy Gus!*

It sounded wonderful, absolutely glorious, as a matter of fact, but something tugged at her consciousness. It was somewhere there, just beyond the creamy gauze. And the more she tried to understand the reason for the unease, the more her feeling of warmth began to abate. The grass was beginning to feel dry and frayed.

*Something's missing.*

The darthano root began to weep sap, tangling her hair.

*No, it's not something, but someone.*

The light from the triple suns was fading now, devoid of dancing fire.

*This is Oneiros. According to the travel packs I've read, I should have a Dream Ambassador accompanying me at all times, so I don't trance out.*

Then the clouds tightened into bristled smudges of fleshy stain. Oddly, they seemed to be taking the shape of a man, and they seemed to be calling to her.

*I'm not on Oneiros.*

The man-shaped clouds vanished as the velvety, pink sky turned an angry red.

*I'm freezing.*

The three suns faded out, leaving her in total darkness, something that was impossible according to the travel packs, and defenseless against the unsympathetic cold. She threw out her hands, trying to feel anything at all, but not even the ground was there anymore; she was in complete darkness and floating in eternity. Perhaps she was on Oneiros after all, and she was trancing out.

*No, the Doctor wouldn't let that happen.*

Suddenly, she felt a pain pierce her left eye. Her hands shot to her head.

*This can't be Oneiros; I've never been there. I've only read about it. Where am I?*

When she brought her hands down, she was back in her room aboard the *Cosmos*, and the pain was gone. Once again, she was lying in her bed, but now she was unable to move. Her mind was glazed in a disorienting fog, the fog she had picked up while dreaming of Oneiros. And somehow, the room seemed different; it seemed immense, beyond crossing even in the totality of a lifetime; yet, she also felt smothered by an equally concentrated sense of claustrophobia.

She was drifting away, lost in her unease, losing consciousness in the warmth of her peculiar bewilderment when, suddenly, an undefinable wave of expansive fear hammered Cassandra into full wakefulness. She tried to yell out, at what she didn't know, but even her vocal cords were paralyzed. She tightened with alarm as she felt a tingle creep up her arm, as if a spider's web had just caressed her flesh. There was a spark in the air, an electrical energy she couldn't explain.

Her head, cocked at an angle which allowed her to see the rest of the room, began to pound with this new galvanized clarity. Unable to blink, her eyes watered as she saw a substance appear between herself and the door, the substance resembling waves of boiling air shimmering off of a hot surface.

At first, the substance was only discernible as ripples of light, but then it gathered moisture, finally blooming into a milky vapor; watching it hang in place like an anemic, diaphanous cloud, she was shocked to feel what she could only describe as a monstrous bleakness radiating from it, almost as if it were in the deepest recesses of despair. As the bleakness overwhelmed her, she watched the vapor whirl into diffuse, transparent fumes then reform into the nebulous figure of what seemed like a man, repeating the process again and again as it drifted toward her.

She tried to back away, tried to press her body against the wall of her room, but couldn't. At the last moment, the mist ejected from its mass two shafts of opaque condensation, giving the impression of menacing arms reaching out further and further, growing larger with every second. Just as the shafts touched the bed, Cassandra broke free of her paralysis and was finally able to scream. As she did so, the mist contracted violently, losing its nacreous appearance and returned to its original humid fluidity before evaporating out of existence completely, draining the room of the despair that had previously filled it.

Terrified, Cassandra jumped from her bed and shot for the door. Opening it, she dashed out and slammed directly into Rollie, knocking him down and sprawling atop his struggling form. The Doctor advanced to help the fumbling pair to their feet.

The Doctor looked frantically at Cassandra and said, "My dear girl, what happened? Why did you scream?"

Cassandra, still alarmed, blurted out, "A ghost! I saw a ghost!"

The Doctor paused for a moment, then said, "A what? Come now, don't be silly. You just had a nightmare."

She said heatedly, "Yes, I did, but it wasn't!"

Bemused, the Doctor chortled, then looked at Rollie and said, "Yes. I see. What do you make of that, Rollie?"

Catching on, Rollie said, "Sounds right to me, Doctor. I couldn't have said it better."

Cassandra said to both men, "You don't believe me," her displeasure becoming apparent. "You think I'm making it up."

Seeing her indignation rise, Doctor Omega restrained himself and said, "I'm sorry, my dear, but you did catch us off guard, you know, what with your shrieking like that, then you barreling out of the room like a rocket ship, nearly taking poor Rollie's head off as he was coming to help you."

Rollie looked sheepishly at her.

Cassandra cooled slightly and said, "I see your point. But, still, I saw a ghost!"

The Doctor took her by the elbow and guided everyone over to the gravcap, then said, "Let's go have a nice cup of relaxing tea and discuss it. Maybe we can make more sense of this in calmer surroundings."

As Rollie followed behind, he said meekly, "But I don't like tea."

The Doctor looked back at him, cocked a nettled eyebrow, and said, "Good to know, Rollie. We'll send out for something a little more to your liking."

Rollie cheered up. "That would be great!" Then he looked confused and said, "I didn't know you could do that."

Without turning, the Doctor said flatly, "For you, Rollie, anything is possible."

As they entered the gravcap and the door slid closed, no one noticed frosty tendrils of mist, the color of pearl, worming their way out from under Cassandra's bedroom door. Nor did they hear the faint sound of a restless scraping coming from inside the room.

Back on the bridge, Doctor Omega stirred his tea absently; he was barely aware of the delicate steam rising from the Tellurian leechweed brew, yet its calming attributes did help him center his thoughts, whether he was conscious of that fact or not.

Cassandra, seated at the console once again, cradled her cup with both hands, close to her body as if she were protecting it, a worried look in her eyes. A disgruntled Rollie stood behind the console and grimaced at his unwanted cup sitting on the end table nearby, wondering how anyone could stomach that smelly muck. *The Doctor can travel light years through space, but he can't muster anything more to drink than this gamy silt?*

As if something had been settled, the Doctor stopped stirring his tea and said emphatically, "A ghost? I think not." With an air of absolute certainty, he turned to the others and waited for his challenge to be met.

Cassandra bristled, just as the Doctor had expected. "It was real, Doctor; I could feel its despair!"

"Despair? That was only residue from your bad dream. What you're experiencing is a delayed form of Deep Space Trance. It's quite clear. You're having hallucinations."

27

"How is that possible? I've been traveling through space/time for years now; it only happens to first-time travelers."

"Or, it used to. Perhaps you're manifesting a new variant. Perhaps you've experienced an anomalous temporal rift within your parietal cortex, almost a time-based personality split if you will, which could have delayed the reaction."

Frustrated, Cassandra put down her cup. "By *years*? With something that drastic, I would have shown symptoms decades ago. A mental timeslip, or a kind of pre-cognitive *deja vu*."

"Possibly, but the typical DST symptoms are manifesting right now, which strongly implies my diagnosis is correct, either way."

Cassandra said tensely, "Unless it isn't, and I did see a ghost."

"Nonsense," Doctor Omega arrogantly exclaimed.

Sensing the agitation between the two, Rollie threw up his hands and murmured, "I'll be exploring the lower decks if you need me," then he departed in the gravcap without the Doctor or Cassandra retreating from their sparring long enough to notice.

Rollie felt foolish after leaving the other two to squabble. Down here, on the second level, he tried to find something to do to make himself productive, but before he could, a wave of nausea suddenly swept over him. He began to gulp air, desperate to counteract the queasiness quickly growing inside him. A sudden sense of abysmal despair overwhelmed him as the stench of something rancid filled his nostrils. His head began to spin as he watched a vapor, the color of pearl, form a few feet away. Backing up against the wall as the vapor drifted closer, a look of terror crossed Rollie's face like a bleak shadow passing over a newborn's crib.

Back on the bridge, the gravcap door slid open onto the sounds of mild bickering. The Doctor and Cassandra were still in the midst of their impassioned disagreement, so much so they barely noticed Rollie had returned, or even left, for that matter, or that he was ambling past them smoothly, almost mechanically, and heading for the console. Once there, he began waving his hands over several of the nested control panes; it was only then that the Doctor and Cassandra broke from their little tiff.

"What are you doing, Rollie," the Doctor asked mildly.

When Rollie didn't respond, and continued his robotic movements, the Doctor repeated his question but still received no reply. Puzzled, he left Cassandra and went to the console. He watched as Rollie's hands danced effortlessly, yet with deliberate purpose, across the control panes at remarkable speed. "Rollie, what *are* you doing?"

As he casually touched Rollie's wrist, hoping to draw his attention, both men were flung away from the console, and each other, as if a lightning bolt had struck them, the Doctor bumping into the nearby wall and Rollie falling to the floor, screaming in terror.

Cassandra rushed to the Doctor who brushed her away, indicating he had felt nothing more than a mild shock and was fine otherwise; with that, she went to a stunned, but now aware, Rollie who looked at both Cassandra and the Doctor with panicked eyes, his mouth working silently as he gasped for breath.

Within moments, Rollie's lungs were able to take in enough air for him to cry out, "It's true! I saw it! I saw a ghost!"

# CHAPTER II

The Doctor clamored to his feet with the aid of the wainscoting's elaborate edge and scampered over to Rollie and Cassandra, then helped Cassandra lift Rollie into the nearby Louis Philippe settee. Still a bit put off, the Doctor gathered himself and addressed Rollie between breaths as he waved his hands about. "Now, what's all these *pitreries*?"

Rollie gasped for air.

The Doctor bent down and tapped him gently on the cheek. "Come now, boy, speak up!"

Cassandra looked fiercely from the settee. "He's trying, Doctor, but he's just been through something quite traumatic! Let him breathe!"

Hesitantly, the Doctor stammered, "Yes, quite right. Do what you can, my dear, while I check the control panel to make sure nothing's been damaged." Satisfied, Doctor Omega returned to the pair and asked if there were any improvement.

"He seems to be calming now." Cassandra made way for the Doctor to sit down beside Rollie.

"Good. Good. Now, my boy, can you tell me what happened?"

Slowly, uncertainly, Rollie said, "I...it...was a ghost!"

The Doctor grimaced. "Forget that nonsense. I'm talking about the shock. That sudden electrical shock. Where did it come from?"

Wide-eyed, Rollie said, "I don't know."

"Surely you know something. What did you touch? In what sequence? And, for that matter, why?"

Rollie whispered, "I don't know. I don't remember. All I remember is seeing the ghost, then the shock that threw us across the room. Nothing else." Rollie regained himself as if he'd become aware of something. "It was some kind of force, some kind of energy."

The Doctor lit up. "Yes, what was it?"

"The ghost. That's what caused the shock."

The Doctor paused for a moment, looking puzzled as he considered Rollie's statement. After a moment, he stood up and looked at Cassandra. "You may have been correct after all. There may be something to this ghosties and goblins stuff you've been talking about!"

Surprised at the Doctor's sudden change of heart, she said, "You believe me? About the ghost?"

"Well, not entirely. There are no such things as ghosts."

"But you just said...."

"I said nothing of the kind. I just said there may be something to it, not that they exist. Two entirely different things."

"Alright. Fine. So, how is there something to it, then?"

"Do you remember my earlier chat with Rollie? About the possible fourth dimensional breach in the Vega sector?"

"Yes."

"Well, that residual pulse may be our culprit."

Cassandra shivered slightly and said, "Doctor, I'm suddenly feeling quite cold."

"What, really?"

Before Cassandra could answer, Rollie said, "Me, too. It's strange; I'm cold, but the air seems thick and oppressive at the same time."

Cassandra plopped into the Doctor's previous spot on the settee and said, "He's right. Something's wrong." Then, her eyes went wide as she said, "I can feel it. The ghost. It's coming back!"

The Doctor grabbed her hand and said, "My dear, do calm down. Nothing's coming back. I feel nothing."

"It's here, Doctor," Cassandra said emphatically, "It is here. Its presence is so heavy, so suffocating." She rubbed her brow as if to wipe an encroaching fog from her mind.

Rollie broke in. "It's almost like a deep depression, Doctor, trying to manifest itself. Make itself real."

Bemused, the Doctor said, "My, Rollie, you've suddenly become philosophical."

Rollie said lightly, "Yes, well, it may not be my natural state, but it does seem to be appropriate right now."

"Indeed it does, my boy. Indeed it does." The Doctor rubbed his chin thoughtfully. "But what we need right now is to understand what's *physically* going on with you two. Physical indicators require physical answers." The Doctor abruptly went over to the controls and examined the radiation indicator. "Aha!" He returned to the settee with renewed intensity. "The residual pulse has boosted slightly from our last reading. Mm, this calls for deep neurological examinations for both of you. Do you feel steady enough to stand? You do? Good. This way, then."

He guided them round to the other side of the bridge and pointed Cassandra to a plain, utilitarian chair and Rollie to a comfy, but resolute, George II wingchair off to the side, then he proceeded to remove something bulky from the storage area immediately behind Cassandra's chair. Just before he could place it on her head, she shifted away, startled.

"What's this, then, Doctor? Do you mind telling me what *that* thing is and what you're doing with it?"

The Doctor sighed. "As you wish. This device is called a cerebro-probe. It does various things; I originally designed it as a first step toward a technology that would allow me to control the *Cosmos* with my mind – a cerebro-enhancer, if you will – but I found it could do many other things as well."

Still skeptical, Cassandra asked, "Such as?"

"Such as diagnose neurological disturbances. Like the ones you and Rollie are experiencing."

Hesitantly, she sat back and said, "Okay, but it better not hurt."

The Doctor rolled his eyes and said, "It won't, my dear. I guaranty it." Then, he slipped the device on her head and switched it on. There was the slightest of hums, a small, green light blinked on, and within one minute, the hum ceased and the light blinked off. "See, Cassandra, not a pinch." The Doctor slid the cerebro-probe gently from her head and placed it back in the storage area.

She smirked and said breezily, "Well, you did guaranty it, Doctor. And, I do feel better. That thing does seem to work."

The Doctor came back to her and looked puzzled.

Cassandra noticed and asked, "Something wrong?"

"Yes, I believe so. You say you feel better now?"

"Yes. Why?"

"The cerebro-probe isn't supposed to heal; it's only supposed to prod and poke, diagnose and occasionally enhance. Nothing more, really. Quite odd."

Rollie chimed in, "I feel fine now, too." Then he continued with a chuckle. "That thing must have some good reach."

"But it wasn't the cerebro-probe, I tell you. It couldn't be."

Rollie continued, "Well, I don't care what it is; that overwhelming depression that was creeping in is gone again, and I don't care what made it go away."

Curious, the Doctor dashed back to the control panel and studied the readings again. "Just as I thought."

Cassandra sat forward. "What, Doctor?"

"The residual pulse has dropped to its earlier level. If I'm correct, both of you may be experiencing a form of dissonant radiation poisoning!"

Rollie tensed. "What? Radiation poisoning?"

The Doctor sputtered. "Well, now, let's not get all excited."

Rollie was astonished. "Let's not get all excited, he says! Really, Doctor?"

The Doctor waved his hands as he said dismissively, "Don't be so emotional, Rollie. As I said, if it's radiation poisoning, it's dissonant. That is, it's discordant, dispersed. An echo, if you will." Then, he smiled and said, "Perfectly harmless, you see?"

Dismayed, Rollie said, "Perfectly harmless? No. I don't see, Doctor."

Cassandra added, "He's right, Doctor. How can it be harmless? Both Rollie and I have been terrified by something, whether ghosts or psychological manifestations; we feel something oppressive, and it's affecting our behavior; it even turned Rollie into a sort of somnambulist, had him fiddling with the controls, and sent out a shock when you tried to stop him. It isn't as harmless as you think."

The Doctor stiffened, regaining his composure. "You're quite right. I've been trying to belay your fears, for your own sake, of course. But now, that doesn't seem to be necessary; you two are sturdier than I thought. Right. In order to move forward, I'll have to gather the data from the cerebro-probe."

Rollie leaned back grandly in his chair. "By all means, gather away, Doctor."

The Doctor raised an eyebrow at Rollie and turned to a screen embedded in the wall and waved his hand across it. It came to life with a green glow, immediately followed by odd symbols, the same shade of green, dancing quickly by. Once complete, the Doctor waved his hand across it again, shutting it off. He turned to the others with a baffled look.

After a moment, an agitated Rollie said, "Don't leave us in suspense, Doctor. What is it?"

The Doctor raised his eyebrows. "That's just it. It's nothing."

Cassandra said, "What?"

"It's nothing. There's nothing there."

Mildly ruffled, Cassandra said, "Thanks for the compliment, Doctor."

The Doctor, suddenly aware of his flub, laughed and said, "No, my dear, I didn't mean there's nothing in your head." Then, he became serious. "There's nothing abnormal. There's no nerve cell damage of any kind. It's almost as if everything that's happening to you is happening *to* you rather than in your mind…"

Exasperated, Cassandra said, "That's what we've been telling you, Doctor!"

"I understand that, my dear. That's why this is so disturbing."

Rollie addressed the other two. "So, what do we do now?"

The Doctor sighed. "Unfortunately, this mission may be too dangerous for both of you. I may have to take you back to Earth and continue on alone."

Cassandra scrambled from her chair. "You're not going without me, Doctor, regardless of the consequences. Remember: you owe me!"

The Doctor's chin went up as he looked away from her. "I can't take that responsibility."

"No one's asking you to. I'm responsible for myself."

The Doctor looked back at her with soft eyes, hesitated, then said, "Yes. Yes, I think you are." Then, he turned to Rollie. "Well, that just leaves you, my boy. We'll get you home to your wife and son and make our way back...."

"Wait just a minute. I'm already in this too deep; I'm not turning back now. Besides, I'm not all that fond of my wife and son, anyway. Or, is it the other way around? Regardless, you're not leaving me behind." Rollie stood up and joined the other two.

Doctor Omega giggled and shook his head. Then, he placed a hand on each of their shoulders and smiled. "It seems we're off on a wilder adventure than I anticipated. Look at us; we're like the Three Musketeers!"

Rollie looked concerned. "Which one am I?"

The Doctor paused to contemplate, then said, "You, Rollie, are Athos!"

"Athos?!" Rollie continued solemnly. "But, he's so melancholy. I'd rather be Porthos. At least he knows how to have fun."

"Precisely," the Doctor exclaimed with amusement as Cassandra laughed.

The congenial banter and giggling continued for several moments, a welcome release for everyone from the present tensions, until the Doctor gradually resumed his concerned, inquisitive bearing.

Sighing again, the Doctor said, "Our little problem still remains, though." He shook a finger in the air. "The issue is, you two are experiencing something seemingly impossible. It's something external. In other words, it's not affecting your parietal cortices, which is what I thought was happening before. Yet, it still seems to be related to the residual radiation pulse and is, therefore, likely the result of the fourth dimensional breach in the Vega system."

Cassandra crossed her arms and said skeptically, "You mean, the residual pulse is manifesting itself *physically* several light-years away?"

"It seems so."

Rollie said deferentially, "Look, I'm no scientist or anything, so my opinion probably doesn't mean that much to you two, but I don't understand how a pulse – radiation or otherwise – can appear physically *anywhere*."

The Doctor pondered for a moment, then said, "Consider radar. It uses radio waves to pick up echoes and Doppler shifts, then translates them, via processing equipment, into observable imagery on a screen, yes?"

"Okay."

"And, my own holovid, for example, is made possible by combining and structuring discrete kirbyon package sequences in such a way as to reorganize local photons, via a transmitter, into holographic images recognizable to the human mind."

Rollie hesitated. "If you say so."

"I think something similar is going on here."

Cassandra followed up. "Are you saying we're receiving messages?"

"Possibly."

Rollie looked puzzled. "Not to be flippant, Doctor, but doesn't the act of receiving messages require a physical receiver?"

"Well, like I said, Rollie, my holovid essentially creates a physical wall of photons perceived as an image; if we get down to the details, the holovid transmitter is itself a receiver. It collects all radio waves the *Cosmos* moves through, processes them, then transmits them as directed into the holovid imagery."

"So," Rollie said, "someone is sending us messages through the holovid?"

"I don't think so, my dear boy. What Cassandra described doesn't even remotely resemble how the holovid behaves."

Rollie raised his eyebrows. "That's true. We both saw the misty ghost, but it was nothing like the holovid imagery. This thing had a palpable realness, like it was right there, next to me, in the room. And it acted as if it saw me."

"He's right, Doctor. It formed out of thin air and felt as real as you do right now. It was terrifying."

"In a way, I understand, my dear, now that I'm getting a technical grasp on it."

There was awkward silence for a moment, then Rollie said, "Okay. We're receiving messages, right?"

The Doctor said, "Again, possibly."

"That leaves us with a few questions, then, don't you think?"

The Doctor replied thoughtfully. "Yes it does." He put his hand to his chin and said, "Question one: If they are messages, who is sending them?" Then he looked at Cassandra, who asked the next question.

"Why are they, safely assuming it's more than one entity, sending them?"

Then, the Doctor answered back, not with a question, but a statement. "Their technology must be incredibly advanced, far beyond our own, if they can manifest a type of physical entity light-years away without the need of a receiver."

Rollie soberly rephrased what had already been said. "Incredibly powerful beings who can send messages as physical entities from across trillions of miles of space." He looked uneasily at the other two and said, "We're in trouble, then, because so far, those messages have been absolutely terrifying."

The Doctor tried to assuage their concerns again. "Oh, do stop, you two. You're being silly. I believe you *want* to be afraid."

Cassandra said, "You're the one who said this trip was too dangerous for us."

Offended, the Doctor replied, "So, you *do* want to go home, then?"

Apologetically, Rollie said, "No, Doctor. It's not that. We're just trying to make sense of it all. Nothing more."

With that, the Doctor loosened a bit and said, "I understand. This can all be a touch overwhelming at times." Taking a deep breath, he continued. "If it makes you feel any better, I don't know for a *fact* we're receiving messages. It could just be an electromagnetic glitch."

Cassandra looked concerned, "Something wrong with the equipment?"

"No, I don't think it's that. There are many anomalous activities in deep space, things not even I know much about. The ghosts, as you call them, could be the result of a unique glitch in the electromagnetic force in this area, for instance. Something affecting charged particle interactions in strange ways. Perhaps a force well which causes like charges to be attracted to one another, for example. Any number of things could be the cause, really. At this point, I just don't know."

Rollie replied earnestly. "What *do* you know?"

"Only three things: It's affecting you externally. It's not likely to be our equipment. And it has to do with that blasted residual pulse. Basically, we're not much further along than when we started."

Cassandra said, "Okay, so you said this pulse is the result of a fourth dimensional breach."

"That is correct."

"Meaning someone has traveled through time and left an electromagnetic trail as a result?"

"Someone, or *something*, may have done that. It doesn't have to be a conscious being, and it doesn't have to be the result of time travel. For example, it could simply mean entropic forces are doing what they do."

Perplexed, Rollie asked, "Entropic forces doing what they do? What does that even mean?"

Doctor Omega said casually, "It means the universe could be coming to an end, and its starting point could be right ahead of us in the Vega system."

Rollie said peevishly, "Doctor, you have the most annoying way of nonchalantly saying the most excruciating things."

The Doctor raised his eyebrows innocently. "I do apologize, Rollie. I meant nothing by it. After all, my conjecture is an unlikely one. In most estimations, the universe has got several hundred trillion years left before it finally fizzles out."

Relieved, Rollie said, "That's good to know."

The Doctor laughed and said, "Fine. Back to point."

Cassandra said, "Okay. Here's a point. Why haven't you been affected?"

Doctor Omega considered this. "That, Cassandra, is a good question. One I can't answer. I do have a slightly different biological constitution than the two of you, though. Perhaps that's the answer."

Cassandra looked doubtful. "That seems unlikely. You're not that different."

Rollie looked between them and said, "What are you babbling about? Different biological constitution? Not that different?"

Cassandra placed a hand on his shoulder and said, "Don't you worry about it right now."

Rollie, appearing mildly cross, said, "You know, I keep getting the distinct feeling I'm being left out of something."

Smiling warmly, Cassandra said, "You are, and you should be glad of it."

"Deep down, I'm sure he is, my dear." The Doctor gazed at Rollie and said, "Anyway, what we don't want to deprive you of is a good night's sleep. Since we're not likely to make much headway on this little puzzle any-time soon, why don't you two scamper off to your rooms for some rest?"

Rollie and Cassandra glanced at each other, appearing hesitant. A moment of uneasy silence fell between them.

"Well, off to it," the Doctor said, leaving empty air for movement which didn't come. He finally said, "Oh, I see. You're still too afraid to be alone."

Feeling self-conscious, Cassandra blurted out, "You would be, too, if you had experienced what we've experienced."

Attempting to be judicious, the Doctor said, "You may be right about that. It would be a startling occurrence." He paused for a moment, hoping this would make them feel as if their point had been taken seriously and appreciated, then he continued. "Why don't you two take up positions on the comfy chairs here on the bridge? Perhaps you can doze a bit while I continue to study our little problem."

Seeming to consider this idea a good one, they agreed, with Cassandra happily taking the Louis Philippe settee and Rollie searching out a foot stool for his George II wingchair.

Relieved to finally be getting some time alone to think through the rather bizarre situation they had found themselves in, the Doctor waved his hand dismissively and said with as much graciousness as he could simulate, "Fine. Fine. If you need them, you can find blankets in the closet over there."

With that, he left them to sleep and took a seat at the console. Settling in, he stared contemplatively at the stars passing by on the holovid. Despite his advanced age and experience, the immensity of space still left him in awe, an awe subdued now and tempered with a deep wisdom which was lacking in his youth, but an awe nonetheless.

Noticing his companions were asleep now, he abruptly put this unproductive meditation aside and considered the question before him as he studied the star field, the billions of points of light, the gaseous clusters, the Vega system itself, which was just off center in the holovid image. He paused for a moment.

Startled, he looked closer. Wishing to confirm what he was seeing, he passed his hand over a control panel, bringing up a navigational grid across the holovid image. Mild surprise crossed his face now as another piece of the puzzle was dropped. Digging deeper, his hands moved quickly over other embedded panes until hard data came in to back-up the visuals.

On cue, the star field image shifted slightly beneath the navigational grid, moving a different cluster of stars closer to the center of view.

"So, it's true," he mumbled to himself as he sat back in his seat. "And, how long has this been going on?"

After a while of intently staring at the holovid without really looking at it, he began to notice something out of the corner of his eye. At first, he thought it was just one of his companions who woke up and was about to claim he couldn't sleep, but the Doctor realized it wasn't that when nothing was said. Puzzled, he turned and saw a slight mist. A pearly haze boiling in the air a few feet away. As suddenly as a blink, he felt deeply depressed. The feeling was escalating at such a remarkable speed it took away his breath and made him dizzy as the mist began to take on a definite shape.

Trying to stand in order to confront the anomaly, the Doctor swayed slightly and slumped back down. "What is this?" He pushed back against the terrible gloom as best he could, but to little effect. "What is this," he repeated, as he rubbed his temples and cocked his head at the solidifying mist and, with shock, watched it slowly take form.

The frothy mist became thicker, more substantial, rippling and churning now, seizing on the silhouetted structure of a human, with grotesquely misshapen arms, legs, and head. Nearly solid at this point, though still rippling and foaming around its edges, the Doctor could see that it was actually a mockery of the human figure, floating in mid-air, with revoltingly shriveled body and limbs and a lopsided, pharaonic head. The words, 'sickening nightmare', flickered through the Doctor's mind just before he blacked out.

# CHAPTER III

Doctor Omega awoke to find Rollie and Cassandra standing over him, patting his cheeks, rubbing his hands, and looking as if they had just had a bad meal.

"What? What's this?" The Doctors eyes fluttered a bit as he waved their hands away. Realizing he was laying on the settee and not understanding how he got there, he abruptly sat up and gently gestured for the other two to move away and allow him to breathe. The Doctor tried unsuccessfully to regain his composure as he said, "Let's not be silly. Everything's alright. A little nap is nothing to get excited about."

Rollie said impulsively, "A little nap? You call collapsing on the floor a little nap?"

Wonderingly, the Doctor said, "That's odd. I don't remember collapsing."

Cassandra added, "You must have collapsed, because we found you on the floor."

"Really? That's interesting." The Doctor tried standing but swayed a little before the others grabbed him and sat him back down. "This is awkward. I seem to be a tad dizzy." He sat back, closed his eyes, and breathed deeply several times before thoughtfully addressing the other two again. "I do believe something's a bit higgedly-piggedly, at the moment."

Rollie said earnestly, "What can we do for you, Doctor?"

"Oh, it's not me, my dear boy. It's our situation. Something about our situation."

Cassandra asked, "What do you mean?"

"Well, that's just it. I don't know." The Doctor rubbed his forehead and said, "Something's missing."

Cassandra continued. "Like what?"

The Doctor glanced at her and snapped fiercely, "Don't be daft, girl! If I knew that, then it wouldn't be missing, now would it?"

Cassandra straightened and folded her arms. "He seems fine now," she said bitingly.

The Doctor gathered himself to apologize. "I just need a moment, my dear. You've done nothing wrong. I do appreciate your help," he said as he rubbed the bridge of his nose. After a moment, he asked, "What, exactly, did you two see? How did you find me?"

Rollie said, "We woke up and found you on the floor over next to the console."

Cassandra corrected him. "A noise woke us up, *then* we found you on the floor next to the console."

Rollie shook his head. "That's right. The noise must have been you falling to the floor."

"So, you saw nothing before that, not *why* I collapsed?"

The two shook their heads in the negative.

"Hhhmm, interesting. Whatever happened, happened over there," The Doctor said as he gestured toward the console. "I think I'm well enough to stand now; let's go see what we can find." The others helped him up and waited for him to steady before they all went over to the console.

"Let's see, this looks fine." The Doctor studied the power gauges, then moved to the structural indicators. After a brief examination of those, he said, "And, these are fine. Nothing out of the ordinary here." Gazing at the radiation gauge, he said, "That's odd. This is higher again." Then, he moved to the course display. "Very

47

odd, this." Then he paused for a moment as a knowing look slowly crossed his face. Then, he shot his eyes to the holovid and punched his knuckles into the palm of his hand. "That's it. I remember, now!"

Anxiously, Cassandra asked, "What is it? What do you remember?"

"You were right all along, my dear Cassandra!"

"Right about what?"

The Doctor's eyes twinkled as he grinned, "About ghosts. I saw it as well. I saw your precious ghost. The interesting thing is, though, I saw it clearer than either of you!" He paused in a self-satisfied way and said delightedly, "And, it was quite grotesque." He concluded with a big smile, "Horrifyingly so!"

"Glad to see you're so giddy about monsters invading the *Cosmos*," Cassandra said acerbically.

"Oh, sorry, my dear, I'm not giddy about *that*. I'm giddy about things becoming much clearer now as a result of me having the same experience as the two of you. Do you see?"

Cassandra pondered for a moment, then said, "It makes sense. Why don't you explain how it makes things clearer, though."

"That I will do. That I will do." The Doctor wagged a finger as he made his way around the console and over to the holovid. Once there, he touched his fingers to his lips and asked calculatingly, "Notice anything?"

Rollie hesitated, then said, "Well, you seem to be a few inches taller, but beyond that...."

"Not with *me*, Rollie! Don't be puerile."

"I'm sorry, Doctor, but I don't go in for this guessing game stuff. We know you're bright; you don't need to prove it to us."

Cassandra sighed and said, "He's right, Doctor. Can you just get to the point?"

Disappointed, Doctor Omega said, "Fine. The holovid image. Look at it. Look at the star field. We're slightly off course."

The two looked at it for a moment, then at each other, then shrugged back at the Doctor questioningly. "And?" Cassandra asked.

"We're not heading toward the Vega Sector any longer. We're heading toward this." The Doctor jabbed an index finger at a dense cluster of chromatically vibrant stars on the holovid.

Rollie came closer to the holovid until he was only a foot away and said, "And, what, exactly, is 'this'?"

"This," the Doctor said, pointing once again at the image, "is the Phantasma Nebula." Not getting a response from the other two, he elaborated. "This should puff you two up a bit. The Phantasma Nebula is, like most nebulae, a loose body of cosmic dust and a few gasses, all of which eventually concentrate themselves into solid forms, such as stars and planets. What sets this one apart is that many travelers believe it to be a haunted area of space."

Cassandra, wide-eyed, said, "That explains the ghosts."

"Not entirely," The Doctor said. "We aren't *in* the Phantasma Nebula yet. We shouldn't have experienced anything for quite some time."

Rollie asked another question. "Why are we even heading toward that instead of the Vega Sector?"

The Doctor cocked an eyebrow at him and said, "You tell me."

"What do you mean?"

"It was your fumbling at the controls that sent us off course. Before that little incident, I had us on a direct line for the Vega Sector and the residual pulse. If you look here…" The Doctor went back around to the front of the control panel and gestured toward the radiation gauge. "The pulse is…" He stopped for a moment, then mumbled, "This can't be right." He flipped on a sub-gauge and called-up a separate reading but remained silent as he studied it.

After a bit, Cassandra came forward and asked, "What is it, Doctor?"

"This reading. This shouldn't be."

"What?"

"The reading says the residual radiation pulse isn't coming from the Vega Sector like we thought, but instead, is coming from somewhere in the Phantasma Nebula. Our source calculations were off from the beginning."

Cassandra was stunned. "By that much?"

Doctor Omega said thoughtfully, "To be honest, it's not as much as it seems at these distances. One small mistake can lead to light years of difference." Then he cheered up. "Besides, I was never that good at math, anyway. But we're on the right course, now. So, there's that," the Doctor said vaguely.

Rollie said, "Well, that's good to know. Wouldn't want things to be thoroughly planned out down to precise decimal points when it comes to space travel, now would we. Takes the fun out of not knowing whether we're going to collide with a star or not on the trip."

The Doctor looked sheepishly at them, then tried to recover by saying, "At least we definitely know where we're going, now."

Cassandra said, "Supposedly, we knew where we were going before, too."

In an ill-humored way, the Doctor said, "Yes, well, no point in lingering on the past. Let's concentrate on the future." Then, he realized something and said to no one in particular, "Despite the questions we've answered, we have new, uncomfortable questions in front of us."

"What questions," Cassandra asked.

"Questions such as: Who redirected us, and for that matter, why?"

Rollie looked worried. "He's right. Not only that, but why did it take so long for him to experience the ghost?"

Renewed, the Doctor said, "Ah, I was wondering that myself, Rollie, and I think I may know why." He checked the gauges again and said, "Yes, as I thought. Not only has our direction been altered, but we're much further along in our voyage than we should be."

"This means what, Doctor," Rollie asked.

"It means two things. One: my constitution tends to be more resilient than your – eh – normal constitutions; therefore, the residual pulse or – as I'm beginning to think of it – the *signal* had no effect on me until we got closer to it, so to speak. And, two: someone, or something, is anxious to make our acquaintance, because the *Cosmos* is heading toward the source of that signal at a gradually increasing rate, without the aid of the ship's own propulsion system. In other words, we're being *pulled* along some kind of tractor beam toward whatever is at the other end. In a way, I'm glad now we took the leisurely route rather than just jaunting directly to the Vega system."

Rollie looked confused. "Jaunting?"

The Doctor said, "Yes, we could have skipped all of this and done a transdimensional jump from our original point to the point in the Vega system where we *thought* the signal was coming from. We would have arrived in a blink, but there's a chance we may have lost the signal if we had. That's why I'm glad we took the old-fashioned way."

Rollie snorted, "The old-fashioned way, he says."

Cassandra broke in, "The idea of something waiting for us at the other end of this tractor beam seems like an unpleasant thought, Doctor."

"Not at all, really," the Doctor pontificated. "Uncertainty is never a good reason to be afraid. Especially according to my calculations. Following the probabilities I've worked out in my travels, uncertain situations yield an eighty-seven point nine percent possibility of a gratifying outcome."

"That's nice to know, Doctor," Rollie said, "but didn't you say you're not that good at math?"

Doctor Omega coughed. "That is correct, but things have changed since then."

"How," Rollie asked.

"I'm much older now," the Doctor smiled endearingly. "Anyway, the beam hasn't neutralized our propulsion system; in a way, it's actually enhancing it by pulling us along." He looked openly at his two companions. "If things get too alarming, we can always break free and make our escape."

Rollie looked at Cassandra. "Sounds reasonable. To be honest, all of this crazy nonsense has been kind of fun." With that, Rollie concluded, "Once again, we're a go, Doctor. Now, let's see what's at the other end of this little tractor beam."

The Doctor gave a hearty sigh. "Excellent!" He furrowed his brow and said, "Now that that's settled, I think the only thing left to us is to occupy ourselves until we arrive at our destination." He shuffled past his companions and said, "Care to join us, Cassandra?"

"For what?"

"I thought we could take in a three-handed game of T'yok T'yok Gree."

"No thanks. The last time we played, I lost terribly and had to babysit Quish for a month. It took me weeks to clean the jelly out of my room."

"Fine. Fine. I just never mistook you for a sore loser, though."

"I was only sore from cleaning up all that jelly!"

The Doctor brushed her comment away and turned to Rollie. "What about you? Care for a game?"

Hesitantly, he said, "As long as Quish isn't involved, whatever that is."

Delighted, the Doctor said, "Not to worry, my boy. Quish is home visiting his pod. He won't be back until he leaves his cocoon and sheds his epithelium, which could take centuries."

Rollie made a sickening face and said, "Oh, well fine, then. Off we go," as he followed the Doctor over to a table on the other side of the bridge, waving at Cassandra in passing.

Cassandra said, "I'll just stay here and keep an eye on the sensors."

"Good idea," The Doctor said absently from the table as he placed a game board in front of Rollie, who was now seated across from him. The board was twenty by twenty, had what appeared to be hieroglyphic symbols randomly etched into the nineteen-by-nineteen center square, with a one inch outer track separating the square from the edge of the board. The outer track was broken into twenty-five identical rectangles, with each rectangle containing its own unique hieroglyph, except for one, which matched a particular symbol in the square.

"This looks simple enough, I guess," Rollie said as he sat forward. "I'm assuming we move our pieces around the board's outer track, and when we hit a particular symbol, we move to the inner board?"

"Well, yes and no." The Doctor gently pressed the corner of the board to his right; instantly, the line work on the board began to glow. Within seconds, the line work, including the hieroglyphs, shot up from the board, making the whole of the playing area itself three dimensional, giving it the appearance of a castle-shaped diamond with what seemed to be seven mansions within its interior. "You see, not only are you playing vertically across the board, you're playing horizontally *above* the board, as well."

Rollie's face drooped as he fell back in his chair and trumpeted teasingly, "I've been double-crossed! What fresh hell is this?! Adding another layer to the game doubles its complexity. Triples or possibly quadruples it, depending on what goes on in horizontal play!"

"Oh, come now, Rollie. Stop being so melodramatic. It's not as bad as all that."

"Not as bad as all that, he says! You're going to turn my brain to jam with this little game of yours. Can't we play checkers or tic-tac-toe? Something more aligned with my abilities?"

"I'm sorry, Rollie, but laying about and napping can't be considered a game, and watching you do that isn't much fun for me. Besides, with a little training, anyone can play this game. It's quite simple, really. Let me explain." The Doctor began gesturing at specific areas and icons. "This is where you start. You go around here and keep collecting points indicated by these hieroglyphs; but, you can only go around three times. If you go around three times without landing on this symbol, you lose your points and start over. If you land on that symbol at any time within your three rounds, you move up to the second level, doubling what points you have. Understand?"

Rollie, still slouched in his chair, sighed, "Yes."

"Good. Now, once you get to the second level, you must try to move to the inner structure, then make your way upward through the seven mansions to the diamond room at the top where safety and peace await. Along the way, you gain points by slaying demons; these points build themselves into the key of virtue, which is the only key which will unlock the entrance to the diamond room. The game is like a maze, really, filled with all kinds of peril on the one hand and tremendous fulfillment on the other."

"This sounds way too brainy for me," Rollie pouted.

"It'll do you some good, my boy." The Doctor suddenly became expressive. "Think of it as knights fighting for a fair maiden's purity, as Beowulf going to battle with Grendel! Or, Siegfried fighting the dragon!" He leaned in with intensity. "It's *life*, my dear boy! The struggle to do right." His eyes began to glow with an inner fire as he whispered, "It's a deadly duel with evil itself." He sat back in his chair as he said, almost to himself, "Yes, a duel with evil incarnate."

From across the room, Cassandra startled a focused Rollie. "You'll have to excuse the Doctor. Sometimes his inner Don Quixote comes out."

Mildly piqued at that, the Doctor said, "Shall we start, Rollie?"

Observing the Doctor's reaction, Rollie said buoyantly, "We shall," then he coyly glanced at Cassandra. "Who goes first?"

"Click your fingers, and we shall see," the Doctor said.

At the exact moment Rollie snapped his fingers, the neon outline of a spinning ball appeared in the center of the board. As its spin slowed, a small glowing dot became visible at its equator. Soon after, the ball stopped spinning, with the dot pointing at Rollie.

"Well, my boy, it looks as though you go first." The Doctor nudged the virtual ball over to Rollie, who didn't quite know what to do with it. The Doctor said, "Spin it. Simply grab it at the top as if it were a real ball, and spin it with your fingers, thus."

After watching the Doctor, Rollie did as instructed and lightly observed the spinning ball until it came to rest, with one of the hieroglyphs from the board glowing into visibility on its north pole. Then, he looked questioningly at the Doctor again.

The Doctor pursed his lips and said, "See your piece at the start position? Touch it, then touch the nearest symbol on the board which corresponds to the symbol on the ball."

"Yes. Right." Once he did that, his piece vanished from its starting point and instantly appeared in the space with the designated hieroglyph. Pleased with himself, Rollie gently launched the ball over to the Doctor. "Your turn, then?"

"Correct. You're catching on, Rollie." The Doctor spun the ball, but before it could come to a stop, sparks flew from the three-dimensional structure before them, causing the two players to jerk backwards slightly, away from the electrical emissions.

Startled, Rollie said, "You didn't say anything about electrocution being part of the game, Doctor."

Perturbed, the Doctor said, "That's because it's not!"

Before he could say anything more, Cassandra called to them from the control console, her eyes fixed intensely upon the sensors. "Doctor, you need to see this."

Turning to her, both men quickly got to their feet and went to her side. "What is it," the Doctor asked, leaning in to examine what she was focused on. "My, this is interesting," he said.

"What is?" Rollie asked.

"Not only is our speed exponentially increasing, but we've gotten light-years closer to the Phantasma Nebula in a much shorter time than we anticipated, even with the exponential increase in speed. A distance that should have taken two or three days to achieve has taken us only an hour or so to travel."

Behind them, the board began to crackle again, tossing off sparks and glowing more intensely. They all turned as it sputtered, throwing their hands up to block the raw energy from the activity.

Stunned, they said nothing as the neon diagrams danced and mingled themselves into the distinct form of a luminous, transparent, humanoid shape, writhing and twisting as if trying to break free from some kind of invisible bond. They all knew it was another ghost, but this time it was using the energy from the board to material-ize itself rather than the ambient energy in the air around them as it had done before.

Once again, it was a hideously deformed shape, similar to what the Doctor had seen, with withered, vestigial limbs and a bloated, pygmaean body, made all the more stunted by the dominance of its grisly, elephantine head. This time, though, it was clearer, better defined, more tangible somehow, even though it was only made of laser light.

The light had dimmed enough for them to lower their hands. As they did, the Doctor observed, "It's lingering. Before, it showed up, then vanished soon after arrival."

"Yes," Cassandra said, "and I don't feel overwhelmed by it this time. I feel its anguish, but I don't feel drained now."

"She's right, Doctor. It's odd; I feel a deep sadness, but I'm still in full control."

The Doctor said, "Yes, you're both correct. I feel the same. Our guest seems to have tempered his energies a bit since his previous visits. This could be a sign of intelligence, or…."

"Or what, Doctor," asked Cassandra.

"Or, it could be a fluke, simply a mindless surge of energy softening us up for roasting," the Doctor said with an absurd, toothy smile.

Rollie suddenly held up his hand. "Wait. Do you hear that?"

The Doctor's smile slid from his face. Hesitantly, he cocked his head toward the faint sound and said, "Yes, yes I do. Just so." He looked at Cassandra. "And you?"

After a momentary delay, she said, "Yes, barely." She looked at the other two for confirmation. "Someone speaking?"

"It would seem so. Or mumbling." Slightly troubled, the Doctor remarked, "Or whispering?"

Rollie looked about and asked, "Where's it coming from?"

The Doctor tilted his head toward the hideous figure hovering over the board and said, "I believe it may be originating from the Medusa shield in front of the gravcap, but actually emanating from our little friend over there."

Rollie said flatly, "It can talk now? Through that shield?"

"It would appear so."

"But how's that possible? The ghost is simply an image made of light. And a shield is just a shield!"

"Well, how can it be here at all," replied the Doctor rhetorically. "As for the shield, it was a gift from da Vinci, who explained to me its rather unique animating qualities. Those qualities appear to be acting as a conduit, or a speaker if you will, giving our visitor a voice somehow."

Rollie raised his eyebrows in baffled acknowledgment. "Da Vinci? *The* da Vinci?"

Ignoring Rollie, Cassandra looked at the Doctor. "Should we try communicating with it, then?"

The Doctor cupped his fingers around his frock coat lapels and said matter-of-factly, "It would probably be for the best."

After a moment, Rollie looked at the other two and said ambiguously, "Right. Who goes first?"

Before the Doctor could answer, Cassandra said, "Wait, look at this," as she drew everyone's attention back to the control panel.

The Doctor centered his attention on the display Cassandra was focused on and said, "My, my... This is interesting. Let's translate this data into visuals and magnify the image onto the holovid."

Cassandra's hands fluttered around the control panel; within seconds, the holovid's image magnified, homing in on a small portion of the Phantasma Nebula.

The Doctor stepped over to the holovid, snapped his hand at the image, and said with gusto, "There it is!"

Lost, Rollie asked, "There *what* is?! It still just looks like a mess of watercolors and some stars."

"My boy, *this*. *This*." The Doctor wiggled his fingers at an infinitesimal smudge within the large sea of color.

Rollie came closer and leaned in. After a moment, he tried to use his palm to wipe away what appeared to him to be a small, greasy blotch, until he realized once again he wasn't staring through a window. Trying to recover from the embarrassment, he stepped back and asked nonchalantly, "Okay. What is it?"

"That is our destination! We're able to pick it up visually because we're now close enough to do so."

"A blurry smear in space is our destination?"

Ruffled, the Doctor said, "It's not a blurry smear. The blurriness is due to the magnification. We're close enough to determine its exact location now, but we've reached our upper limit of visual amplification at this distance. We're still a few light-years away from it."

"Fine. *So, what is it*?"

"A planet. All of the readings indicate a solid mass, roughly spheroid – *very roughly spheroid* – with approximately one hundred sixty million square miles of surface." Puzzled, the Doctor continued. "Yet, its density is relatively low, indicating the lack of a metallic core, which would make it quite difficult for life as we know it to exist there."

Cassandra cut in glibly. "*As we know it* are the operative words, then."

"Indeed they are, Cassandra," the Doctor smiled back at her.

Suddenly, a brief, garbled shout filled the room. It quickly dissipated into a faded crackling, followed by silence.

The Doctor and his companions looked at one another in surprise then turned to face their neon intruder. It was still as it was, misshapen and glowing brightly.

The Doctor said, "We've apparently hit a nerve."

"Or maybe several," said Rollie.

Cassandra asked, "What do you make of it, Doctor?"

"I'm not quite sure. It could be a warning."

"About what?"

"A warning to not go to the planet."

"Does that mean that thing isn't an envoy from there?"

"Possibly."

Rollie asked, "What if it's not. What if it *is* a warning? What do we do then?"

The Doctor said off-handedly, "Not go to the planet."

"So, we're not going after all," Rollie asked.

"Of course we're going. Don't be silly."

"But you just said -".

"I said if it were a warning to not go to the planet, then we wouldn't go to the planet. We don't know that it's a warning, and we're not even sure if our little invader even has anything to do with that planet."

Frustrated, Rollie said, "You must be joking. So, you think this is all a coincidence?"

"It could be, but I doubt it. I have a suspicion that this poor creature before us is, indeed, associated with that planet in some way. And I believe, he does want us to continue onward. I also believe that inarticulate shout we heard wasn't a warning but merely the earliest convenient attempts at audible communication, something this odd, little kobold isn't accustomed to, at least in this form."

Cassandra broke in. "So, that takes us back to our previous question."

The Doctor replied, "Which is?"

"Who goes first?"

"That is correct." The Doctor pondered for a moment, then said, "I do have a universal translator, but I think it would hardly be adequate in this sublingual situation. Rollie really is definitely out of his league on this one. You, on the other hand, do have a gift for – and experience with – empathic discourse."

"I would hardly call it 'discourse', Doctor. It's more like an associative link. It's not exactly a gift, either, and it was more of a transitory contact."

Rollie asked, "What are you talking about? Contact with whom?"

"Quish," Cassandra said with a deadpan expression. "For some reason, he mentally bonded with me briefly."

The Doctor chuckled. "My dear, he wanted to mate with you!"

Cassandra snorted, "Which is impossible, Doctor! He's a plasmoid, and I'm human. Two totally incompatible physiologies!"

The Doctor continued to goad. "Ah, but the chemistry was there. You could have made beautiful music together."

"You're disgusting, Doctor." Brushing away the current indignities, Cassandra said, "Can we get back to the situation at hand?"

The Doctor sobered up and said, "Yes. You are right. So, that really does leave us with you, Cassandra. I'm sorry, but you are the only one with the experience in this area, regardless of how slight. Furthermore, it did try to communicate with you *first*."

She sighed and said dismally, "Of course it did."

The Doctor proffered his hand in a gentlemanly way, indicating an open path to the invader.

"Thanks, but I'd prefer to not get any closer than I have to."

"But proximity may be key to vigorous communication. It has been so far."

"I just don't want it to be *too* vigorous, that's all."

"Not to worry, my dear. We're right here if anything happens."

Still reluctant, she hesitated, then moved toward the creature and stopped a few feet away. She waited awkwardly, then said, "Nothing seems to be happening, Doctor."

"Give it some time." Then, the Doctor clucked, "Maybe try raising your hands to it."

"What's that supposed to do? I talk through my mouth, not my hands."

The Doctor smiled knowingly and said, "Quite correct," then looked at Rollie and said, "Must be the undue influence of Rollie and his comic book movies."

With mock offense, Rollie cocked an eyebrow, but said nothing.

Cassandra crossed her arms. "Now what?"

"Try opening your mind to it."

"What does that mean?"

"It means exactly what I said. Stop being difficult," the Doctor snapped. "Relax your mind and allow any thought to enter it. Perhaps it can only communicate effectively through thoughts right now."

"I'd rather just say 'hello'."

"If you wish, *do so*. That's as good a place to start as any, I would guess. It could be just that simple. But, please, do try something before our little friend decides to leave us!"

She wavered for a moment, then shrugged her shoulders and spoke haltingly. "Hello?"

In response, the neon monstrosity began to writhe, its lighted silhouette twisting and expanding, with its ghostly limbs bending back on themselves, folding into its larval body only to sprout again from its already lopsided, grotesque head; seconds later, they melted back into its head and erupted obscenely from the unfortunate creature's bloated belly and chest, this time more like tentacles than human limbs. Its mouth, seemingly covered in electrified mucus, was working hideously now, as if it were trying to speak, yet nothing came out.

Both mesmerized and terrified, Cassandra stared speechless at the thing.

The Doctor whispered, "Cassandra." When he received no reply, he tried again. "Cassandra?" Still no reply. He tried again, but louder and more firm this time. "Cassandra!"

As she snapped to, a low hum began to fill the bridge. As it became more pronounced, an unsettled Cassandra made her way back to Rollie and the Doctor. She looked uneasily into the Doctor's eyes. "What's happening, Doctor. Something's changed."

With concern, the Doctor draped his arm around Cassandra and said, "Yes, something has changed, and *is* changing. This thing, whatever it is, may not yet be prepared to communicate with us fully, biologically, psychically or in any other way. Yet, it does seem to desperately want to communicate with us." He halted for a moment, then said, "Listen. The hum is increasing!"

The three backed away and took refuge behind the console as the hum amplified to an uncomfortable level and smoothly changed to a voice intensifying into a high-decibel yell coming from the Medusa shield. It was beginning to sound human to them now but like one they felt was in some kind of unimaginable agony, just as they had felt before. The Doctor and his companions covered their ears as the sound became a thunderous roar, and the otherworldly entity began to fluctuate in size and light intensity. Along with the howl, its silhouette pulsed and distorted erratically, growing to fill its half of the bridge, then just as quickly, it shrank back to its previous size. With one last crack of electrical energy, the phantasm splattered into a million sparks with such brightness, the Doctor and his companions had to cover their eyes until it had passed.

The three came out from behind the console and looked at one another, astonished.

Rubbing her ears, Cassandra said tartly, "You were correct, Doctor."

The Doctor looked at her with exaggerated confidence. "I usually am, you silly thing." Then, suddenly thrown, he asked, "Correct about what?"

"Proximity being the key to vigorous communication."

After brief consideration, he said with another expansive smile, "In this case, perhaps *too* correct, if there is such a thing."

Dismissing the current conversation, Rollie broke in. "Say, what's this blinking light?"

The Doctor and Cassandra looked down at the console display Rollie was gesturing toward. Startled, and still glaring at the readings, the Doctor said, "This is remarkable."

Rollie, worried he may have gaffed again, glanced between the other two and asked, "What is?"

The Doctor looked up at the holovid and said, "That." The image filled over half of the holovid and completely occupied its lower left-hand corner. It was a solid mass, gray and purple in color, knobby and broken through its surface, and oddly rugged along its edge.

Rollie asked, "What is it, and how did it get in our way without us knowing about it?"

"It didn't get in our way. It brought us here, and far more quickly than we anticipated. That, my dear Rollie, is our destination. That is the planet our little ghost is likely from, and the location we've been pulled toward this entire time!"

## CHAPTER IV

The Doctor was silent for several moments, lost in thought over the immense power that would have been needed to pull the *Cosmos* into orbit so quickly without the use of jaunting while also dampening to zero the bone-breaking effects of such movement in Newtonian space. It was mind-boggling, even for him. He moved in closer to the holovid and further studied the details of the planet.

Rollie joined the Doctor and exclaimed, "That's a planet? Looks more like a diseased walnut, if you ask me."

The Doctor's mind puckered at the suggestion as he glanced at Rollie. "Charming. If you'd noticed, Rollie, we didn't ask you." He then turned his attention back to the image as he swiftly jabbed his index finger at various parts of the planet's surface, watching as numbers appeared where he tapped. The numbers indicated depths and heights of the various locations as well as distances between geographic areas.

After a moment, he said, "Hmm, the terrain is highly irregular. Look at this, for example. These crevasses here, here, and here; they're longer and deeper than the Grand Canyon and bleed off into smaller canyons. They all seem to be regularly spaced, which means there are bound to be more like them on the other side. And, these shallower fissures appear to be filled with rounded, unevenly-shaped pipelines or penstocks, almost like lava tubes, that taper off into the higher-elevation landmasses and deep into the crust. This is going to make finding a good landing site quite difficult." He turned back to the console. "What do you make of it, Cassandra?"

"Despite all of that regular geographic spacing, it's obvious none of it is man-made. I'm guessing, our ghost-producing intelligence is somewhere inside the planet."

"Do you detect any life below the crust."

"I'll do a life scan now." Cassandra gently touched a few embedded panes, then looked at the Doctor, stunned.

"Well, what is it, my dear?"

"The sensors say there's life down there."

"Yes, well, we were expecting that, weren't we?"

"Yes. But this is indicating the planet is teeming with life."

"Alright. Then our caller has set up an underground heaven for living organisms. I wouldn't put that beyond the abilities of a being that can do what he's done so far."

"But the sensors are also saying the only hollow spaces within the planet are few and relatively small, too small to accommodate that much life. And, furthermore, they're filled with what appears to be underground seas."

Intrigued, the Doctor said, "Well, well. Our host is aquatic, then. Interesting."

"It is interesting, but how do you explain the sensors indicating the extraordinary amount of life without the space to accommodate it?"

The Doctor pondered for a moment, then said, "You may be thinking too much like a human."

"Ah, you're guessing the intelligent lifeforms down there are not only aquatic but microscopic, as well!"

"That very well could be the case. We've both encountered infinitely stranger beings, have we not?"

Cassandra crossed her arms and nodded knowingly. "That we have."

The Doctor then looked quizzically at her. "But what do you make of these so-called lava tubes?"

"Tunnels, maybe. That lead from the surface to the interior?"

Not wanting to be left out, Rollie said eagerly, "Created by microscopic fish? How could they make tunnels that large?"

"That, Rollie, is a good question," the Doctor said. "But, as Cassandra said, none of this looks artificially made. They could be just what they look like, lava tubes. Tubes which have been adapted for use by interior aquatic life."

"But, for what reason? And, if they're water creatures, how and why would they come to the surface?"

Cassandra looked at the Doctor. "He's right. How and why?"

The Doctor spluttered. "Well, I. They could…. Well, maybe they get to the surface riding the tidal forces." Rollie seemed to accept that answer, but Cassandra had doubt in her eyes. Realizing his gaff, the Doctor said, "Yes, right. No satellite to cause tidal forces. If that's the case, then there would be no lunar stresses to cause volcanic activity, either; which would mean those lava tubes aren't lava tubes after all."

Rollie spoke up. "Maybe they are lava tubes that resulted from volcanic activity that happened long ago, back when this planet had a moon."

The Doctor's eyes brightened as he smiled at Rollie. "Excellent, my boy. Excellent!"

Cassandra added, "That is excellent, but why would aquatic creatures want to come to the surface of the planet, where there is no surface water?"

"That's a good question. One I feel we won't have an answer to until we go down to the planet and meet our host, face to face."

Rollie asked, "Can't we just wait for him to materialize up here again?"

The Doctor said, "Considering he brought us to this point, he knows we're here; he's chosen to not reappear, which is probably a good indication he wants us down there."

Rollie raised his eyebrows, accepting the Doctor's explanation.

The Doctor returned his attention to Cassandra. "In which case, will you please scan the planet for the most reasonable and level area to land in?"

"Will do," she said as her hands began working vigorously at the control panels.

As she did that, the Doctor continued to examine the planet, enlarging and reducing the image several times. Finally, he leaned back a bit, as if to get a better view, and said, "That's odd."

Rollie glanced at him casually. "What is?"

"Look at this." He reduced the image so the whole planet and its surrounding space were visible. "Look at the entire area. Not a sign of debris anywhere. Wouldn't there be an asteroid belt if the planet's moon – or moons – had broken up?"

Rollie looked thoughtfully at the holovid. "Maybe the break-up happened so long ago, the debris floated away."

"Debris of that kind wouldn't just float away. At minimum, it would form an asteroid belt somewhere near the planet because of the gravitational pull. And at most, it would have formed a ring around the planet for the exact same reason."

"Well, maybe there was an asteroid belt or a ring at one time, but it happened so long ago, the asteroids hit the planet because of the gravitational pull you're talking about."

"Good point, my dear boy, but there isn't a sign of asteroid impact anywhere on the planet. Not a crater to be seen."

Perplexed, Rollie asked, "What does it mean?"

The Doctor placed a hand on Rollie's shoulder. "It means your previous theory of volcanic activity being the result of an ancient lunar presence has been debunked. There never was a moon here."

"Okay. But what about the gravitational pull from other planets?"

"There are no other planets. It's not even a star system, because there is no star."

"What," Rollie exclaimed. "No star?" He gazed, wide-eyed, at the holovid and held his hands out to it. "Well, then, how can we even see it? Where's the illumination coming from?"

"That, Rollie, is another good question." The Doctor brought his hand to his mouth in concentration and said nothing for several minutes. Finally, he spread his fingers in a half-guess gesture and said, "Perhaps the geographic makeup of the planet makes it self-illuminating. Like irradiated rocks in a mine."

Rollie scratched his head. "Is that even possible?"

"Anything's possible. Whether it's probable or not, I just don't know. I've never come across an entire planet illuminated by glowing rocks in any of my travels, so I would guess it isn't the probable answer. Yet it seems like the only answer we're left with."

Both were silent for a few moments until Rollie snapped his fingers. "That's it!"

Startled, the Doctor asked, "What is?"

"Bear with me for a second. Hear me out. You said the lifeforms on this planet – or *in* this planet – are aquatic, right?"

"That appears to be the case. Go on."

"Well, back on Earth, we have a few aquatic creatures that create their own light, don't we?"

"Why, yes we do," the Doctor said, his face opening up.

"Cassandra said this planet is teeming with life, didn't she? What if this planet is absolutely saturated with self-illuminating aquatic life."

Hesitantly, the Doctor said, "Yes, it could be. It's possible." But then, he shook his head. "Just possibilities again. Furthermore, how could the planet be saturated – as you put it – with these lifeforms when there's no surface water? And the illumination they would provide wouldn't even come close to being able to light up the planet like that." Agitated, he continued. "We have two unsubstantiated theories, wildly divergent from one another, which makes both highly suspect. The only thing to do is land and explore. First-hand examination always surpasses theory." He turned his attention to Cassandra and asked, "Have you found a suitable spot, yet?"

With a final tap of her fingers, she said, "Indeed I have." She gestured toward the holovid and said decisively, "Right there."

The Doctor examined the quadrant and said carefully, "Yes, I see." Then, he pointed. "A relatively flat surface here, with a gentle slope on the side leading down to one of the narrower branch tunnels that connects to the larger lava tunnel here. Good, good. It also seems we can access some of the nearby shallow valleys from here, as well." He turned to Cassandra and said, "Good choice, my dear!" Then, he raised his hands to both and said with a wide, effervescent smile, "Shall we land, then?"

Cassandra shook her head, mimicking the Doctor's enthusiasm, and said, "We shall!" Cassandra acknowledged the coordinates on the console and activated the landing procedure. Instantly, the *Cosmos* began to move toward the planet.

The Doctor said, "Well, it shouldn't be long now."

Lost in thought, Rollie asked, "What do you think they'll be like, Doctor?"

"The beings from this planet? I think both you and Cassandra may have hit on it; most likely, they're aquatic creatures."

"I don't know if I like that."

"For goodness' sake, why not?"

"I'm allergic to seafood."

Both laughed for a moment before Cassandra called their attention to the holovid. "It looks like our friend is at it again." The others looked at the screen and saw the ship wasn't headed toward the location Cassandra found in the northern hemisphere but instead was headed toward the planet's equator.

The Doctor said, "It appears you are correct, Cassandra. Interesting."

Vacantly, Rollie asked, "What's this all about?"

The Doctor replied, "Obviously, we don't know what it's about, other than our ghostly visitor wishes us to go to his planet's equator. Perhaps that's where he's located. Perhaps that's where his welcoming committee is. Or perhaps it's something else entirely. We won't know until we get there, which should be relatively soon. Might as well make ourselves comfortable until we land." The Doctor gestured toward the seats around the console. They all chose a spot and settled in, with the Doctor saying to Cassandra, "Continue reading the sensors, just in case." Cassandra nodded in reply while Rollie cocked a concerned eyebrow in his direction. The Doctor, seeing this, said reassuringly, "Oh, I doubt there's anything to worry about. Simply a precaution and, also, a good data-gathering habit."

Rollie relaxed slightly and said, "Good enough."

After a moment, Cassandra said, "We're going in fast, but steady. Entering upper atmosphere in three, two, one...." At that instant, they felt a tingling sensation and saw the electrical displays blink out for half a second.

Startled, Rollie asked, "What was that?"

The Doctor said, "That's a good question," then he looked to Cassandra for an answer.

"I, I'm not certain," she said, slightly out of joint. After checking various sensors, she said, "Whatever it was, it seems to have passed. Everything's reading normally now."

Satisfied, the Doctor said, "Fine. A mild glitch of some kind." He patted the console gently and said, "The dear old thing is a bit touchy at times. Ah, well; proceed with the landing."

Cassandra said, "I don't need to. The landing is being taken care of for us." She acknowledged the console displays which indicated descent. Astonished, she said, "We've already landed."

The Doctor looked at the displays then at the holovid and whispered uneasily, "Remarkable. We *have* landed." Regaining his composure, he said robustly, "Absolutely remarkable, wouldn't you say," as he quickly glanced at the other two. He patted the console again, this time with satisfaction. "Well. Now, that we've arrived, what are the readings?"

Cassandra blinked herself back to the moment and said, "Nothing, really, other than what we found before. The planet seems to be absolutely loaded with life form indicators." She looked from the console to the holovid and waved her hand at it casually. "All we can see from here, though, is what appear to be bald, rolling hills and canyon drop-offs."

The Doctor looked at the holovid, squeezed his lower lip between his index finger and thumb, then said, "Yes, numerous canyons. Really, it looks like a sea of limitless canyons, punctuated by rounded mesas, one of which we appear to have landed on." With one fluid move, as if refreshed, the Doctor stood up and said, "Well, shall we go meet our host?"

Cassandra followed suit and said, "By all means."

Rollie stood as well, although less enthusiastically, and said, "After you two. I don't want to be the first one vaporized by some alien ray gun."

The Doctor pursed his lips. "Don't be silly, Rollie. No one uses ray guns anymore; they went out with jet packs." The Doctor looked at Cassandra, and they both began to giggle.

Rollie looked down his nose at them. "Alright, you two; enough of the ridicule. There's a good chance you'll need me on this trip, and you'll be sorry you laughed at me when you do."

The Doctor shook his head in a fatherly way and said, "You're quite right, Rollie." He touched Rollie's shoulder, then continued. "We're sorry right now." He looked at Cassandra as they both giggled again.

Conceding defeat, Rollie shooed them over to the gravcap, which took them to the ship's exit. After disembarking, the Doctor took a sweeping look around. "This is extraordinary. The canyons go on for as far as the eye can see, in every direction. Not a tree or a mountain in sight, and no visible artificial structures of any kind, yet it all seems repetitiously similar, almost manufactured. The entire planet must be like this, or at least this hemisphere."

He moved over to the edge of the mesa they had landed on and called to Cassandra and Rollie, "Over here." They came up to him as he gestured to something a few feet away and said, "There's a trail, or at least a natural berm, over there going down into the canyon; the decline seems to be gradual enough for us to easily reach the bottom. Thankfully, this particular canyon is shallow, with the bottom only about twelve to fifteen feet away." He rubbed his chin briefly and added, "Not only is the canyon shallow, it's also quite narrow. Not even pushy enough to be a canyon, really; more like an arroyo." He looked at Rollie and said, "Which gives your theory about bioluminescent organisms more credence." Then, he turned to the berm and said, "Let's proceed."

Once at the bottom, the Doctor scanned their surroundings again and went over to the arroyo wall. "This truly is fascinating."

Cassandra followed him over. "What is?"

"This. Look at the walls. They're almost perfectly smooth. And gray-green in color, with just a light touch of red and purple mixed in. Reminiscent of soft pastels, in a way."

Cassandra said with curiosity, "They are smooth. There must have been an incredible hydrological force running through here once, and for an extended period of time, too."

With equal curiosity, the Doctor said, "Yes. Possibly for thousands of years. But, the top of the mesa was like this, as well."

Rollie interrupted as he ran a finger under his ascot. "Is it just it me, or is it unbelievably humid?"

The Doctor turned to face him. "Now that you mention it, yes, it is quite humid." Then, he glanced about the empty arroyo. "You would think, with this much moisture in the air, there would be some form of plant life."

Cassandra followed his gaze as she slowly said, "Yet, there's nothing."

Suddenly aware, Rollie looked about. "There aren't even any rocks or pebbles. Or sand. You know; like the normal debris you'd find in a riverbed. It's just smooth terrain all around."

The Doctor looked upward. "And there's a strange green glow to the sky, and to a lesser extent, to the air all around us. Due to microscopic algae, perhaps?"

Cassandra glanced about. "The multitude of life form readings the sensors picked up?"

The Doctor said, "That's quite possible. The intelligent life here may not be *in* the planet, as we originally thought, but floating in its atmosphere!" He looked at Rollie with delight. "This may be another confirmation for your theory about bioluminescent organisms."

With a sour face, Rollie said pathetically, "Oh, no."

Cassandra asked brusquely, "What now?"

Rollie placed a hand on his stomach. "The marine life. The algae. We're inhaling it. I'm going to be sick."

The Doctor raised his eyebrows as he looked at Cassandra. "Oh, dear. He is correct, you know. We may very well be ingesting an intelligent alien life form. One that invited us here." Then, he said with some concern, "How ill-mannered."

Cassandra said, "Well, there's nothing we can do about it now."

The Doctor drew up and said, "That is true. Nothing to do now except press on and find the spokesman of this algae brigade and get to the bottom of things." With solid conviction, he looked about, then licked his index finger, and put it in the air. Shaking his head with satisfaction, he said confidently, "This way."

Incredulous, the queasy Rollie and dubious Cassandra shrugged as the Doctor guided the two from the landing site.

After a short distance, Rollie said, "Wait a minute."

Irritated, the Doctor turned to him and said, "Good heavens, we've just gotten started. Please don't tell me you have to stop for a bathroom break."

Slightly piqued by the Doctor's sudden snappiness, Rollie said, "Really, Doctor, I'm not a child. I was simply going to point out the floor of the arroyo."

The Doctor looked at his own feet. "The floor?" Then, he looked back at Rollie. "What about it?"

Rollie hesitated for a few brief moments, deciding whether to release his information; then, he sighed and said, "The floor of the arroyo is squishy."

The Doctor and Cassandra looked at him blankly. The Doctor said, "Squishy. *Squishy*?" Then, he looked at his feet again. He took a few steps and watched as indentations formed, filled with an oily, grayish-clear liquid, then sprang back, absorbing the liquid again. He stopped and looked at Cassandra. "Odd. It's true. It's quite spongy. I didn't notice this before."

Cassandra shrugged. "Dense moss? A fungus, maybe?"

Rollie was dubious. "Covering the entire surface of the planet?"

Cassandra spread out her hands. "We've only seen this area, which is about nine hundred square feet, at most. This could be the only spot it's in. But, it could also be the plant life we would expect to see in this kind of exceedingly damp environment that we're not seeing in any other form, other than possible algae."

"You may be onto something, Cassandra." The Doctor went over to the wall and pressed his hand against it, watching the grayish-clear liquid leach out; removing his hand, he saw the spongy material spring back into place, reabsorbing the aqueous substance into its cushiony material again.

He took a hankie from his pocket and wiped his hand. After sniffing the hankie and making a face, he placed the hankie back in his pocket and said, "Intriguing. It's blanketing every surface of this area, including the mesa above. And, it doesn't have that aquatic smell, like a sponge from the ocean or something covered in planktonic cells. As a matter of fact, it doesn't have any smell at all, which is even more intriguing. The surfaces appear to be covered in a slimy biofilm. Let's get moving and see if it ends anywhere along the way."

A short time later, the Doctor stopped immediately after a gentle bend in the canal and waved the others over to his side. He pointed a few feet ahead to a small, cracked bulge in the canal's doughy surface, no bigger than knee high. "Look. What do you make of it?"

Cassandra said, "It looks almost like a miniature lava dome. It even looks like it's extruding a kind of milky-red lava from the cracks."

"It does, doesn't it," the Doctor said, fascinated. "But there's no steam."

"You're right."

Rollie pointed. "And there's another, much smaller one just beyond this one."

The Doctor stretched to get a better view. "Yes. Look. That same milky-red lava." After a moment, the Doctor said, "There doesn't seem to be any danger from them at present. Let's get closer so we can examine them."

Once at the mounds, Doctor Omega knelt before the largest one and pulled a small metal tube from his pocket. He pressed one end, and what appeared to be a short palette knife extended from the opposite end. The Doctor noticed Rollie's inquisitiveness and explained, "This is an omnilyzer. Just as its name implies, it analyzes everything. Right now, I have it set to analyze molecular structures." Seeing that Rollie was satisfied with that answer, the Doctor took a sample of the flowing liquid and waited for the result. Shortly, the omnilyzer beeped, indicating it had finished its job. The Doctor stood and said, "Well, we now know why there's no steam."

Cassandra looked at him. "We do?"

"Yes. There's no steam, because these are not lava domes."

"What are they, then?"

"They are biological in nature. I'm guessing some kind of neoplasms."

"And the milky-red fluid?"

"Biofilm mixed with blood."

Rollie scoffed. "Blood from moss?"

The Doctor said in a calm voice, "I've encountered such things on other planets. Mixes of animals and plants. Typically horrible, monstrous things. But they have happened." He cleaned the omnilyzer and placed it back in his pocket. "That also explains why we haven't felt any volcanic rumblings. No volcanic activity, no tremors. Simple as that," he said with a bit of perkiness.

Just at that moment, the ground began to gently tremble. Almost offended, the Doctor looked about and said to his surroundings, "Well, you needn't be so impertinent."

Cassandra raised an eyebrow and said, "What do you make of that, Doctor?"

He thought for a moment, and said, "Perhaps it's some form of activity that resembles volcanic behavior but is something else entirely. As far as we can tell, there aren't any geological pressures in the planet which would produce seismic disturbances, yet we just felt one."

A worried Rollie said, "It feels like we're about to get another one!"

The ground trembled again, but more vigorously this time, and was accompanied by a low, persistent rumble. As the shaking increased, they tried to maintain balance by reaching for one another while they stumbled over to the opposite wall to steady themselves. Once there, they observed the larger of the two neoplasms cracking open even more and bloody biofilm oozing from the gash. The milky-red substance pooled at the base of the dome, filling a natural moat, before it ran off into a shallow channel in the arroyo floor, apparently heading downstream and in the direction from which they had come.

Above the thrumming, the Doctor said, "Look. It's not just the neoplasm. That channel is fracturing into a fissure that's spreading the length of the arroyo, and it's releasing a viscous river of biofilm as it does so."

Rollie said with confidence, "Going back is out of the question, then." Gesturing in the opposite direction of the flow, he said, "There must be another berm somewhere up ahead. The one we came down can't be the only one."

The Doctor shook his head. "Right you are." Then, he invited Rollie to take the lead.

Rollie shrugged. Stepping around the other two, but staying as close to the wall as possible for stability, he hesitantly set off up the arroyo. As they slowly progressed, more bulges began to gradually appear around them, expanding then contracting, almost like bubbles in a thick, rolling liquid. Some popped, spurting bloody smetana while others simply hemorrhaged sluggishly before collapsing back into strangely smooth surfaces, sealing their cracks as if nothing had happened. Another tremor hit, causing the travelers to stop for a moment and press themselves against the wall again.

The Doctor looked back and noticed the channel fissure advancing toward them more quickly now. While still looking at the approaching fracture, he put his hand on Rollie's shoulder and said, "My dear boy, I think we should pick up the pace a bit."

Exasperated, Rollie said, "Tell that to these ridiculous tremors! We can't very well go running off, willy-nilly, while the ground is shifting beneath our feet and these filthy bubbles keep spewing their filthy goop at us!"

"That's understandable, Rollie, but look." The Doctor pointed at the nearing fissure.

Rollie's eyebrows went up as he suddenly grasped the situation. "Right. Off we go!" Locking hands, the group dashed away in single file, dodging and swaying as they went. After a short time, their speed and agility became ineffective against the seismic activity and hematic muck gathering around them. Now, horrifically hobbled by their environment, they became desperate and frantically searched for anyway up and out of the arroyo. Staring ahead, Rollie saw what he thought could be their path to salvation. He shouted, "Up ahead, about twenty feet," and looked back at the Doctor.

Hoping to see a clear access way to the top, the Doctor glanced past Rollie's shoulder and saw nothing. Crisply, the Doctor said, "What? It's nothing but the same smooth surfaces."

"Look. The wall." Rollie pointed to barely noticeable ledges in the arroyo wall, so smooth and slight one had to focus to see them. "It's not a berm, but we may be able to use them as hand and foot grips for climbing out of here. It's the best I've seen so far, and it seems to be our only choice, anyway."

Annoyed with the slim prospects, the Doctor said agitatedly, "Very well. Let's get to it, if we must."

They frantically dashed to the wall, and Rollie precisely pointed out the holds to them, then motioned for Cassandra to begin climbing. She hesitated, explaining she could take care of herself and that the Doctor should go first because of his age. Piqued by the affrontery, the Doctor began to bicker with her, demanding she go first. Frustrated, Rollie interrupted. "One of you go, please! We don't have time for this!"

Noticing the quickly advancing biofilm, the Doctor capitulated and began to climb with the help of Rollie and Cassandra. Struggling, he soon reached the edge and clawed his fingers into the soft surface to pull himself over the top.

Once there, he anchored himself and hung his arm over the side to help bring up Cassandra. Then, they both put their hands out to help Rollie up, but before he could get past the first hold, the ground shook violently, causing him to fall back into the arroyo.

Wrestling with the powerful seismic waves, he finally got unsteadily back onto his feet. He stood for only a brief moment before he realized something terrifying. He couldn't move his feet now, because he was beginning to sink into the arroyo floor as if it were quicksand.

# CHAPTER V

Quickly realizing the enormity of his situation, Rollie did what came naturally; he panicked and began thrashing about, causing himself to sink even deeper into the quaggy marl. *This can't be happening*, he thought. *How did I get myself into this?*

With lightning speed, his life began racing through his mind. Early, serene memories of his mother consoling him when he was bullied by schoolmates; his mother consoling him when he received a mediocre grade in dance class; his mother consoling him when a girl he liked rebuked his clumsy, youthful friendship; his mother planning his daily high school activities and picking his clothes for the following day; his mother packing his lunch before he headed off to his college classes; his mother negotiating the salary for his first real job.

Then, suddenly, he stopped, slightly embarrassed. *This is getting me nowhere.* He looked about for something to grab, some kind of leverage, but only saw the shallow holds on the wall. Realizing they were his sole source of possible escape, he reached for them, but came up short by mere inches; he stretched again just as the tremors struck, causing him to swerve away slightly.

One more lunge, and he was finally able to sink his fingers into the spongy wall holds. With immense effort, he began to twist himself free of the ground's sodden grip, but as one foot pulled loose, the other sank deeper, the imbalance sending his free foot right back into the muck.

Desperately, the Doctor and Cassandra stretched to meet Rollie's grasping hands, their fingers almost touching, but each action drove his legs further into the soft floor of the arroyo and further away from escape. A last, hazardous lunge from Doctor Omega, and his hand met Rollie's with a resounding slap; Cassandra quickly grasped the Doctor about the waist, anchoring him as he attempted to reel Rollie in like a large, cumbersome fish. Realizing he needed more leverage, the Doctor twisted round and dug his heels into the edge of the escarpment and gave a final, forceful tug with the assistance of Cassandra.

Free of the sucking mess below, Rollie let the Doctor's hand slip from his own, sending the Doctor and Cassandra backward into an awkward heap, and began to claw at the yielding wall like a drowning man hungry for air. Frantically finding the holds, he bolted up the side of the arroyo and over the top to collapse next to his startled companions just as the river of biofilm filled the sinkholes he had just escaped from.

Before they could pick themselves up, another round of tremors came, though less vigorous this time. They seemed to be tapering off now. As they diminished, the Doctor rolled his hand at the other two, signifying that it was safe to rise.

Rollie patted himself to make sure he was intact and said with a half-ironic tone, "Well, that was a close one."

Cassandra said, "Yes it was," then, she unsuccessfully attempted to wipe away some of the slimy fluid which had covered her body during the struggle. She looked disgustedly at her hands and said, "This really is revolting."

The Doctor looked at the slime covering his own clothes, grimaced, and said to both, "Stating the obvious won't alleviate the situation."

Ignoring him, Cassandra casually added, "This slime reminds me of cleaning up after Quish."

The Doctor stiffened, then looked sharply at her, suddenly becoming aware of something. "Quish, you say?"

Confused, she said, "Yes, Quish. Remember? He left a tremendous amount of slime about."

Suddenly energized, the Doctor said, "My dear, I was wrong. Sometimes stating the obvious can be useful."

Rollie chimed in. "What are you going on about, Doctor?"

The Doctor took Rollie by the elbow and guided him back to the edge of the arroyo as Cassandra tagged along. He spread his hand toward the floor of the arroyo as if presenting something revelatory to them and said, "Ah! Just as I suspected! What do you see?"

Cassandra squeezed between their shoulders as Rollie thought for a moment, then said, "The floor of the arroyo; it's completely smoothed over again. The crevasse is gone and so is that magma-style fluid."

Pleased, but still wanting more, the Doctor gently prodded, "And…?"

Rollie hesitated again as he intently scanned the area below them. After a few seconds, a look of surprise appeared across his face. "The arroyo is wider now. Not by much, but it is perceivable!"

"Exactly, Rollie!"

"But I still don't quite understand any of this."

Cassandra added, "I have to confess, Doctor, I'm not quite there yet, either."

With crackling energy, the Doctor clarified. "The slime, my children! It covers everything. No, correction. It emanates from the planet itself; not just from the surface but from its interior. Just like Quish, this organism-rich slime originates in the interior then migrates to the surface, if you will."

Still not quite getting it, Cassandra said, "And that means what?"

"It means, not only is this slime, and the other bio-film we just encountered, organic, but," he tapped his foot on the ground, "this spongy coating is also organic, almost like a skin; the slime is originating in the interior of the planet and makes its way through this spongy skin to coat the surface. In other words, this entire planet isn't just a planet; it's a whole, living organism!"

# CHAPTER VI

Cassandra said, "You're joking, aren't you Doctor?"

"Not in the least. It explains everything. Not only is the planet teeming with life, as your readings indicated earlier, it *is* the life itself. And it's growing, if the expanded crevasse is any indication."

Rollie said incredulously, "A living, growing planet? It's not possible."

Pleased with himself, the Doctor said, "Apparently it is, my dear boy. We're standing on it. We're standing on a living being the size of a planet; an enormous living maze of a planet, which explains why our indicators said the planet was teeming with life!"

Rollie and Cassandra were speechless, so the Doctor continued. "The planet itself was communicating with us, and its enormous size indicates an astronomical amount of neuro-electrical energy, which explains how it was able to interact with us from light-years away."

Rollie and Cassandra looked in awe at their surroundings, then at the ground beneath their feet. Wide-eyed, Rollie said half under his breath, "Incredible."

The Doctor continued. "And, now that we're here, we should be able to communicate directly with it."

Cassandra said honestly, "And how do we do that?"

The Doctor said, "Well, we – eh – we. I have to admit, I'm not quite sure."

Then, the Doctor stopped for a moment, suddenly perplexed by something. He raised his hand as Rollie was about to speak again, then pulled his omnilyzer out and activated it. Without saying a word, he scraped it across his coat, collecting a sample of slime, then pressed the activation button. After a moment, the omnilyzer finished, and Doctor Omega read the results silently as his eyebrows raised. "Intriguing."

Both Rollie and Cassandra looked at him with anticipation. Noticing, the Doctor said firmly, "Well, it appears the slime isn't just any old slime. According to the omnilyzer, it's cerebrospinal fluid." Then, he added ironically, "In other words, this isn't just some ordinary, run-of-the-mill organic planet. It seems we've landed on something akin to an enormous brain." The Doctor corrected himself. "No, it isn't akin to an enormous brain; it *is* an enormous brain!" Looking at his surroundings with fresh eyes, he continued. "Which means those canyons and arroyos out there aren't canyons and arroyos, per se."

Confused, Rollie said, "Then what are they?"

Rollie and Cassandra followed the Doctor's gaze and looked across the landscape, all the way to the horizon, as the Doctor continued. "From our new perspective, it's obvious those smoothly rolling hills, like the one we're standing on now, aren't shallow, uniform mesas after all, but are instead the gyri of the brain!" Noticing their lack of understanding, he rephrased the statement. "The cerebral cortex, or the outer tissue layer, of the brain folds on itself and produces ridges and furrows. Ridges like the one we're standing on and furrows like this arroyo here."

Cassandra said, "This is mad. Not even I've ever heard of anything this incredible."

The Doctor said, "True. It's remarkable. Almost beyond comprehension. I say almost, because we're obviously experiencing it. But at least this new, outlandish revelation gives us a path to communication."

Rollie asked, "How's that?"

"We now know it's a brain, and as such, there must also exist two vitally important areas within the brain called the Broca and Wernicke, which are central to language use. What we have to do is find the area which connects the two, and tap into it, thereby facilitating direct communication with our strange host."

Cassandra said, "Where do we find this connection?"

Rollie thought for a moment, then said, "Didn't the brain draw the *Cosmos* directly to this spot?"

The Doctor said, "Yes it did."

"It's been trying to communicate all this time, so wouldn't it have had a reason to draw us here, possibly related to communication?"

The Doctor picked up on what Rollie was saying. "Right you are, my boy! Very good! Our host did land us on what would be considered the side of the brain, where the Broca and Wernicke areas would be located, so the connective region must be here as well."

Cassandra asked, "Since everything looks pretty much the same, how will we know it when we see it?"

"We won't actually see it. It's beneath the cerebral cortex, hidden by it. We just need to stimulate the correct general area for communication to be effective."

"All right, then," Rollie said. "What next?"

The Doctor said, "Since this is the general area we probably need to be in, we should look for the deepest furrow, which would bring us closer to the connective tissue hidden beneath."

Rollie pointed to the arroyo they had just escaped from and said, "We need to go back down there?"

"This one seems to lead to deeper ones over in that direction so, yes, I would say so." He smiled, then said,

"You first, my boy, then you can help myself and Cassandra down."

Surprising the Doctor, Rollie shrugged his shoulders and agreed without much grumbling. He scurried over the side and easily dropped the short distance to the smooth floor of the furrow, his feet slightly compressing the spongy surface when he landed; then, he proceeded to help Cassandra down, followed by the Doctor. Once together, they headed off in the direction they had been going before the crack appeared and the magma-like biofilm began to flow.

Not long after, they came to the first turn in the labyrinth, forcing them to take a left. Rollie noticed that this part of the furrow was seemingly identical to the previous section, although there was a more pronounced downward slope here. They moved on, eventually making another turn, but to the right this time, which took them into a slightly wider and even deeper furrow.

After a few more uneventful turns, and a noticeable drop in elevation, Rollie, who was in the lead, brought everyone to a halt just before the next turn in the furrow. He looked back and said to the Doctor, "Did you feel that?"

"No. What did you feel?"

With a questioning look, Rollie then turned to Cassandra. She said, "No. I didn't feel anything, either."

Satisfied, Rollie said, "I thought I felt a slight tremor. Must have been my imagination."

Before they could continue on, they all felt a noticeable rumble at their feet. Rollie looked at the other two and said to the Doctor, "Should we turn back?"

Worried, the Doctor said, "Yes, this spot will have to do, I'm afraid." As he said this, he pulled a cylindrical device, about one inch in length, from his coat pocket and pressed a tiny button at its base. Two needles, an inch in length, extended from its tip, and what looked to be a small, thumbnail-sized tuning fork popped from the center of the cylinder's body, aligning itself at a right angle to it. Just as the tuning fork appeared, another more violent tremor occurred, causing the trio to sway and almost lose their footing.

Along with the tremor came a rumble, low and barely audible, that seemed to come from everywhere. Its timber quickly increased, becoming a wave of deep, audible force that vibrated through their bodies, causing them to shudder. Regaining his composer, Doctor Omega quickly plunged the device, needles first, into the fleshy wall of the furrow, burying it up to the tuning fork, then said above the din, "I just hope the signal will be strong enough."

Cassandra said loudly, "What signal? For what?"

The Doctor said, "The signal I'll be sending to the Broca and Wernicke areas via the arcuate fasciculus!"

"The what?"

The Doctor said tensely, "The connective tissue between the two areas associated with communication, my dear!"

Breaking into their conversation, Rollie turned back and yelled over the increasingly oppressive thrumming, "We better go; looks like we're about to get a flood of biofilm again!"

Before he could take a step, the Doctor, who, along with Cassandra, had also turned back, grabbed Rollie's arm, stopping him, and said loudly, "Not yet! This seems to be a different phenomenon. There doesn't seem to be a crevasse forming anywhere along here. And then, there's that."

Rollie's eyes followed the gaze of the other two. They watched as just a few feet in the direction from which they had come, at the previous turn in the furrow, the edge of a shadow appeared, slowly swaying back and forth, growing larger and moving up the opposite wall. Something was coming from the next furrow over, and judging from its shadow, it was humanoid in shape.

As they slowly backed away, they covered their ears against the increasing baritone of the thrumming, but it did no good; the drone moved through them, vibrating so intensely they nearly passed out. Just before they reached unconsciousness, the thrumming broke into what seemed to be a human scream, which quickly drifted away into distant echoes.

Bewildered, they watched as the shadow reached its full length on the opposite wall, and the being casting it slowly swayed into view. To their horror, they had been mistaken; the creature was only vaguely humanoid in shape and was unlike anything Rollie or Cassandra had seen before.

Fearfully, and looking a bit overwhelmed, Cassandra called out, "Doctor, that thing, it's emanating so much violent energy, so much rage! I can feel it! It wants us dead! What is that thing?"

As the group slowly backed away from the revolting creature, the Doctor hesitated, then said with finality, "Possibly our doom."

# CHAPTER VII

The creature resembled an upright insect from the deepest recesses of Hell, with two thin legs separated by an elongated, oval abdomen which came to a point at the bottom, tipped by continuously working pincers. The abdomen was connected, via what looked like a thick spinal column, to a long, narrow rib cage coated thinly by some form of leathery skin. Beneath the skin, internal organs could be seen moving about, fulfilling the individual functions required to keep the creature alive.

From this emaciated thorax extended undersized, delicate arms, bony and too short for the torso, which ended in something akin to lobster claws and which also resembled the creature's feet. The mouth, situated just below two serpentine eyestalks terminating in blood-red, translucent globes, was a short, sharply pointed beak surrounded by gyrating tentacles dripping a green, gelatinous saliva. The head itself was split widely in two, with a pulsing, slug-like organ supporting the eyestalks and filling the cavity of the cranium.

Looking for a way out, the Doctor saw that the ridge above was at least, in distance from them now, double Rollie's height, and there were no berms or vague footholds in sight for them to use as they had previously done. Eyeing the slowly approaching creature again, he said tersely to his companions, "It appears the only way to go back is to go forward."

With that, they all turned and quickly made for the next bend in the furrow, which took them right, into a much longer, gradually widening fissure. Although the extra space gave them a certain sense of respite, they continued their urgent pace, knowing their danger was far from over. A few minutes later, after reaching the halfway point of the furrow, they glanced over their shoulders and saw that the creature, while losing ground because of its slow pace, was still methodically following them, clicking its insect hands menacingly in their direction. Eventually reaching the next juncture, which turned left this time, they stopped for a moment, feeling the monster was at a great enough distance now to allow them to briefly rest.

The Doctor quickly observed their surroundings and said, "Considering the slowness of that creature and the fairly extensive width of the furrow, we may be able to use a little dexterity to get around it and make our way back to the *Cosmos,* using the path we arrived on."

Rollie nodded and said, "That sounds reasonable, and a lot better than continuing on and getting lost in this ridiculous maze."

Rollie and the Doctor looked at Cassandra, who nodded in agreement with their estimation.

The Doctor said, "Right, then. We'll proceed on my mark," but before he could continue, another hideous figure came squirming around the bend from the previous furrow, and it was moving a bit faster than the first creature, quickly closing the distance between the two.

Perturbed, the Doctor said, "Well, this will not do. Not at all." Unlike the first monster, this second one lacked entirely the basic resemblance to any humanoid form. Essentially, it had the appearance of a man-sized worm, completely lacking arms and legs, with its body terminating into a plump tail at its back end and presumably a head, punctuated by a large, continuously working circular mouth filled with hundreds of pointed teeth, at its front end; housed within its widely cleaved head, just above the mouth, was a lump of smooth flesh with sprouted eyestalks extending forth blood-red orbs, an organ surprisingly similar to the repulsive cranial tissue of the first creature.

Watching the oncoming monsters, Rollie said urgently, "That plan's scratched," then he turned to the Doctor and said, "Looks like you were right before. The only way back is to go forward!"

The Doctor said, "Indeed," then promptly led the other two to the left, around the turn, and into an even wider, yet equally deep, furrow; but this one had an offshoot to the right, about halfway down its length. As they came to it, the Doctor said, "Either our options are improving or they're doubling our dangers." A cursory examination showed that the offshoot was a dead end, the path closing itself a mere few feet in.

Deciding not to dally, they pressed on and reached the end of the main furrow, turning right into the next one, which was as wide as the previous one, but which had a few offshoots this time, and also seemed to be slightly rising in elevation, taking them a fraction closer to the ridge and escape from this deadly labyrinth.

The Doctor pointed to the closest offshoot and said, "Let's see if that one goes anywhere, so we can get out of this main artery. Maybe we can lose those things and then backtrack once they pass us."

They all dashed ahead, breathing heavily by the time they arrived at the opening. Peering in, they saw that it went back a few feet, then made a sharp turn to the right.

The Doctor said, "This will have to do. Follow me."

Hesitantly, the Doctor walked in, leading the other two. Once they came to the right turn, they noticed, going forward, the opening above them had narrowed so dramatically that the two ridges had merged into a ceiling of spongy cortical tissue which had essentially reduced the radiance from the surface by half, although a lesser bioluminescent glow from the walls and floor continued to illuminate their path.

"Remarkable," the Doctor said as they made steady progress.

Cassandra, who was right behind him, asked, "The glow?"

Doctor Omega said, "Yes, that, but this pathway seems to be narrowing dramatically, as well."

Rollie, who was guarding the rear, said in a stern whisper, "Quiet. Those things may be closing in." Acknowledging the truth in the statement, everyone fell silent as they moved on.

After a short time, the Doctor came to a halt, stopping the other two, then whispered, "I believe we may have gotten ourselves into a trap. This furrow is narrowing to an alarming degree. There's another turn up ahead, so I have no idea if it's going to get tighter or open up into a larger area or even take us deeper into the brain." Then, he looked at Rollie in the dim light and asked, "Do you hear them coming?"

Rollie said, "I'm not certain. I'll have to go back a few feet and check."

The Doctor waved his hands and said, "Do so, but please be careful."

The furrow was so narrow now that Rollie could not fully turn around, so he had to do an awkward backstep, one foot behind the other, while looking over his shoulder at where he was going. At one point, he stopped briefly and listened. With a look of uncertainty, he carried on until he reached the area where he could comfortably turn and face the way he was moving.

After only a few more steps, he had reached the bend, then halted. He slowly leaned out and peered around the edge. To his shock, the giant worm was at the entrance, projecting its grotesque head into the furrow, wiggling its eyestalks into the cavity, as if it were examining for their presence. *How did that thing know we were here*? Rollie whipped around and headed back to the Doctor and Cassandra. Once he got to them, he waved his hand aggressively at the Doctor and hissed, "Go! Go! They're coming in!"

They moved forward as quickly as they could, now having to walk sideways, pressed up between the walls of the narrowing pathway. The space at the turn widened just enough for all of them to stop and huddle together so they could see where they were going. They were grateful to see the path slightly widen before them but were unpleasantly surprised by the steep decline the furrow was taking, seemingly leading them deeper into the interior of the brain. Hearing a wet shuffling noise behind them, they quickly moved on, anxious to put more distance between themselves and their pursuers.

Only a few paces in, they had to use the walls and each other to steady themselves, due to the slippery floor of the furrow and its striking downward slope. As a result of the biofilm also covering the walls, the grip they were hoping to achieve was difficult to attain, leading them to grab desperately for one another, making their actions even more precarious. In their attempt to pick up their pace while also holding on to each other, and digging their free hands as deeply as possible into the moist cortex, they inadvertently stumbled into one another, sending the group tumbling down the slope and rolling around a turn where they awkwardly fell into a pile, quickly coming to a stop.

Getting up, the Doctor said, "Well, that was embarrassing," as they all futilely went through the motions of wiping slime from their clothing. Soon enough, they gave up, then took in their surroundings.

Rollie said, "This new furrow is almost cavernous compared to that coffin we were just in."

The Doctor looked about sharply and said, "Hmm, yes. You're right. We're deeper in, right about where the connective tissue between the Broca and Wernicke areas should be. Granted, the arcuate fasciculus is much deeper into the body of the tissue, but we are significantly closer to it now. Good luck is with us after all, it seems."

Rollie and Cassandra smirked at one another.

Ignoring them, the Doctor waved a finger toward a narrow pathway about a hundred feet ahead and said, "Look at that. It appears to slope up and out of here, going to the surface."

Changing his tune, Rollie said, "Well, that is a bit of good news."

As if to dampen the uptick in positivity, they felt the minor stirrings of another seismic rumbling. Concerned, Rollie said, "We'd better move on; I don't want to be stuck down here with those things coming after us and this rumbling starting up again."

Doctor Omega said energetically, "Right you are, but first, I want to insert another antenna down here, closer to the underlying communication tissue."

Cassandra said, "Another one?"

"Yes. This location is far better than the previous furrow, where I inserted the first antenna, since it's much closer to the parts of the brain used for communication. I can use the first antenna to boost the signals from the *Cosmos* to this antenna, which will be much more likely to reach the interior of the brain."

As he said this, he quickly pulled an inch-long tube from his pocket, identical to the first one, pressed a button on the end, and once again, watched the two-inch-long needles project from the other end. Just as before, a small tuning fork popped from the body of the cylinder and came to a right angle to the cylinder's body. He then dashed over to the nearest wall and plunged the device into the spongy cerebral cortex, needles first, all the way up to the tuning fork.

Instantly, another rumble came, stronger than before. As the shaking intensified, the baritone thrumming accompanying it grew into a resonant booming before bursting into what seemed to be a sepulchral scream again, quickly evaporating into nothing.

Unsteadily making his way back to the other two, the Doctor put his hand on Rollie's shoulder and pointed off to their right, a few feet away. Rollie and Cassandra watched as the wall of the furrow bulged slightly then compressed back to its original shape, only to bulge again, but this time going further out before recompressing.

Cassandra, looking worried, said to the Doctor, "Another neoplasm dome?"

The Doctor frowned and said hesitantly, "I don't believe so. A neoplasm wouldn't expand and compress like that. This is something else entirely, and it's got me worried."

Rollie said, "It's got *you* worried?"

The Doctor ignored him as he watched the area expand again. But this time it didn't compress; instead, the area slowly separated from the rest of the wall, finally breaking away from it, leaving an ugly scar behind, which miraculously healed before their eyes. This separate piece immediately began to take definite shape and detail. Its main bulk was like a large barrel; and, extending from this barrel, around the top and bottom, were numerous tentacles, all whipping about. At the top, centered between the tentacles there, and buried deeply into the creature's flesh, was another one of those oddly smooth organs with projecting eyestalks supporting large, red orbs which they had previously seen on the other two monsters.

Shocked at the sudden manifestation of this creature, the trio turned and ran for the narrow pathway ahead of them, digging their hands into the soft cerebral cortex for leverage as they struggled up the moist floor toward their salvation.

Just before reaching the surface, Doctor Omega looked back over his shoulder and saw the huge worm that had been chasing them earlier finally come sliding wetly down the incline into the large furrow, followed immediately by the insect creature, which landed near its companion.

Then he saw, off to the right, not far from the tentacled monster, another creature taking shape in the wall. Startled, and before he could discern its shape, he rushed his companions out to the surface, where they thankfully found themselves standing in the open, atop one of the cerebral ridges.

Catching his breath, Rollie scanned the horizon and, in short time, found the *Cosmos*. Stunned, he pointed at the ship and said, "Look. Over there. We must have traveled a good quarter of a mile in that rotten maze!"

The Doctor said, "It would appear so. Now, we must find our way back along these ridges. And do it promptly, before those beasts crawl up after us."

Thinking rapidly, Rollie said, "You two work out a path. I'll try to give you some time." Then, he made his way back to the path they had just left so he could keep watch for emerging creatures.

After a few moments' examination and discussion, the Doctor said over his shoulder, "Right. I think we've got it!"

Just as Rollie turned to rejoin them, the insect creature's claw clamped around his ankle, causing him to yell out. In the sudden rush of adrenaline, he brought his other foot down onto the bony wrist of the creature, snapping its claw loose, and sending the monster tumbling back into its companions at the bottom of the furrow. Rollie easily kicked the disembodied claw aside and joined the Doctor and Cassandra, saying cheerfully, "It wasn't as bad as I made it sound. The yell mostly came from surprise. Shall we go?"

The Doctor raised his eyebrows and said, "Yes, we shall." He took Cassandra by the elbow as they both led the way, with Rollie limping behind.

Not long into their serpentine journey back to the *Cosmos*, Rollie looked over his shoulder and saw the creatures finally emerging, one by one, from the furrow they had just left. He informed the Doctor, who then picked up their pace.

About halfway to the *Cosmos*, Rollie began to notice, down in the crevasses they were traveling past, there were diffuse shadows gliding about, then disappearing. After a few of these, he mentioned it to the Doctor.

Curious, the Doctor checked to see if they had put enough distance between themselves and the pursuing creatures then, satisfied, he came over to Rollie and asked, "Where are these shadows?"

Rollie pointed back a couple of feet, down into the furrow they were right next to. "The last was right there."

Scanning the area quickly, the Doctor said, "Yes, well, I see nothing now, and those dreadful beasts back there are closing ground between us rather rapidly, so let's move on, but be cautious."

The other two nodded in agreement, but within moments, they came across a long vine, covered in clusters of leaves, stretched in front of them, covering half the ridge, forcing them to use the other half of the ridge to avoid it. Its leaves were a smoky black, as was the vine itself, and there was a delicate, almost seductive, scent resembling rose arising from it. In passing, the Doctor voiced his suspicions, saying sternly, "That, obviously, doesn't belong here. Keep as far away from it as possible. We have no idea what it's capable of."

Once on the other side, with their backs to it, the vine crawled toward them, then shot up, wrapping itself around Rollie's waist. He called out, "Doctor!" Then, he grabbed desperately at the vine only to have hundreds of small, razor-sharp teeth bite into his skin. Each of the hundreds of leaves was similar to a Venus flytrap, but with needle-sharp fangs in place of the eyelash prison bars.

The Doctor and Cassandra whipped around and saw another vine hurl up out of the furrow and take hold of Rollie's torso and shoulders, digging another several hundred fangs through his clothes and into his flesh. While naturally fragile and easily breakable on its own, the tensile strength of the coiled vine was doubled and tripled, depending on the number of coils looped around him, making Rollie's escape nearly impossible.

The Doctor and Cassandra watched in horror as more vines instantly launched themselves from the crevasse and wrapped around Rollie's entire body, becoming ever tighter in their grip, finally leaving only his wide, terrified eyes visible to them. Rallying from their shock, the Doctor and Cassandra moved to help Rollie, but before a step could be taken, he suddenly yelled to them through the vines, "No! Stay back!"

As they halted, they were stunned to see the vines force Rollie to his knees and wrench him backward, knocking him completely to the ground, then suddenly drag him over the side of the ridge to the furrow below. They rushed to the edge, but were only met with Rollie's nauseating screams of pain and terror, which died away to an awful silence.

# CHAPTER VIII

Cassandra pleaded, "Doctor, we've got to save him!"

Catching motion out of the corner of his eye, the Doctor turned and saw the creatures that had been pursuing them were now too close for any rescue action to be taken. And, judging by his screams, it seemed to him that Rollie was beyond help at this point. Attempting to placate her, he said tightly, "I understand, my dear, but there's nothing we can do for him now. We must get away from these creatures and back to the *Cosmos* if we hope to do anything for Rollie!"

Cassandra reluctantly agreed as the Doctor immediately turned back to their path and led her away, with Rollie's screams still echoing in their minds.

On their route back, they encountered, and successfully fought off, more disturbing creatures, all of different and repulsive build, yet each having the same slug-like organ with eyestalks somewhere on its body. Exhausted, the two finally reached the *Cosmos* just as their original pursuers were within feet of catching them. With their last bit of strength, the Doctor and Cassandra kicked and yelled at the horrifying beasts, hoping to keep them at a relatively safe distance as they dashed into the ship and secured the lock before collapsing against the wall.

Now within the *Cosmos*, the tension Cassandra felt evaporated as she began to cry. Placing his arm around her shoulders, the Doctor said regretfully, "I understand, my dear, but there was nothing we could do for him. We'll have to try a rescue later."

Through her tears, Cassandra said forcefully, "Rescue? You know as well as I do, Rollie's dead. I can't believe we just left him to die such a horrible death." Then, she broke down again.

Sensing she was correct, he slowly guided her to the gravcap and gingerly said, "Come now, we mustn't give up hope. Let's go to the bridge where we can collect ourselves and consider our next steps."

Back on the bridge, Cassandra took the seat at the control console, next to the Doctor. The small, red warning light before them blinked rhythmically as the Doctor adjusted a dial which brought up visuals on the holovid of the ship's entrance, showing the creatures milling about, as if they were uncertain as to what to do now that their prey was out of reach. Soon, the red light stopped blinking as the creatures seemingly moved on and left the two in peace.

Trying to alleviate her sense of helplessness, Cassandra began absently checking various gauge readings as the Doctor considered their situation. After a moment, he said, "You know, there's something odd about those creatures."

Cassandra kept fiddling with the gauges in a distracted manner as she said, "Are you sure they were even real? They could have been more illusions, you know."

The Doctor said tersely, "And how would you explain Rollie's abduction?" He caught himself, and pursed his lips, realizing his mistake.

Cassandra abruptly stopped working the gauges and looked harshly at him without saying a word.

He hesitated, then began again, attempting a more delicate tone. "Considering what we know so far, the illusion theory doesn't sound quite right this time, don't you think?"

She said flatly, "Why not? Too much like your earlier DST theory?"

Delicately peeved, he said, "Well, for one thing, we know the neoplasms were real, and the biofilm. We had direct contact with those. And, for another thing, none of the ghosts we've encountered were even remotely as real as those creatures out there appeared." His tone went down, becoming gentler. "And, finally, we know Rollie was real."

Cassandra shrank slightly and said, "After all of this, I'm beginning to think there's no such thing as reality."

The Doctor leaned in and cupped her hand in his and said in a grandfatherly way, "My dear, you can never do that. Of all things in the world, the one thing you can never question is objective reality." Then, he sat back and almost brightened up. "Why, once you do that, you invite all manner of insanity to infect your mind!"

With that, Cassandra became a little more buoyant and asked, "Alright, then. But, if those horrid creatures *are* real, why did this living planet call us here just to have them attack us," she became hesitant, then continued, "and take Rollie away?"

The Doctor replied cautiously. "*That* is a good question." After a pause, he said ambivalently, "Because it needs our help, and it doesn't know how to communicate that need."

Cassandra dismissed the idea with a doubtful look. "More likely, it brought us here to kill us."

His bold confidence returned, the Doctor said, "Nonsense. It could have done that long before our arrival."

"It could have, but would it? Perhaps this Big Brain we're on is psychopathic and likes to do its killing up close and personal."

"Really, now, for a being this intelligent and powerful, even if it were inclined to be nothing more than a murderous beast, proximity wouldn't be a determining factor in such vile behavior; in fact, the situation would be to the contrary if it *were* a mindless beast. Distance would mean nothing to it, in that regard. No, we're dealing with an entity of great awareness and brilliance which means us no harm. But what those creatures are out there, I have no idea." As he gestured to the holovid for emphasis, he noticed the red warning light was beginning to blink again.

Startled, they looked up at the image and saw a figure approaching the ship. It was definitely humanoid in shape but looked out of sorts and disheveled as it staggered in their direction.

Perplexed, Cassandra's hands began working the console as she stared at the holovid and said, "That doesn't look like the others." Becoming more excited, she said, "That looks like a human, an actual human!"

Now, fixated on the holovid, the Doctor said eagerly, "As a matter of fact, it does." Then, he turned abruptly to Cassandra and said with a half-smile, "My dear, let's get to the ship entrance immediately! It appears Rollie has returned to us!"

Exiting the gravcap, the Doctor and Cassandra quickly made their way to the entrance door. Once there, the Doctor anxiously brushed his finger along the length of a dark panel embedded in the wall. Instantly, the door opened just as Rollie stumbled up to it and stopped, swaying gently, his severely lacerated face devoid of understanding.

The smiles the Doctor and Cassandra had sported slid from their faces once they saw Rollie up close; he was covered in blood, his clothes were torn, and his features were mottled with swollen ulcerations where the deadly vine's fangs had obviously torn deeply into his flesh.

Most repulsive of all, though, was what they saw at his side, squirming in the iron grip of his right hand. It was about the size of an average forearm, smooth-skinned, and glistening with slimy moisture; its skin was gray with black spots that tapered off from its head down along its back; what appeared to be its head was only discernible from its body because of the darker color and the long stalks projecting out several inches from it, and the dark red globes supported by them. The Doctor hesitated for a moment when he realized the squirming thing was one of those slug-like organs he had seen previously embedded in the other creatures.

Startled, the Doctor stepped forward to help him into the *Cosmos*, and said with distress, "My dear boy, get in here this instant!" But, before he could get to him, Rollie fell, face-first, like a dead weight into the ship. Immediately, Doctor Omega kneeled at his side, did a cursory examination, and said, "He's alive but completely unconscious. We must get him to the bridge, now, so I can thoroughly examine him."

Scanning about for any attacking creatures and seeing none, the Doctor grabbed Rollie's shoulder and began tugging at him, then noticed Cassandra stood back reluctantly.

Vexed, the Doctor noticed her worried attention was focused on the writhing thing held tightly in Rollie's hand, then said, "Cassandra, even while unconscious, he does seem to have that horrid creepy-crawly in check for the moment. But the more we dawdle, the sooner that situation could change. Please, do lend a hand before it gets loose!"

Apologetically, she agreed and helped the Doctor drag Rollie the rest of the way into the *Cosmos*. From there, the Doctor closed the door and retrieved a folded canvas bag from a nearby compartment and placed it over the slug-like creature, covering it and Rollie's hand entirely, then tied it closed. Once done with that, he turned Rollie over onto his back and gestured for Cassandra to help drag him as quickly, but also as gently, as possible over to the cravcap.

Back on the bridge, they took Rollie to the same area where the cerebro-enhancer was stored and placed him on a gurney which also doubled as an examination table. The Doctor made sure to lock it into an adjacent brace so it wouldn't roll away under the movement. Cassandra retreated slightly, giving the Doctor space to work, and watched as he retrieved what looked like a magnifying glass attached to a thin, metallic armature which unfolded from the wall as the Doctor brought it over to Rollie.

The Doctor said crisply, "Right, first things first. We'll soon find out exactly what our little friend here is," as he untied the twitching canvas bag and swiftly pulled it from Rollie's hand, causing Cassandra to flinch slightly at sight of the repulsive creature again.

The Doctor hovered the magnifying glass over the thing and pressed a button on the glass's rim. Instantly, the instrument became an ex-ray machine, showing the internal structure of the twisting creature. Twice, the Doctor passed the glass over its body, the first time rapidly, the second time slowly.

Once finished with the second pass, the Doctor switched off the glass and said in a satisfied manner, "Excellent."

"What is?"

The Doctor turned to Cassandra. "The creature, my dear. I've encountered a vaguely similar mollusk life form in the Eridani star system." He then turned back to Rollie's hand, studied the creature briefly, as if deciding a chess move, then hovered his index finger just above a particular spot behind one of the creature's eyestalks and, once certain, shot it down without further delay, applying a brief, but productive, pressure. Immediately, the creature stopped moving.

Startled, Cassandra said, "Did you kill it?"

"Hardly, my dear. I could have done that easily enough by taking the barbaric route of stabbing it with a scalpel or spraying it with a bit of sodium sulfuride in order to melt it away. No, essentially, what I did was momentarily paralyze its nervous system, primitive as it is."

"Just by touching it with your finger?"

The Doctor held up the finger he used and said, "Exactly. Martian aikido, my dear. Devastatingly effective, but not deadly." He then turned back to Rollie and applied pressure to a particular spot on his right wrist, causing his fingers to relax and release the creature, letting it fall stiffly to the table.

As Cassandra watched the Doctor place the now paralyzed thing in a large jar and set it aside for later study, she said distractedly, "Mars, I remember reading about Mars during my school years."

"I'm sure you did, in historical records no doubt, since it was destroyed long before your time. Odd that such a peaceful form of defensive martial art was invented on such a warlike planet."

The Doctor then went around to a cabinet and withdrew several antiseptic cloths, then returned to Rollie and began wiping the blood from his face. After a moment, he held out a cloth to Cassandra and said, "You can begin by removing what's left of his shirt and cleaning his torso and arms."

She promptly came over and pulled away the fragments of shirt that still remained, then started meticulously wiping away the blood.

Seeing this, the Doctor said sharply, "You don't have to be so precise. The cloth is antiseptic, and we haven't much time to waste. Fall to, my dear, fall to!"

Applying herself more vigorously, she began to see that the wounds weren't as bad as she had previously perceived. Realizing this, she made short time of clearing the blood away, then paused, and addressed the Doctor inquisitively. "If his wounds aren't all that severe, they wouldn't have been enough to make him unconscious, would they? There does seem to be a lot of blood, but not enough to do harm, and now that the wounds have been cleared, they seem to be little more the small needle punctures."

Bent over, examining Rollie's shoulder, the Doctor said, "Very observant of you, Cassandra, and quite correct." Then he straightened and held up surgical forceps which contained within their clasp one of the small Venus flytraps they had seen earlier on the attacking vine. "And this little devil may clarify the situation."

He brought out the omnilyzer again, turned it on, and used it to gently scoop out a small sample of viscous fluid from between the plant's clamping, bristly petals. After a moment, he said, "Aha. Here we are."

"What does it say?"

"Oddly enough, this organism is genetically similar to Earth's own mandragora plant."

"Why is that odd?"

"Because, one, it's more morphologically similar to the Venus flytrap than the mandragora and, two, it's from an entirely different planet in an entirely different galaxy."

Cassandra crossed her arms and said, "That is perplexing." She thought for a moment, then said, "So, in what way is it genetically similar to the mandragora plant?"

Doctor Omega looked at the omnilyzer again and explained its readings. "It has a similar alkaloid output; that is, it produces a toxin which creates symptoms similar to atropine poisoning, but, which seems to be weaker in its detrimental effects. I would guess, the worst it can do is induce short-term unconsciousness and, possibly, hallucinations."

"And there it is. I told you we were hallucinating!"

"There's one small problem with your theory. You and I haven't been bitten by that nasty thing."

"True, but couldn't the atmosphere of this whole planet be saturated with the toxin?"

"It is possible, but it's not likely." The Doctor waved his hands dismissively and said, "Why must you run off into fruitless conjecture? Let's deal with things as they are, not as we fantasize them to be."

Cassandra said modestly, "Well, from what I've seen, things can get pretty fantastic."

The Doctor smiled. "I understand, my dear, but we must keep a level head about this." He then turned back to Rollie, passed the examination glass over him, and finally said, "All indications are he's fine, other than for these minor wounds. I'm going to give him a mild stimulant, which should counteract the dulling effects of the toxin and gradually bring him around in the next few minutes."

Cassandra shook her head in agreement and waited for the Doctor to request her assistance. She didn't have to wait long.

Within seconds, Rollie's eyes fluttered open, and he sat up, straight as a rail, with eyes shockingly wide, as he shrieked in terror, as if suddenly waking from a horrifying nightmare. His scarred hands covered his equally scarred face as he screamed, "Help me! Please, help me! I can't stop it!"

His breathing began to calm, and his hands began to lower, as the Doctor placed his arm around his shoulders in a show of comfort; the Doctor said, "We're here, my boy. It's me, the Doctor, and Cassandra is just over there." The Doctor moved his head, indicating his desire that Cassandra shift to the other side of Rollie and provide support if he should happen to pass out again.

She did as requested, but Rollie sluggishly bobbed his head and said dreamily, "Yes, the Doctor. I need help." Then, he stopped and became sharply focused. "The Doctor!" Rollie turned to him and grasped him by the shoulders. "The Doctor! It's you!"

Startled, the Doctor said, "Yes, it *is* me! Who else would it be?"

Rollie sagged slightly, releasing the Doctor, and said distractedly, "Yes, yes. It must be you." He ran a hand through his hair and said, "I don't understand. What happened?"

Cassandra leaned in and said, "You were attacked by that vine creature, and it dragged you away."

Rollie faltered for a moment, then became lucid again and said, "Yes, I remember now." Puzzled, he said, "But, how did I get *here*, and where's my shirt? And what are all these scars on my hands?"

The Doctor said, "The scars are from the plant bites. They're not deadly, and they'll heal relatively quickly. Somehow, you got away from that creature and made your way back to the *Cosmos*." Then, he paused and laughed slightly. "Your shirt, well, that was shredded by that thing, and what was left we had to remove in order to clean your wounds."

At ease now, Rollie said, "Alright. That makes sense." With an air of tired whimsy, he looked at both of them and said, "I don't want to be too demanding, but can I get a shirt, please?"

Set into motion, Cassandra said, "Oh, certainly," as she headed to the gravcap, and Rollie's room down below, in order to retrieve appropriate clothing.

While away, Rollie said carefully, "Doctor, there's something I need to talk to you about."

Sensing the gravity in Rollie's voice, he said devotedly, "Of course, Rollie. You can talk to me about anything."

Rollie dithered for a moment, then finally said, "I don't want you to think I'm crazy, but...," Then, he stopped.

"But what?"

"Well, I just hate saying it."

"Rollie, my boy, just say it."

"Alright. Here it is. After I killed that thing out there, that vine creature, and got away from it, everything went a little blurry, and I could've sworn I heard a voice in my head. No, not a voice, exactly; more like a presence. It wasn't like anything I'd heard or felt before. And it was pleading desperately for help."

"Pleading for help? Help from whom?"

"From you, Doctor. It desperately needed *your* help, specifically."

"Help with what?"

"That's just it. I don't know. It was all so hazy and unclear at that point."

Cassandra returned with a shirt and said genially as she handed it to him, "I didn't think a replacement ascot would be necessary right now."

Rollie smiled warmly and put the shirt on. "Thanks. I might survive without it."

Following the brief pleasantries, the Doctor said, "I do have one question, though."

Rollie rose from the examination table, began tucking his shirt in, and said, "And that is?"

"Our rather large mollusk over there, how did you come upon it?"

Rollie turned and looked at the jar containing the creature he had been holding. It was beginning to twitch back to life again. Rollie diverted his attention to his right hand and said distantly, "Yes. I vaguely remember. The vine thing, its body was nothing but a mass of condensed, writhing creepers and thousands of small, working mouths. And, burrowed deep into the beast was that thing." Rollie leaned against the table and said, "It was hideous. For some reason, I felt the overpowering urge to rip it from its roots, so I did. Everything after is a blank."

"Then came the presence you spoke of?"

"Yes, somewhere in there. It started with that urge, then it overcame me with that tremendous despair again."

The Doctor stroked his chin and said, "Fascinating." He looked at the other two and said, "Now that we have Rollie back, I do believe it's time we attempted contact with our host."

Cassandra and Rollie moved to the side as the Doctor returned the table to its wall niche. He then suggested the two settle themselves onto the nearby George II wingchair as he attempted his experiment. He removed the cerebro-enhancer from its storage area, put it on the adjacent laboratory workbench, and connected it to a mini-A/V display, which immediately projected a virtual screen, similar to the larger holovid, above the workbench. On a small keyboard, he typed in a code which connected the A/V unit to the first antenna.

Once the connection was confirmed, the Doctor said, "Here we go." He then pressed a button which sent out a single test pulse to the first antenna then waited for the pulse to bounce back, once it made its trip to the second antenna and into the interior brain tissue. After only a few seconds, the pulse was received. The Doctor exhaled happily and said, "It worked! My cerebro-enhancer received the return signal!"

Cassandra said, "That's great! What did it say?"

"Nothing yet. We've only established a connection, letting our host know we're ready to communicate. How long it takes him to respond, I can't tell. It could be a bit, you know. The larger an organism, the slower its neural activity usually is."

Before the Doctor could say anything else, the virtual screen began to flicker. A weak popping sound occurred, followed by several sparks. The sparks increased as a bulge appeared in the center of the virtual screen. Worried, The Doctor ran his fingers across the keyboard, hoping to stop the flying sparks, but found he couldn't.

Realizing the reaction had taken on a life of its own, he backed away, stepping closer to his companions, putting ample distance between himself and the virtual projection, which had quickly gotten bigger and was extending at least a foot from its origin now, and forming a tumorous knob at the end closest to them.

The Doctor said, "My, I wasn't expecting this." Concerned now, he joined Rollie and Cassandra as they huddled together and backed further away.

An oppressive sense of despair filled the room, with Cassandra being the first to perceive it. Rollie glanced at her. "I feel too," he said knowingly.

Cassandra moved in closer to the other two and said, "What's going on, Doctor?"

Blinking against the sparking lights, he said, "If I were to guess, I would say that our host is manifesting himself again."

At that moment, there was a bright flash, causing the three to shield their eyes. Just as abruptly, the light faded, allowing the Doctor and his companions to slowly lower their hands.

Blinking away the remnants of the sparking light, they clearly saw standing before them a fully developed human, but one that was menacing in nature and eerily spectral.

# CHAPTER IX

However semi-transparent and intangible the entity appeared to be, it was quite obvious to the Doctor and his companions that it was still capable of inflicting some kind of force upon them, or at least it very much felt that way to them at this moment. And, remembering their recent encounters with the earlier monsters, that feeling was amplified even more.

The Doctor turned his attention away from his worried companions and focused on the apparition. Despite being diaphanous, he could see clearly that the projection was that of a humanoid male, large in stature – *nearly seven feet tall*, he thought disquietingly – with a significantly regal disposition. Accentuating the impressive composure was a shock of lions-mane hair, a luxuriant beard and mustache, and opulent robes, trimmed in gold and blue designs.

The phantom sparked again, seeming to electronically glitch, the Doctor observed, before it began to shimmer in and out of focus. The Doctor leaned back to his companions and said over his shoulder, "It seems to be phase modulating, trying to lock on to the correct frequency, if you will." Then, he turned his full attention back to the phantom. "Fascinating," he said with a twinkle in his eyes. "Absolutely fascinating."

"That it is," Rollie said, surprised, as they all were, by their new visitor's strikingly human form. "None of the other boogeymen we've encountered so far looked anything like a human, except in general shape, so why this one now?"

"Concerning our astral friends, I would guess it's due to proximity and strength of the relay signal being directly pulsed into the brain's communication tissue. This may be the brain's actual complete form or, at least, how it perceives itself," the Doctor said, lost in thought.

Cassandra said, "Actual form? Isn't this giant brain we're on its actual form? If not, where's it keeping this body it's projecting at us, then?"

The Doctor said brightly, "I'm not sure. This being could be dimensionally bisected, its body in its own dimension and its brain stuck here in ours, with both still connected on a psychokinetic level. Or, it could be a vast, formless, cosmic entity in our own dimension attempting to materialize a physical form for itself, perhaps in order to make itself more amenable to us. As of now, though, I just don't know."

Cassandra seemed unsatisfied by his answer as she said, "Well, if we don't know exactly what it is, what do we do with it, then?"

The Doctor pondered this for a moment, then said, "Nothing."

"Nothing," Cassandra said doubtfully.

"Yes, nothing. Frankly, there's nothing we can do right now. This particular incarnation seems to be calibrating itself, attempting to fix itself to this specific spatial window. It seems to be exhibiting a stronger, more directed, intent than our previous visitors."

"In other words, it's tuning in to the right frequency so it can communicate with us," Rollie said alertly.

"Splendid," the Doctor said enthusiastically. "Splendid! Rollie, you're surprising me more and more!" Turning his attention back to the ghostly vision, he said, "Considering its progress, stabilization shouldn't take much longer now, then we'll finally get to the bottom of all of this."

With their conversation ended, they fell into a silence that was tinged with apprehension. While they worked to hide their stress, the Doctor could see on his companion's faces the strain they were under. The odd situation they were in, and the pressure which came with it, were taking their toll, even on Cassandra, who had encountered far more of this type of thing than Rollie. Her fragility was understandable, though, considering she had mid-level empathic abilities, but Rollie holding together so well, and seemingly thriving, was surprising.

The seconds seemed to crawl by until, at last, a final spark issued from the shimmering image. But, with that final spark, the pervasive feeling of ominous dread intensified, wrapping the Doctor and his companions in a chilling unease. Now they noticed the figure settling into a steadier electronic glitchiness which repeated the same, brief movements over and over again.

A disturbance beyond the dread and glitchiness began to scratch itself into existence, a muffled sound which gradually became coherently tonal. It gave the Doctor the definite impression of hushed, indistinct whispers which, at first, seemed to be originating in his own head. He was correct to assume the others felt the same.

Startled, Rollie and Cassandra gestured questioningly as they looked at the Doctor. Overcoming the intense feeling of despair and melancholy enveloping them, Rollie glanced about and said, "What's that noise, Doctor? Where's it coming from?"

"It sounds like a voice, my boy. And, the best guess is, it's coming from our friend here."

"But his lips aren't moving!"

"They don't need to. Remember; this is just a visual manifestation; it has no physical embodiment."

Just as Rollie was about to blurt out the impossibility of the situation, he caught himself, a look of comprehension brightening his face. He pointed at the Doctor knowingly. "The Medusa shield!"

Without taking his intense focus away from the projected figure, the Doctor said, "Correct, my boy."

Just then, all three began to acknowledge a vague discomfort, a tingling sensation coming from behind, as if a slight pressure were pushing against their backs, drawing their attention. With this, the Doctor gave Rollie a directed glance, at which time, Rollie knowingly turned and rushed to the other side of the bridge. Returning quickly with the shield, he placed it at an angle against the table near the holographic giant, then briskly rejoined the others.

They waited eagerly for the giant to speak now, but it remained frustratingly resolute in its detachment and repeated misfiring. The mumbles continued, but they were no more coherent than before.

The Doctor tapped his chin. "Interesting."

Cassandra looked at him curiously. "What is?"

"He's not talking. Or at least, he's not articulating."

Rollie puffed irritably, "If you ask me, someone not doing something isn't terribly interesting."

The Doctor stopped tapping his chin. "In this case, I think it is, precisely because it's disconcerting."

Rollie's eyebrows rose up effortlessly, like two weightless balloons. "Well, you've got me there." Frustrated, he continued with a frown. "How do we get this thing to budge? Is there something wrong with the shield or the cerebro-enhancer?"

The Doctor abruptly turned to Rollie. "Unthinkable! How dare you even consider such a thing!"

Embarrassed, Rollie pulled back slightly as they all fell into an awkward silence, uncertain as to what to do next.

Seeing the bewilderment from the other two, the Doctor said with a sharp burst of confidence, "Right! This ought to do the trick," as he rushed over to the cerebro-enhancer.

Rollie shouted, "Doctor, what are you doing?"

Dashing directly through the holographic giant, the Doctor arrived at the device, then turned and said with gusto, "Knocking some sense into this obstinate thing, that's what!"

"But, you said it was unthinkable to even *think* there was something wrong with it," Cassandra innocently pointed out.

Again, the Doctor faced the device. Quickly formulating a way out of his self-imposed contradiction, he said cryptically, "True. But the problem isn't with the cerebro-enhancer. It's with the signal." Then, he gave it a good smack on the side. That done, he promptly returned to the others and said with anticipation as he rubbed his hands together, "Right, here we go."

In reply, the lights, along with all the systems of the *Cosmos*, shut down with a mechanical rasping sound similar to that of a 19th century phonograph on its last spring. Realizing he would see nothing in the darkness, Rollie looked about anyway and saw exactly that, then asked only half-mockingly, "Where, exactly, *have* we gone, Doctor?"

In the pitch-blackness, Rollie couldn't see the Doctor grimacing at his lighthearted sarcasm, but he could definitely hear it in his answer. "Nowhere, Rollie. We're still on the bridge."

"Oh, right," Rollie said sheepishly.

Drawing his attention back to the matter at hand, the Doctor said distractedly, "Now, where exactly is that pesky fuse box? I don't remember where I placed it after the renovations." Lost in thought, the Doctor didn't notice the slight glow which began to appear in the room.

Never really being lost in thought, Rollie *did* notice and pointed it out. "Hey, look at that." While he still couldn't see her, he could feel Cassandra next to him as she said, "Yes. Something's happening."

Breaking his concentration, the Doctor sputtered, "What? What's happening?"

"There's a glow," Rollie said.

"What? A glow? Where?"

Cassandra spoke hurriedly. "Everywhere! Just look!"

Presently, the Doctor could narrowly make out her shrugging silhouette behind him as he said in a surprised tone, "Yes, yes. You're quite correct." Momentarily, the mechanical rasping sound returned, growing in pitch, accompanied by the lights and the rest of the electrical systems of the *Cosmos*. "Ah, there we go. I told you. It just needed a little coaxing," he said with a satisfied tone.

By the time he finished, the mechanical rasping had stopped, and the lights were back on in full force; at once he could see Rollie and Cassandra looking timidly passed him, in the direction of the cerebro-enhancer. Puzzled, he turned and saw the giant was now in a slightly different stance; he was no longer glitching, and he had the stern look of a wrathful, imperious deity right out of the darkest recesses of mythology.

The Doctor was expecting something of this kind to happen, yet it still stunned him when it did. The proximity, size, and the palpable domineering energy emanating from the entity projected before them now as a hologram was overwhelming, and it somehow made one slightly nauseous, especially when combined with the still present sense of despair which had never really gone, even though it had lost some of its intensity.

Admittedly overwhelmed to a limited extent, the Doctor considered it wise to approach the being discreetly. With faint deference, he said, "Yes, well, this is interesting. You can move now, eh?"

In a reply which knocked the three back a shade, a thunderous voice boomed from the shield as the giant's lips moved. "You are Doctor Omega, I presume?"

# CHAPTER X

The Doctor and his companions glanced at one another nervously as he stammered in surprise, "Why, yes, I am." Regaining a bit of composure, the Doctor absentmindedly held out his hand to the hologram and said with breezy pleasantness, "Nice to meet you!"

The giant simply folded his huge arms and glowered with what the Doctor clearly understood to be an unpleasant mixture of contempt and incredulity. Shaking off the unpleasant feeling, the Doctor gathered himself and addressed the giant with a more confident tone. "I seem to be at a disadvantage, sir. You know who I am, but I do not know you. Since we are guests here, would you mind introducing yourself?"

Immediately, a projected wave of concentrated emotion washed through the Doctor and his companions, giving them the distorted impression they had shrunk to microscopic, inconsequential levels before an all-powerful god. The wave faded shortly after, but it left behind an intentionally distinct feeling of immense insignificance.

Rollie leaned into the Doctor and whispered, "He seems quite antagonistic, which tells me he's not the one who brought us here. As a matter of fact, that tells me he's probably trying to keep us away from whomever did bring us here."

Cassandra tapped Rollie on the shoulder and said sincerely, "I don't think you need to whisper. Considering this being's immense power, I'm sure he can hear you at any decibel level, and he may even be able to read your mind, although I'm not sure about that one."

Rollie stared into her eyes for a moment then said without pretense, "You know, you're right." Hesitantly, he moved his gaze to the Doctor and said in a normal tone as he gestured at the hologram, "What are we going to do about Goliath here? He's obviously trying to block us from something."

In response, the Doctor furrowed his brow and said, "After a fashion, Rollie, I do believe you're correct."

"After a fashion? How so?"

"Well, first of all, I don't believe he can read our minds, otherwise he would be responding to things we haven't expressed or done yet but were actually considering."

Rollie pondered this and said, "Sounds reasonable. Unless he *can* read minds, and he's simply outmaneuvering us."

The Doctor cocked an eyebrow at him. "My boy, you're becoming far too clever for your own good. Keep it up; it may come in handy." He winked at Cassandra, and his face brightened, then he lightly returned to his explanation. "Secondly, he may not be able to read our minds," he emphasized, "but he does, obviously, have the power to influence us in uncomfortable ways, as we've already seen. Related to that, he also seems to be able to sense our emotions, judging from the influences I just mentioned."

Cassandra piped in waggishly. "I'll say he can."

"And, lastly, he definitely has a passion for pageantry which, along with everything else, indicates he's hiding something. But the fact he's likely the one who brought us here, and the fact he hasn't vaporized us yet, indicates one other very important thing."

"And, what's that," Cassandra asked.

"He's afraid."

Rollie gawked. "Afraid! Him? You must be joking. Afraid of what?"

The Doctor patiently replied, "Let me see if I can find out," as he signaled to Rollie that he was going to try another approach. He directed his attention back to the giant and presented a more docile bearing as he spoke. "Your High Lordship and Grace. It is with great honor I come before your Infinite Majesty. Your call has been zealously heeded by your humble servants. How may we assist you, Your Magnificence?"

For good measure, he tossed in a subtle curtsy which was more discreetly acerbic than genuine. He hoped Rollie and Cassandra, if they were aware of this, would be able to keep the emotional response to that awareness tamped down and inaccessible to their host's emotional probings.

The air around them became malicious and cold, like the tips of a thousand penetrating needles, before erupting into a rush of boiling fury. The three, once again, were engulfed by a flood of emotions which were clearly not their own as that imperial voice roared at them once more.

"YOU DARE MOCK ME?"

The trio huddled together in uncharacteristic trepidation, experiencing a maelstrom of fear, anger, and most importantly, overwhelming despair being projected at them. With profound willpower, the Doctor was the first to get control of himself and break free from the crippling entanglement. The others, he saw, were less successful.

Out of options, he turned to the giant and, with his own true anger coming to the surface, he waved his fist at the hologram and shouted, "Stop this madness! For the love of humanity, stop! My companions can't tolerate this assault! Don't you understand? They'll die if you keep this up!"

The giant's features softened slightly. "Humanity? Madness?" His eyes filled with realization as his voice trailed off. "How did I come to this, me of all beings? How did I allow my emotions to overcome my intellect?"

The Doctor looked at the giant with hopefulness as he said coaxingly, "Yes, that's it. You, of all beings. Maybe if you tell me who you are, I can help you figure out how you came to this. Yes?"

The giant, steadying himself, slowly became aware of the Doctor again. The emotional storm now passed for Rollie and Cassandra, and they recovered as the giant said resolutely, "Yes. I remember now. Yes. I will tell you who I am, and you will help me."

"That is correct. I will help you if you just tell me who you are."

The giant exhaled as if to release a lifetime of built-up tension and said, "I am... *Mentacron*."

The Doctor's eyes widened, but he said nothing.

Puzzled, Rollie's fingers wrapped around the Doctor's shoulder. "Doctor? What's wrong? Doctor?"

The Doctor blinked and said in a confused fashion, "That's not right at all." Then, he became more focused and said emphatically, "Well, this can't be. This won't do, not at all."

"What won't do," Cassandra asked from behind.

The Doctor fanned his hands and said, "This can't possibly be Mentacron."

"And, why not?"

"Because Mentacron is only a figure in mythology. And, besides, the myth says he disappeared generations ago, never to be heard from again. If this were true, he would have lived several times the average lifespan by now."

Rollie let go of the Doctor's shoulder. "Okay, where did this Mentacron person disappear?"

"Every child knows that! Somewhere near the Phantasma Nebula. As a matter of fact, the more fantastically inclined have conjectured that it was Mentacron's vanishing which caused the so-called hauntings there in the first place."

Rollie looked at him knowingly. "Which nebula, again?"

"The Phanasma Neb...." The Doctor continued sheepishly. "Oh, dear. This *is* the Phantasma Nebula, isn't it."

Rollie folded his arms. "Yes, it is."

Exasperated, the Doctor shot back. "Yes, but that doesn't mean he's Mentacron. He was just a mythological being, written about in fairy tales."

Rollie said, "That doesn't mean he wasn't actually alive at some point. The fairy tales had to start with some grain of truth."

The Doctor was about to partially concede that issue when, again, he felt a wisp of overwhelming sadness, only for the mood to dissolve away a moment later. He rubbed his forehead in confusion, then noticed the being calling himself Mentacron had completely vanished, apparently taking his black ferment with him.

"Oh, dear. I wasn't expecting that," he said with surprise.

Rollie stepped around him and stared at the place where the hologram had been. "Hey, look here; the cerebro-enhancer is off!"

His airy dismay replaced by an unexpected curiosity, the Doctor came to Rollie's side, gazed at the device, and said clinically, "It would seem so."

Cassandra joined them and gave the Doctor a questioning look. "What do you make of it? Did he turn it off so he could escape?"

Carefully, the Doctor said, "Hardly. We can't possibly be a threat to him. I'm gathering the cerebro-enhancer has been off since the power went out, and the thing never came back on. I believe it was at that moment he was able to fully synthesize his essence into the neurophysical pattern we saw, thus self-actualizing his form."

Appropriately stupefied, Rollie probed. "And that means...?"

The Doctor unhesitatingly addressed both of his companions. "I'm guessing he's capable of manifesting and departing without the aid of our devices now."

With hands on hips, Cassandra asked, "Is that good or bad?"

"That's hard to say at the moment. But, if I were to guess, I would say it's good." The Doctor looked at their doubtful faces and clarified. "Think for a moment; he left on his own volition and without annihilating us, which is good, because it shows he doesn't see us as a threat. Furthermore, that also indicates he needs us. For what, though, I have no idea."

Puzzled, Rollie frowned, then addressed the Doctor's points. "Let's say you're correct. Why would he leave at all, then? Why wouldn't he just stay and tell us what he needed so we can be done with it and go home?"

"As I said before, I think he's afraid." The Doctor saw the continued skepticism in Rollie's expression and almost took it as a challenge, even though he knew it wasn't meant to be. Rollie's reaction vaguely reminded him of an annoyingly precocious and overly inquisitive child from his youth; namely, himself.

Dryly, the Doctor smiled inwardly at the thought and continued. "Consider the predominant emotions he's been projecting at us. Despair and sadness, with a touch of anger here and there. That indicates a sense of hopelessness about something he has no power over, something which threatens him, perhaps."

"What could possibly threaten *him*?"

"Well, taking into account Mentacron's nearly godlike abilities, I would have to say an immensely powerful being of some sort." He finished ominously, "Someone quite terrible, I would assume."

Surprised, Rollie tilted his head slightly. "So, you believe he *is* Mentacron, now?"

"Taking your arguments into account, and my own observations, I would say the possibility is quite high that this is, in fact, *the* Mentacron. Which, to be honest, takes my breath away."

Cassandra stepped closer. "But, why? He's got to be something pretty special to impress you, Doctor."

"That he is."

Rollie asked, "Exactly who is this Mentacron, anyway? How do you know him?"

The Doctor said introspectively, "I don't know him personally, or at least I didn't until recently. Oh, but I know *of* him, and it seems like I always have."

With curiosity piqued, the Doctor's companions encouraged him to resume.

"As I've previously stated, Mentacron holds a high place for myself and many others in the universe. In our mythological tales, he was a towering giant of intellectual and scientific pursuit; so much so, he was depicted as giving his entire life over to scholarship and the accumulation of knowledge. Not for himself, of course, but for the benefit of all Creation. Erudition, the life of the mind, was his whole purpose for being. The Mentacron stories showed how any problem could be overcome if one were simply to apply enough mental effort." The Doctor broke from his revere and addressed his companions soberly. "The problem, though, is if this truly is Mentacron, then those stories were all lies."

Shocked, the other two replied in near unison. "What are you talking about?"

Bleakly, the Doctor said, "The Mentacron of the stories, and I would presume of actual history, would never be in despair; he would never be confronted by a problem he couldn't solve. His intellect was too great for that."

Cassandra gently touched his arm. "Perhaps he does have a solution to his problem."

"Why would he bring us here, then?"

Rollie said, "He said earlier he wanted your help."

The Doctor brightened slightly. "That is true. But how could we help him? If he's threatened by something, it has to be at least as powerful as he is, which means we're little more than insects compared to that threat, whatever it is!"

Rollie rubbed the back of his neck. "It is rather perplexing, isn't it?"

The Doctor placed his hands amiably on his companion's shoulders and turned them toward the control section of the bridge. "That it is, my boy. This is something we need to ponder over, long and hard. And I know just the thing to get our little gray cells moving. Another cup of Tellurian leechweed tea!"

Rollie's knees buckled a little at mention of the horrific concoction, but he did a fairly good job of maintaining his composure as they headed to the control panel, the other two grinning all the way at his expense.

After heartily downing his second cup of tea while seated at the console, the Doctor said, "Rollie, my dear boy, you haven't even touched yours."

Rollie, standing off to the side, grimaced. "Uh, yes, well. I will."

"But you can't now. It's cold. It's jellified. Tellurian leechweed is undrinkable when it gets cold. You know that."

Rollie said under his breath, "It's undrinkable before it gets cold, too."

The Doctor looked at him pleasantly as he poured a third cup for himself. "What was that?"

Rollie jolted to attention. "Yes, that's true. It's jelly when it gets cold. I was planning on eating it later, with a spoon." Noticing the Doctor didn't seem convinced of that one, Rollie changed his excuse. "Come to think of it, Tellurian leechweed is a bit too strong for me. Tends to give me an upset stomach."

The Doctor smiled coyly as he took a sip from his third cup of tea. "Ah! Well, we don't want you having a tummy ache, now do we."

Rollie rubbed his abdomen and said dubiously, "No. That wouldn't be good. Not in the midst of this mess."

Cassandra, sitting in the console chair next to the Doctor, interrupted. "Are you referring to the tea or the Mentacron situation?"

With the faint prod from Cassandra, the other two stopped the playful banter. The Doctor put his empty cup down and looked at her approvingly. "So, my dear, what's your take on 'The Mentacron Situation,' as you put it?"

She thought for a moment, then said, "We have to get him back here. Without that first step, there's little we can do."

"How do you suggest we do that?"

Uncertain, she looked to Rollie for support.

Feeling stuck, he finally said, "We could call him."

Amused, the Doctor said, "I doubt he has a phone."

Rollie sighed and said, "Thank you, Doctor, for your mockery, but that's not what I meant, and you know it."

"Yes, you are correct. I apologize." The Doctor looked sheepish for a moment.

"What I meant was, we can use the relay system and the cerebro-enhancer to send out a signal again. It worked the first time."

"That is a good point, but I'm not sure it will work again. He seems to be long past needing our equipment to materialize at this point, which also means he can probably hear our conversations right now. That being the case, he probably already knows we need him back here. For goodness' sake, he knew it before he vanished."

"True. He's the one who brought us here in the first place."

"Exactly. What we're dealing with here isn't a matter of the inability to make contact. Our problem is with understanding. He's afraid, and we have to alleviate that fear. The question is, how do we go about doing that?"

Cautiously thinking through the idea, Rollie said slowly, "Well, in a way, I don't think we have to. I mean, he brought us here, right? He obviously knew of us – or at least of you, Doctor – right? So, bringing you here, he must have trusted you from the beginning, right?" Making a spontaneous decision, he abruptly stopped addressing the other two and began speaking to the ether. "See here, Mr. Mentacron. You must trust the Doctor. You've heard our conversation, and you know it's all true. If you want our help, you have to return and tell us what you want."

They waited for a moment, but nothing happened. Frustrated, Rollie threw up his hands and mockingly addressed the ether again. "Fine. Be childish. I find it quite funny Big Bad Mentacron is afraid. You're not so smart now, are you, you coward!"

Straight away, the group felt a wave of nausea which couldn't be accounted for by any reasonable means. Fighting through it, the Doctor said wryly, "That seems to have done the trick, Rollie."

With a look of queasiness spreading effortlessly across his face, Rollie said, "That it does, but now I wish it hadn't."

Cassandra, being empathically sensitive, appeared more distressed than the others when she said to Rollie, "You look as though you've just had a cup of Tellurian tea."

"You look like you just married Quish," Rollie said, sounding much sharper than he intended. Frowning, he apologized, and she accepted distractedly.

The sensation of nauseousness rapidly shifted to one of intense fear, jolting everyone psychologically, Cassandra in particular. "Doctor, I can't take much more of this. Can't you get Mentacron to stop this foolishness? Don't you have some way to block these psychic intrusions?"

Before Doctor Omega could answer, they all detected an elusive vibration in the floor of the bridge, and were immediately overtaken by a distinct impression of fear; this dread was promptly replaced by an unexpected feeling of overwhelming doom, which was so sudden and kaleidoscopic a shift in emotions, it made the Doctor and his companions noticeably unsteady. It was then the whole ship began to shake, at first subtly, then more vigorously.

The feeling of doom quickly vanished, leaving behind a tingling, light-headed bewilderment as the shaking intensified, accompanied by the familiar low rumble, which quickly escalated into a shriek of unrelenting despair before dissolving away. They all steadied themselves by leaning on the bridge console as Rollie asked the Doctor, "Is this what I think it is?"

"I believe so, my boy. Another brainquake, if you will. But, this time, we have a good idea who is doing the screaming!" After a moment, the quake subsided, and the group relaxed. Then, the Doctor said decisively, but with a tinge of worry, "Mentacron's brain has expanded again."

Rollie asked, "Do you think his little tantrum triggered it?"

"It's possible. But perhaps something else is going on here. What that is, though, I don't know." The Doctor scratched his forehead and said lightheartedly, "It seems I've been saying that a lot recently."

Before long, the red warning light on the console began to blink. Curious, they gazed at the holovid, which was now focused on the inner entrance to the *Cosmos*, and were surprised to see the door was wide open.

The Doctor's eyes glazed with shock. "This can't be!" After a brief moment of stunned silence, he concluded ominously, "It's not possible to break my baryonic code."

At that point, they noticed a shadowed figure out-side the *Cosmos*, just beyond the entrance and off to the side. And it was slowly making its way into the ship

.

# CHAPTER XI

At first, the figure was indefinite in shape and detail, but as it began its slow, tentative breach of the ship, its features became more distinct.

Cassandra shuddered as she watched an incredibly long, jointed, and terribly thin biological structure, black in color, leisurely project itself into the doorway and delicately wrap itself around the edge of the door frame. Two more followed, giving the impression of attenuated, spidery legs probing a web for captured, struggling prey. In an identical, unhurried fashion, three others came forth and grasped the opposing frame, making it evident these were the horribly elongated fingers of two monstrously large, spindly hands.

As the thing gradually pulled its hulking mass into the lower deck, its features became clearer. The arms, like the hands, were shiny-black in color, the skin tightly drawn across distended veins and narrow, lengthened bones. To Cassandra, they resembled rotted, worm-infested twigs.

She recoiled and said sickly, "It's horrid."

Rollie, still gaping at the holovid, said, "That it is. And we haven't even seen the whole thing yet. Look!"

As he spoke, what they could only presume was its head sluggishly came into view. It was roughly humanoid in appearance, but it was overly large and disfigured with doughy tumors of various sizes, giving it the quality of a wart-covered lump of moist flesh. What would have been a lower jaw on a human was, here, replaced by a mass of stunted, thickly swollen tongues, squirming with slow deliberation while secreting a greasy mucus.

The Doctor instantly recognized what he saw next; it was the same type of slug-like creature Rollie had brought back to the ship and which they had all seen nested in the heads of the previous beasts, with the two bulb-tipped stalks once again projecting out from the end of its body, presumably replacing the wretched host's original eyes. It was now obvious to the Doctor that this slug-like creature was some kind of homogeneous parasite, perhaps a grotesquely large amoeba of some sort capable of perfect division, of perfect replication, with all duplicates being capable of autonomous action at some basic level yet still being beholden to a larger, over-arching instinct. It was also obvious to him now that this mollusk-creature burrowed into the cranium of each alien being, replacing the host's central nervous system with its own. It must be so, he thought, otherwise there would be no need for such precise uniformity in the organisms he had seen.

With great effort, the monster pulled its vile bulk a little further into the lower deck, its bloated body dripping slime while its long, spidery fingers probed the walls and floor, almost blindly, like the tentacles of an octopus searching for food.

Once its appendages touched the gravcap door, a sudden change in its behavior became obvious; its probings became more insistent, as if it somehow knew this was the way to the bridge, and that was where its prey awaited it. With another mighty expenditure of energy, the beast pushed vigorously with its other hand, which was still behind it and up against the ship's interior wall near the outer door frame, forcing its fat, thickly-veined midsection to compress as it slid around the frame and into the lower deck, suddenly expanding again on the other side like a greased bag of gelatin.

As they watched the monster's moist, skeletal fingers desperately probe the gravcap door further, the Doctor said in an ambivalent tone, "Not to worry. I've locked the gravcap entrance from the control panel, here."

Cassandra took her eyes off of the repulsive thing and looked at the Doctor sketchily. "Through the same baryonic internal system that locked the outer exit? The system it has already broken through?"

The Doctor's brow furrowed. "Well, yes. That's about all I can do at the moment. I could shoot a high-intensity electrical pulse through the outer hull of the ship, but considering that thing is already partially inside, the pulse would carry through its body to the interior and right up to the bridge, knocking us unconscious or even possibly killing us! At least the lock will give us a little time to work something else out."

"Good point." Cassandra hesitantly turned her attention back to the holovid and instantly became queasy. The thing was just now pressing its lower half through the ship entrance with the help of two more spidery appendages wrapped about the door frame, appendages that were similar to its hands but slightly larger. From their positioning, they seemed to be attached to spindly legs which were multi-jointed and able to turn at what would be excruciating angles for a human, up above and behind its enormous, tumor-infested abdomen. It was now almost fully inside the ship.

As the Doctor and Cassandra watched the holovid intently, and with great trepidation, Rollie's face began to glaze over. He became distant as he listened to a faint whisper, a gossamer sound carried on a non-existent wind. Without knowing why, he thought it was the Doctor directing him to immediate action.

"Yes," he said in replay to the whisper, "Yes, it may work."

Surprised, the Doctor and Cassandra turned to him questioningly, but he ignored them and quickly moved forward with focused intent. Puzzled, the Doctor and Cassandra looked at one another then back at Rollie as he moved to the shield and took it up with both hands then headed toward the gravcap. Startled by this sudden burst of unexplained maneuver, they ran after Rollie and reached him just before he arrived at the gravcap door.

The Doctor grabbed his shoulder and pivoted him back toward them, saying, "Here, my boy! What are you doing?"

Still glazed, Rollie said dreamily, "What you told me to do." Then, he twisted free of the Doctor's hand and activated the gravcap door before they could stop him.

As the door slid open, the Doctor said, "But what do you mean? I told you nothing."

Without replying, Rollie resolutely stepped into the gravcap, with the other two following cluelessly behind.

After the door closed, the Doctor tried to communicate again. "Really, my boy, what *are* you doing? We can't go confront that thing with only a shield. We must think of something else." He tried to take the shield, but Rollie held it firmly and stared mildly at the gravcap door as if he were the only one there.

Then, Rollie said raptly, "Yes, I understand. Like this." He took a braced stance, as if he were preparing for battle, holding the shield up in front of himself, using the forearm straps to ensure a firm hold. Satisfied, he said grimly, "I'm ready."

The Doctor stepped in front of him and exclaimed, "Now, wait just a minute, Rollie. What is all this about?"

He slapped the wall to the side of the door, which suddenly stopped their descent. He wagged a finger at the door and said to Rollie, "We cannot confront this beast with only a shield! We must find another way! Don't you understand?"

Rollie held his stance like a statue as the gravcap finished its descent, startling the Doctor once it resumed its movement. Just before the door slid open, the Doctor and Cassandra, considering this their only option now, moved behind Rollie and hunched together for protection, desperately hoping he knew what he was doing.

When the door opened, one of the large, spidery hands instantly shot in and wrapped its repugnant fingers around the gravcap door frame. The moment it did this, Rollie countered with his own aggressive move forward, shoving the shield in front himself while simultaneously slamming the finer edge of the shield into the beast's gripping fingers, breaking their bony structures and sending the beast into a fit of blazing agony. It pulled back as Rollie pushed forward.

A dazzling radiance began to emanate from the shield as he forced the creature to retreat, inch by inch, until it was finally part way through the ship exit. The creature seemed stuck now, its bulk compressed by the door frame. It became more frantic as the radiance grew brighter with Rollie's every step. The gleam seemed to have quickly become some kind of vital force, discharging an undefinable living energy of its own.

Within moments of this change, the creature quivered and became sluggish. It tried desperately to look away, to escape, but with its massive bulk being compressed by the exit, it had nowhere to go. It quivered again, spasmed slightly, then stopped moving completely. The three watched as the monster's slimy flesh lost its suppleness. Its multitude of tongues stopped rippling about, and the eye stalks on the parasite in its skull ceased their wavy probings. An odd solidness crept over, and through, the beast. With that, the light from the shield blinked out, and Rollie relaxed.

Noticing the shift in atmosphere, the other two relaxed as well, with the Doctor saying in a surprised tone, "Well, Rollie, you did it! How in the world did you think of that?"

As if waking from a hypnotic sleep, Rollie looked curiously at the Doctor. "Think of what?"

The Doctor spread his hand toward the shield, which was now leaning quietly against Rollie's leg. "Why, that! How did you know it could do that. I didn't even know it was capable of that sort of thing."

Rollie glanced down blankly at the shield and said simply, "You told me."

"No, no I didn't. I had no idea the shield actually had the fossilizing powers of the mythological Medusa. I knew it could do other remarkable things, but not that."

Still slightly detached, Rollie shrugged, but offered no further explanation, not because of obstinance, but because he *had* no explanation. Or at least none for which he had a clear understanding yet, although there was something obscure tickling at the back of his mind.

The Doctor stroked his chin and grimaced. "Yes, well, we'll discuss this later." Then, he gestured toward the ossified beast blocking the main door of the *Cosmos* and said, "We must do something with this first." They gathered up a few laser hammers from the utility room and went to work turning the petrified creature into rubble which they then transferred to the outside of the ship.

Once they finished and the door was closed, the Doctor removed a panel and disconnected a couple of wires, making it impossible for the door to open again until the wires were restored. Replacing the panel, he rubbed his hands together in a satisfied manner, returned the laser hammers to the utility room, and led the others back to the bridge, taking the shield with them.

Leaving the gravcap, Doctor Omega hung the shield back in its original location, directly opposite the gravcap door, saying, "I don't think we'll be needing this for now, considering Mentacron seems to have developed the ability to manifest and communicate without our equipment." Then, he ushered the others back to the control panel, where he had them take a seat while he stood nearby and thought through the situation. After several moments, he addressed Rollie. "You say I told you what to do?"

"Well, I thought it was you. Or maybe not. There was a voice in my head. No! Not a voice, really. It was a whisper, very faint. Now that you mention it, maybe not even that. It was more like a progression of ideas that, together, made up a kind of wordless command, or series of commands. It was odd; I was aware of everything, but at the same time, it seemed a little like a dream."

The Doctor tapped his chin. "This is starting to make some sense, now."

"How's that," Cassandra asked.

"It was a psychic command, or at least a series of instructions. Who, exactly, has been tapping into our minds recently?"

Cassandra said openly, "Mentacron."

"Exactly!"

Confused, she asked, "But why would Mentacron give Rollie instructions on how to stop the very thing he sent to kill us, the thing he already controls?"

"That, my dear, is a good question. Another is, if he really does want our help with whatever his predicament is, why did he send any of those monsters to harm us in the first place?"

Instantly, everyone felt a rush of unchecked emotion, but not like before. This felt cleansing in a way, and almost refreshing. A look of surprise spread across the Doctor's face. "Why, I think our visitor is returning!"

They felt a familiar tingle in the air as a distinct charge began to spark on the other side of the console where the holovid was currently positioned. A large humanoid figure, presumably that of Mentacron, began to take shape, forming out of the naturally occurring energy particles within the room. Apprehensively, Cassandra and Rollie stood and joined the Doctor; the three stepped back a trifle even though they subconsciously knew the move gave them no real safety from any aggressive act the giant might choose to take.

Once materialized, Mentacron occupied a tremendous amount of space, enough to completely block the view of the holovid. His voice, although as commanding as before, now had a certain hollowness to it, which the Doctor could tell was derived from a tremendous struggle to maintain emotional balance. The words, which he addressed to Rollie, were also accompanied by a degree of humility which was lacking previously. "You were correct before. I'm being childish." His head lowered, almost imperceptibly. "I am a coward."

Awkwardly, Rollie said, "Well, maybe not a coward, exactly...."

The strained deference masking Mentacron's face did little to soften the cool pride in his eyes. "I do need the Doctor's help, and I have been experiencing uncustomary moments of doubt, but I will not accept your condemnation nor your pity."

The Doctor gently moved Rollie back as he stepped forward, addressing Mentacron. "We have no pity nor condemnation for you. How can we, if we have no idea what your problem is?" He hesitated, then continued carefully. "Would you mind telling me why you need my help? And why have you been sending creatures to harm us. but then instructing Rollie on how to stop them? Or were they not doing your bidding after all?"

"You are partly correct. You see, my diminishing psychological strength is a symptom of my illness."

The Doctor's face brightened with sudden awareness of a breakthrough. "Ah! Please elaborate."

"My grip on sanity is beginning to wane. In this deformed state, I have no limitations and, as a result, I'm losing control of everything, my humanity included!"

"What do you mean?"

"I mean, I've become a monster. No, I've become more than that."

Doctor Omega's face darkened slightly. "You mean a monster beyond just the physical form you possess now?"

"Yes. Not just in physical form. You see, this brain you are resting upon is all that remains of my incarnate being. I have become a vile aberration, a near deity, if you will, an unbridled power so immense that I will, if left unchecked, inevitably destroy the universe."

# CHAPTER XII

The Doctor read Mentacron's face and saw beneath the stoic demeanor a dark and calamitous psychology. It was apparent to him that Mentacron was under immense, incomprehensible pressure, a distress which would instantly obliterate the mind of a lesser being.

Mentacron continued. "In a way, I have been sending those alien monsters to attack you, to stop you, partly because of my own conscious selfishness, and partly because of my mounting lack of control. It's that mounting lack of control that holds sway, unleashing the latent, selfish impulse I've tried so desperately to suppress."

As he listened to the confession, a shadow passed over the Doctor's own face. Mentacron laid his entire history before them, hoping it would make them understand. He spoke of the vigorous search for knowledge in his youth and how that eventually became an all-consuming pursuit once he realized how it could help others. With this altruistic goal in mind, he spent the first part of his considerably long life searching, archiving, and assimilating mathematical and scientific concepts at a fantastic rate, soon outdistancing his own people's greatest minds. Forced to leave them behind and move out into the void, he found, in due course, other planetary systems with beings who also shared his passion and expertise. But, as time went on, his ability to acquire and assimilate knowledge increased at such an alarmingly rapid rate, the ideal of using that knowledge to help others gradually vanished into forgotten memory. Slowly but surely, he had learned all he could from others and, so, he began to naturally turn inward, probing concepts and ideas far beyond anything anyone else could dream of, devoting himself entirely to an abstract existence. Until one day, he discovered the Theta Sequence, the fundamental lifecode of the universe. A series of fractal equations closely related to, and hidden within, the Fibonacci Sequence.

With this last revelation, the Doctor blanched. Mentacron paused. Although he was a hologram, he was still able to sense his surroundings, and he knew that this key bit of information he had just given them would require a certain amount of time to be grasped.

Noticing the Doctor's concern, Rollie asked, "What is it, Doctor?"

"The Fibonacci Sequence, my dear boy," the Doctor said tensely. "Apparently, the Theta Sequence, the crux of all of this, is buried inside the Fibonacci Sequence!"

Rollie was mystified. "Alright, but what does that mean?"

The Doctor half turned to him. "The Fibonacci Sequence is a series of numbers; the sum of each number is the added total of the two previous numbers! Don't you see? It's an endless spiral; it's encoded into everything. And it manifests as the sub-quantum particles I told you about, the kirbyons, which are apparently directly connected to the Theta Sequence! It's intimately tied into the branch of discrete particle physics I've been uncovering and which makes possible quite a bit of the technology on the *Cosmos*."

Cassandra cut in. "Yes, that's right!" Then, she frowned. "But what does any of this mean? How does a series of numbers and equations have anything to do with, well, any of this?"

The Doctor thought for a moment, simultaneously piecing the data together himself for the first time while also trying to explain it to his companions. "As I said, the Fibonacci Sequence is the mathematical description of growth, even of life, if you will. Since that's the case, the Theta Sequence must be the bridging formula just below the Fibonacci numbers!" He rubbed his forehead and said absently, "How did I not see it before?"

"That's all well and good, Doctor, but what is it bridging to?"

The Doctor spread his hands. "Us. This. The material world!" The Doctor focused intensely for a moment, then said darkly, "Mentacron found a way to tap into the fundamental, secret language of the universe, the very source code that makes existence possible. Not only that, but he found that once it was applied through a mechanical interface, the growth became – unstoppable." He turned back sharply to Mentacron and asked in a half-accusatory tone, "That *is* correct, isn't it, sir?"

Mentacron looked at him with a delicate relief. His chin came forward slightly, bearing a subtle witness to the inconceivable guilt and mental strain he had been enduring for eons. Then, he said in a close sigh, giving the faint impression he had finally been set free and found someone who understood, "Yes."

Appeased, the Doctor relaxed. "Right. Now, we've hit the proverbial nail on the head."

Mentacron gathered himself and said, "Not quite. To be more precise, the Theta Sequence is simply the key which turned on the engine, the kirbyon accelerator which I had created to explore and, yes, *exploit*, this arcane, first physics. The product of that device is the Gamma Wave. *That* is the primordial lifeforce. And, once activated by mortal hands, it cannot be deactivated."

Rollie grimaced. "It looks like you've been tampering with something you never should have been tampering with."

Mentacron gave Rollie a steady look. "I know that now."

"Why didn't you know that before?"

"A blinding lack of wisdom. I was in pursuit of raw knowledge, ungoverned by humility; I didn't realize that fact until it was too late."

"But can't we just turn off the mechanical interface thingy you were talking about?"

"Turn off the kirbyon accelerator? No. It was absorbed into my system eons ago. Furthermore, I did try turning it off at one point, after I had already stepped into its radiation field, once my brain began to grow like a monstrous cancer; it was then I realized, to my horror, that once I activated the Gamma Wave, it could not be deactivated."

Cassandra said doubtfully, "So, you're saying you – or your brain, or whatever you are now – will just keep growing until you take up all the space in the universe?"

The Doctor gave her a disapproving look as Mentacron replied piercingly, "Do not provoke me!"

Immediately, the Doctor stepped in and tried to answer Cassandra. "No, it's not likely to happen that way. It's more likely that he will eventually consume a considerable portion of the universe before reaching a critical mass, at which point what's left of his physical being will simply dissolve away at the atomic level." He glanced at Mentacron, looking for approval. Mentacron nodded, then encouraged him to continue.

The Doctor looked back to Cassandra and proceeded carefully, unsure of this next theory. "However, his psyche, or he as a cosmic cloud of powerful intellect, will go on expanding, absorbing every consciousness he comes in contact with until there will be no sentient being left in the universe, other than himself." He glanced back at Mentacron and asked, "Yes?"

Sadly, Mentacron said, "This is correct."

After a moment of numb silence, Rollie spoke up. "How do you expect *us* to help *you*?"

Mentacron hesitated, knowing this next phase would be the most difficult for them to handle. Then, he said steadily, "The only way I can stop the death of the universe is by absorbing the mind of Doctor Omega."

# CHAPTER XIII

Rollie felt a rising tension within Cassandra as she impulsively clasped his arm. He touched her hand reassuringly, then gently pulled away and stepped around the Doctor, taking a protective stance in front of him. He addressed Mentacron firmly. "What do you mean when you say 'absorb' the Doctor's mind?"

The Doctor peeped around Rollie and said bluntly, "I think he means just that – absorb my mind and assimilate it into his own."

Rollie glanced back over his shoulder and regarded the Doctor's surprisingly poised expression, then asked "But wouldn't that kill you?"

The Doctor interlaced his fingers and said remotely, "I believe it would. Unfortunately."

"You can't really expect us to let that happen?"

"That may be a situation we might not be able to avoid."

Cassandra joined in. "You can't mean that!"

The Doctor turned to her and said in a fatherly way, "Consider our situation, my dear."

"I have, and your death isn't inevitable, as far as I'm concerned."

"For my sake, I hope it isn't!" The Doctor stepped around Rollie and addressed Mentacron. "And how do you propose to go about this mind absorption you've referred to? Will it result in my death?"

"Yes."

Stunned by Mentacron's frankness, the Doctor spluttered, "Yes, well, you don't have to be so definite about it."

Unmoved, Mentacron continued. "The procedure will require the use of an encephalopod, one of which you have over there." He gestured toward the area in which Rollie had been examined after his return to the ship. Nearby was the jar containing the large, squirming mollusk the Doctor had removed from Rollie's grasp during the examination.

Instantly, the Doctor realized the procedure to which Mentacron was alluding would necessitate the ingestion of his central nervous system by the encephalopod. From this, he correctly surmised that the encephalopds he had seen attached to the earlier monsters were simply duplicate extensions of Mentacron's own nervous system, and that by absorbing his brain, his own consciousness and intellect would forever be a part of Mentacron's, leaving his body behind as nothing more than a shambling, animated corpse totally subject to Mentacron's will.

He also correctly guessed that the alien zombies they had encountered up to that point, acted as antibodies, in a way, fighting off unwelcome intruders, which explained why he and his companions had been so aggressively attacked during Mentacron's moments of psychological weakness.

Putting the final pieces together, the Doctor concluded that the other creatures had been drawn into Mentacron's orbit, just as he and his companions had, with Mentacron hoping they possessed the scientific knowledge he needed to solve his problem. But, after absorbing their minds, he realized none had the intellectual capabilities he required. Once this became apparent, he chose to use them for another function and keep their cadavers as a legion of protective guards.

Presently, the Doctor gathered himself and asked, "So, you detected my kirbyon drive from all the way out here and realized I was the only one capable of understanding your predicament, am I right?"

"Yes. It appears, other than my own, your kirbyon experiment is the only other one in existence. And, therefore, you are my only hope. My ability to throttle the Gamma Wave is waning. It takes almost all of my attention, leaving no mental strength to find a way to stop it entirely. By joining your intellect with mine, I hope to put an end to this nightmare."

Rollie grabbed the Doctor's shoulder a little too firmly and said, "Really, you don't expect us to let you go through with this!"

The Doctor bit his lower lip and said, "I'm hoping I can find another way around it, but there might not be."

Cassandra looked pleadingly at him. "No, you can't do it!"

He gently took her hand and smiled dimly. "I'll do my best." He thought for a moment, then turned back to Mentacron. "And, what happens to my friends here? If I go through with it."

"I will guide the ship safely back to their planet. Or, I should say, *you and I* will safely guide it back to their planet."

"And, if the procedure fails?"

Without hesitating, Mentacron replied, "Then, the universe is doomed, and their safe return home becomes irrelevant."

Cassandra crossed her arms and said, "That's rather cold, isn't it?" Presently, she drew closer to Rollie, who had draped a comforting arm around her shoulders.

The Doctor asked, "Is there no way to do this without the total absorption of my brain?" It was then he noticed the beginnings of mounting stress on Mentacron's face.

Mentacron said testily, "None that I know of, otherwise I would have offered a different way."

The Doctor looked about hesitantly, then became somber. "This isn't good, not at all." Anticipating the rather brutal thoughts of his companions, he let them know, doing away with Mentacron would be impossible. "It's safe to assume our friend here has already tried that, most likely early on, before his cerebral growth got out of hand. If I were to guess, I would say he probably attempted it multiple times, only to be instantly revived by the unrelenting Gamma Wave." Unsettled, he shook his head. "The whole thing is so horrible, yet I still don't know if I can go through with the procedure, even though I know I must."

Mentacron burst through the indecision with a rumble. "We have to do it *now*! The Gamma Wave is reasserting itself!"

Both Rollie and Cassandra rebelled against Mentacron's demand and implored the Doctor to not cooperate with such a suicidal act, insisting that he and Mentacron could surely come up with an alternative solution without resorting to such a drastic measure.

After much prodding, and aggressive appeal to his natural desire to live, the Doctor came to a hurried decision. "I will not go through with this abominable demand! I think my companions are correct. If we just try, I know we can find an alternative approach which will stop the Gamma Wave."

Upon hearing this, Mentacron broke. His face contorted as a thunderous cry erupted from deep within his chest. Sparks began to fly from the hologram as he spread out his arms and a glowing orb appeared in his midsection. Within seconds, his image and cry shriveled down to a point, then vanished, leaving a fading crackling sound behind. The Doctor's companions huddled close to him as they all gazed about in shock.

The Doctor said, "That's not good."

Still close to the Doctor, Cassandra asked dryly, "You think so?"

He glowered slightly, and said in an even tone, "It isn't funny. All indications are, we're about to experience another brainquake. I just saw the stress in his face and, it seems, his recent disappearances tend to indicate an immediate loss of control over the Gamma Wave." He looked at both of them menacingly. "It should hit at any moment."

At that same second, the *Cosmos* began to shake. As a group, they moved over to the console and steadied themselves as the trembling from the brainquake intensified. The Doctor kept an eye on the gauges, making sure nothing went too far off normal calibration. Suddenly, there was a convulsive movement of the ship which caused them to almost lose their footing. The Doctor glanced at the stabilizing indicator, adjusted it slightly, and read the gauge again.

He said distractedly, "It seems something large has struck the *Cosmos*!" His gaze moved from the gauge to the holovid. "And, so it has. There it is."

His companions followed his line of vision. Rollie said, "What is it? I don't see anything other than some yellowish substance filling the screen."

While working various switches, the Doctor said, "It does seem that way, doesn't it? Let's get a look at it from another angle." He recalibrated the holovid sensors and picked up a view of the ship from several feet away, from an objective vantage point.

What they saw stunned them. The ship was sur-rounded by many of the zombified aliens they had en-countered earlier, but the most disturbing one of all was a large, formless jelly they had not come across before.

It was a massive, semi-translucent, amoeba-like creature which had apparently slammed into the ship, almost entirely covering it while firmly attaching itself to the hull with its numerous sucker cups. If it generated enough pressure, the Doctor knew it could very well crush the ship like a tin can if nothing was done to stop it. The other creatures had taken up positions around the exposed areas of the ship and were pounding against it, adding to the already acute instability created by the in-creasing shock waves of the brainquake.

Rollie gawked at the scene. "What do we do about *that*," he asked as he pointed at the gelatinous monster.

As the Doctor was about to reply, the ship jerked violently, forcing the Doctor and his companions to brace themselves. Before they could recover, another tremor started, setting off the stabilizer alarm and nearly tipping the ship onto its side. Desperately grasping the control console in order to prevent his sliding away from it, the Doctor raised his hand in a frantic gesture and slammed it down hard on to a specific embedded control pane.

The abrupt sound of sparking electricity crackled the air as the ship began to right itself. Once the ship was settled back in place, and the stabilizer quieted, the Doc-tor explained that he had just sent an electric shock through the outer hull of the ship, hoping the counter-measure would pacify the attacking creatures and, hope-fully Mentacron, enough to calm things for a moment.

Within seconds, though, another brainquake desta-bilized the *Cosmos*. The seismic tremors were closer together now, telling the Doctor that Mentacron would soon permanently lose his grip on the Gamma Wave, and what was left of his sanity. To gain more time, the Doctor adjusted a gauge and slammed the same control pane again, sending an even stronger electric shock through the hull. Instantly, everything quieted, and the ship settled. The smell of ozone and burning flesh was so intense, it somehow permeated the ship's hull. The Doctor and his companions straightened as their eyes glanced furtively about.

Rollie, his hands cautiously splayed before him, asked in the stillness, "Is it over, now?"

The Doctor took on an even tone. "I think not."

They all looked at the screen and saw that the amoeba had turned a darker yellow, probably from being partially singed by the shot of high-voltage electricity. Yet, it still clung to the ship. And even now, the other creatures were pressing in on the *Cosmos* once again with their own smoldering bodies.

The Doctor noticed a burnt halo of cerebral cortex surrounding the ship at its base. It was at that moment he began to realize the electrocutions were not only *not* slowing down the brainquakes and making them less potent, but they were ultimately going to make things even worse by hampering Mentacron's own psychological strength and ability to maintain his tenuous control over his ever expanding, and all-consuming, life force.

Instantly, as if in sync with the Doctor's thinking, the ship began to tremble again. They clumsily reached for the console once more as the brainquake grew in amplitude. The vibrating continued to grow in ferocity, sending objects tumbling away and causing welded joints to pop while filling the bridge with the sound of groaning metal.

The Doctor's features darkened with concern as he kept an eye on the wildly active gauges. Rollie noticed this as he tried to keep up with the Doctor's anxious gaze; his agitation also increased as he saw the calibrating numbers blur by, revealing the stabilizer's mad effort to maintain the ship's balance.

Realizing Cassandra would probably be worried as well, he reached for her hand, hoping his touch would calm her while also giving himself relief, knowing she was well and by his side. When he didn't find her hand, he turned, and discovered she was gone. Immediately, time slowed for him as he intuitively swiveled around to look toward the side wall encasing the gravcap.

Then, he felt as though he were in a dream where nothing was real. He saw Cassandra's body crumpled on the floor, up against the gravcap wall, her head at an awkward angle, with blood trickling onto her shoulder. When he called her name, it almost sounded like a startled reprimand rather than the uneasy expression of concern it was meant to be.

Without hesitation, he released the console and allowed the current tilt of the ship to take him to her. Once he made contact with the wall, he quickly dropped to his knees and put his arms around her, shoring her up and softly patting her face, trying to bring her to consciousness.

Underneath the distress, he could feel the tremors diminish and the ship begin to level itself again. Responding to the stabilization, her head slumped to one side, exposing a spot of blood-matted hair. His renewed efforts to wake her became more fevered.

As the ship finally settled, the Doctor began expertly checking gauges, estimating in seconds any damage to the *Cosmos*. Finding nothing serious, he hurriedly turned his attention to Rollie and Cassandra.

Swiftly moving over to them, he asked, "How is she, my boy?"

By this time, Rollie had stopped trying to wake her. He had already checked for a heartbeat and found none. After a moment, he said in a muted tone, "She's dead."

# CHAPTER XIV

The Doctor stiffened, looking confused. "Why, that's nonsense." He waved his hands energetically and said, "Here. Move aside, and I'll look at her."

With a vacant stare, Rollie shifted to the side to give the Doctor room. When he did, Cassandra slid softly to the floor, like a feather gracefully drifting to the ground.

The Doctor checked for breathing and found she wasn't. He, too, felt for a heartbeat and found nothing but stillness, despite the skin being warm beneath his touch. Stunned, he rose from her as he passed an unblinking gaze over Rollie. His eyes large with disbelief, he muttered, "This can't be." As he became more distant, he said to no one, "It's impossible."

Rollie fell back against the wall with a thump and held his head in his hands. "She's dead, Doctor. Mentacron killed her."

Allowing himself only a brief moment of grief, Rollie quickly evolved from despondence to rage. Using the wall as leverage, he awkwardly got to his feet and roared at the air. "You murdering wretch! You vile, murdering wretch!" His emotions taking over, he clinched his fists in a blind fury. In an act of almost blazing instinct, he staggered like a feral beast to the other side of the gravcap and jerked the Medusa shield from the wall, then turned to the gravcap door, which automatically slid open before him.

The Doctor called to him with a stern authority which surprised even himself. "Rollie! Put the shield back on the wall and get back over here! Now!"

Rollie briefly hesitated, then made for the gravcap again but with a slightly tempered aggression this time.

Once more, the Doctor commanded him to halt, but in a less edged tone. At this, Rollie was compelled to stop and listen to what the Doctor had to say. "Rollie, don't you realize I'll need your help moving Cassandra's body. If you go out to confront those creatures like a mad bull, you most likely won't survive. And where would that leave Cassandra?"

The Doctor's words struck at the heart of Rollie's rage, causing his heated anger dissipated; Rollie reluctantly put the shield back on the wall and shuffled back to the other side of the gravcap as the Doctor said, "We must move her before another quake occurs. I know you don't want her body to be harmed any further."

Rollie nodded weakly and placed his hands gently under her shoulders while the Doctor secured her feet. Gingerly, they moved her body to the nearby settee and wrapped it with a blanket the Doctor had gotten from a storage cabinet.

From there, they were going to take her shrouded figure to her room on the lower deck, but the Doctor hesitated, suddenly realizing the next quake he had expected hadn't arrived yet.

Without warning, he sensed something behind him. He turned and saw the distressed figure of Mentacron towering behind the console, again, his face badly disguising the titanic psychological tug-of-war he was experiencing. The Doctor could tell he was barely keeping the Gamma Wave from completely breaking loose at this point.

Once Rollie saw Mentacron, his rage returned. He stepped from Cassandra's body and advanced toward

Mentacron, thrusting out an accusatory finger and snarled, "You! You killed her! Why?"

Mentacron closed his eyes for a moment in an acknowledgment of guilt, then opened them again and said as calmly as he could, "Yes, it is my fault, but it wasn't intentional. It was an unfortunate accident, a result of my dwindling stamina."

Rollie came closer. "Your dwindling stamina? How easily you absolve yourself, you bloodthirsty swine!"

Doctor Omega stiffened as he watched Mentacron struggle to gather his strength; Mentacron thrust out an angry, open hand toward Rollie. A green ray of sparking plasma shot from his palm and struck Rollie, completely engulfing him and stopping him in his tracks as if he were a statue. Mentacron, looking severely weakened, lowered his hand and somberly observed his work.

Startled, the Doctor took on the diffident expression of one who is fully aware of his inferior position. Nevertheless, he expressed his concerns with as much confidence as he could muster. "See here, what have you done to Rollie? This is not acceptable! Release him at once!"

Despite being visibly haggard, Mentacron's voice still projected a certain rumbling power beneath the deadened words. "He hasn't been harmed."

"Regardless, release him!"

Mentacron wavered for a moment, then acquiesced.

The green glow enveloping Rollie shimmered away with a crispy sound, similar to bacon frying in a pan. For a fleeting moment, Rollie was confused as to his whereabouts, but the diminishing pops of static electricity caused him to regain his senses. Catching sight of Mentacron again, he tensed up and prepared for another verbal blast.

Just before he could get going, though, the Doctor exclaimed, "That's quite enough! Your nipping at his heels won't bring Cassandra back!" He leaned in closely, muttering, "And it may even get us killed." He finished with a softer tone, accentuating every word. "Cassandra wouldn't want that, now would she?"

Rollie's blood cooled in due course. He sagged slightly and nodded at the Doctor. "You're right. I need to think more clearly."

The Doctor eased up and said, "We all do." Turning to Mentacron, he said, "We'll need a few minutes to remove Cassandra to a more discreet location, preferably to her room down below." His tone lowered. "It would be the respectful thing to do at the moment."

Mentacron reluctantly nodded agreement.

The Doctor went over to the gurney on which Rollie had been examined, detached it from its brace, and wheeled it over to the settee where Cassandra's body lay.

Together, he and Rollie lifted her shrouded figure onto the gurney and guided it to the gravcap, which took them to the lowest level of the *Cosmos*. Neither spoke as they went. Once there, they rolled around to the other side of the area and entered her room, then proceeded to place her body on the nearby bed.

As the Doctor prepped the gurney for the return trip to the bridge, Rollie gently pulled the covering from Cassandra's face, brooding for a moment as he stared at her serene features. The Doctor, out of the corner of his eye, observed Rollie bend forward discreetly and press an evanescent kiss upon her cold, unresponsive lips.

A green, static discharge from Rollie's previous plasma encounter passed impalpably between them as their lips touched; it quickly vanished, registering no significance for either the Doctor or Rollie.

Presently, the Doctor addressed Rollie, reminding him of their extreme situation and the grim duties awaiting them. Rollie hesitantly agreed and returned to the gurney, helping the Doctor wheel it from the room. Rollie gave one final glance back, then slowly closed the door. Their senses clouded by grief caused them to miss the appearance of a pale, green glow which had begun to softly cocoon Cassandra's body.

Back on the bridge, the Doctor turned his attention back fully to Mentacron again and said, "One of my friends is dead now, because you couldn't control yourself."

Mentacron lowered his chin slightly. "In a way, this is true. However, controlling the Gamma Wave is becoming more difficult with every passing second. Nonetheless, I am truly sorry for your loss."

Rollie replied, this time with coolness. "That's all well and good, but it's not good enough."

"My companion is correct, Mentacron. If you don't exert a stronger hand against the Gamma Wave, and further harm comes to us, I'll refuse to help you."

After a moment, Mentacron said, "Agreed. I will continue to do what I can. But we both know your position is untenable. If we don't act soon, or you refuse to help, the annihilation of everything will be on your head, Omega."

# CHAPTER XV

Rollie grimaced at the Doctor and blustered, "You can't fall for that; it's emotional blackmail! How can we even be sure he's telling the truth. I mean, look at what he's done to Cassandra!"

The Doctor put his hands to his temples and shouted, "Enough, Rollie, enough of this caterwauling!" He lowered his hands and said quietly, "He's right. We mustn't be foolish and allow ourselves to lose control. Mentacron barely has a grip on his own mind at this point, and once he loses it fully, we're all doomed. He's not lying about that, or anything else. He has no need to. I must go through with this, regardless of the circumstances. Otherwise, the universe will cease to exist!"

"But you can't! You'll die. He said so himself."

"I understand that, but I may have another way." Doctor Omega turned to Mentacron. "How much time would you say we have before you reach critical mass?"

"All I can say is soon. I can feel my psyche slipping away as we speak. Perhaps one or two more quakes, and it will be too late."

"Alright. My plan may work, but I can't be certain. If it doesn't, I promise you, I will go through with the encephalopod operation."

Noticeably relieved, Mentacron said, "Very well. Take your path. But do it quickly. I don't know how long I can hold off the next quake, or even the creatures near the ship."

Rollie huddled up close to the Doctor. "I don't know about this. All of this seems incredibly dangerous."

"True. But the entire universe dying off seems a bit more deadly, wouldn't you say?"

"Yes, I would, but I'm just worried about you. I've just lost Cassandra. I don't want to lose you, too." He paused briefly, realizing how maudlin he was sounding, then tried to soften it with a bit of weak drollery. "After all, I would look pretty silly, being the only one arriving back home in this thing, and having to answer all of those annoying questions about how I did it."

The Doctor smiled reassuringly and said, "That you would, my dear boy. That you would. But, you may have to anyway. If I can't make my idea work, then I'll have to go through with the encephalopod operation, like it or not."

Finally giving in, Rollie asked, "So, what is this grand idea of yours?"

Almost forgetting the circumstances, the Doctor perked up and said, "Ah, I'm glad you asked! I'm going to reprogram the cerebro-enhancer."

Rollie gave the Doctor a blank stare. "Alright, but what's that supposed to do?"

The Doctor pursed his lips. "Rollie, how do you not see it? By reprogramming the cerebro-enhancer to be a neurological interface, I can use it to safely meld my mind with Mentacron's while avoiding the need for an irreversible brain absorption."

Rollie made a face. "Is that even possible?"

The Doctor frowned, momentarily surprised by the question. He had come up with the solution quickly, while under extraordinary duress. Under such conditions, he simply assumed it would work. "Of course it will work," he blurted out. Then, he held his chin and said hesitantly, "I *hope* it will work." Finally, he waved his hand confidently and said, "It will definitely work."

"Really? Have you ever done it before?"

Again, the Doctor was hesitant. "Well, no. But, I do know this technology inside and out, considering I invented it. I do understand what it can and cannot do, and I'm certain it can do what I've described."

"I hope so, because if it can't, I think we're all done for."

The Doctor said somberly, "Right you are, my dear boy." Breaking the moment, he said, "Now, let's get to it. Come along and help me set up the cerebro-enhancer."

Rollie followed the Doctor over to where the piece of equipment was stored and helped him set it near a holographic display base. The base, Rollie discovered, was small, too small, he thought to be anything other than a quirky expression of Modernist design projecting up intrusively from the work surface. He knew, though, that this couldn't be the case, considering the Doctor's obvious preference for archaic and outmoded aesthetic ornamentation.

Presently, he observed the Doctor bringing out a couple of wires and using them to connect the cerebro-enhancer to the display base. While assisting the Doctor in this process, he maintained a subtle awareness of Mentacron whom, he could tell, was observing with great tension everything they were doing.

Once the Doctor had finished his connections and pressed a few buttons, a mini-holovid appeared just above the base. Realizing he lacked the expertise to assist further, Rollie stepped aside. In an odd way, he was thankful he could now give over most of his thoughts to the passing of Cassandra; in addition to helping him work through the sudden and devastating loss, it also aided in partially crowding out the overwhelming sense of doom constantly emanating from Mentacron. Strangely enough, it gave him a calming sense of hope. Despite this, he couldn't help but detect an agonizing, half-hidden wildness in Mentacron's eyes. There was something magnetic and subtly dangerous about them, something unnerving which forced an occasional, furtive, and begrudging glance from Rollie. It was obvious to him that the volcano was about to erupt again, yet he tried to put it out of his mind and let thoughts of Cassandra come to the fore.

The Doctor perceived none of this as he focused all of his attention on adjusting wires within the enhancer and tapping furiously on a miniature keyboard attached to the device, all ultimately resulting in the transformation of the enhancer into a highly powerful interface which would be capable of directly linking his mind to Mentacron's.

As the Doctor toiled away, another sense of foreboding forced Rollie to glance at the holographic giant not far from them. All thoughts of Cassandra vanished as he watched a screen of crackling static replace the enormous, distressed shape of Mentacron; with a sudden spark, the shape flared out of existence again. Startled, Rollie raced to the Doctor's side, placed one arm around him while using the other to brace both of them for the coming assault. "Hold on, Doctor; we're about to get another brainquake," he barked. The tremors started immediately after Rollie's declaration and escalated quickly thereafter.

While he thankfully accepted the protection, the Doctor continued to work beneath the defensive shielding Rollie supplied, knowing full well what may happen if he indulged in even the minutest of delays. Ignoring the quakes which were increasingly rattling the ship, his eyes intensely skimmed the mini-holovid and keyboard while his fingers rushed through the coding process.

This raw burst of activity convinced him they may possibly have a fighting chance, now. With a crisply precise tap, he made the final keystroke and waited pensively for a clear indication the reprogramming worked. The seconds which followed were agonizing in their intensity but, after what seemed like an eternity, the Doctor saw the first flash of a green light, which indicated success.

Amidst the harsh tremors, he shouted, "I've got it," then, he rapidly disconnected the wires and indicated to Rollie he needed assistance onto the gurney. From there, he had Rollie help him fit the enhancer snugly over his head. Once he felt the enhancer was suitably in place, he gave Rollie an encouraging glance and activated the device.

At that moment, the Doctor's head jerked oddly to the side and froze there, with his eyes wide open and glassy, as if he were a robot which had suddenly been deactivated.

# CHAPTER XVI

For a moment, Doctor Omega had difficulty determining his exact position, whether he was lying or standing. And, he was in total darkness, which naturally prevented him from orienting himself in relation to other objects. While it seemed gravity had no bearing at present, he could still, oddly enough, feel the general weight of his own body. This discordant sensation produced a fleeting nausea. Then, instantaneously, he felt himself moving at a rapid speed in a particular direction, although he couldn't determine which direction that was.

A microsecond later, he stopped without the aid of deceleration or the inertial shock which would normally accompany such a jolting event. He was beginning to realize that he was immaterial consciousness here and that this place, he reasoned, must be a subatomic liminal space accessed by the interface and the cortical relays he had earlier placed along the path to the Wernicke area within Mentacron's brain.

In other words, there was no physicality here, only sensation. To him, this reasonably meant he was on the verge of making direct contact with Mentacron's mind, and that very awareness temporarily terrified him now. Yet, not long ago, the idea of being able to do such a seemingly impossible thing would have thrilled him beyond measure. His quest for scientific knowledge, while not being remotely on par with Mentacron's was, nonetheless, also at an exceedingly high level. But, considering his current encounter with the legendary figure, his understanding of the dangers of such an excessive pursuit was beginning to take on greater clarity.

After what he felt was a short while, he began to sense a pinpoint of light off in what he could only currently comprehend as the distance. In this ambiguous territory, it was hard for him to tell exactly how near or far things were, or whether they were simply large or small, since he quickly understood that the traditional perception of geometric space was quite inadequate to describe such an enigmatic and totally unfamiliar realm. Still, he did his best, which was better than most, and he hoped it would be enough to get him through.

He perceived the light growing larger, until it filled the entirety of the liminal expanse. The light seemed to have a humanoid essence dispersed throughout it. Without knowing how he knew, the Doctor was instantly aware that the being was a child. He could feel its tormenting fear, which was almost a living thing unto itself.

Before he could mentally probe it further in order to determine who or what it actually was, the child's essence disappeared and was replaced by the impression of a disquieting thing which resembled nothing the Doctor had encountered before. While it seemed to be towering incomprehensibly above him, it could also, he realized, be directly upon him, making it seem larger than it was. But, he understood just as well, that both interpretations could hold the same weight of truth at the same time in this extraordinary place.

The object itself, he sensed, was madly grotesque in its abstraction, broken up as it was into three-dimensional cube shapes, projecting out to differing degrees, in differing directions, from what he presumed to be the core of its form. The Doctor couldn't discern any features beyond that, and he still wasn't quite sure if the thing were alive or not; yet there was something about it which indicated it was. But, once again, he accepted both were simultaneously possible in this psychosphere.

Just as he was about to put out an invisible hand to touch it, the light flicked off as if a switch had been thrown, leaving in its place total darkness and the sudden, piercing clash of horrified screams coming from every direction.

The Doctor's mind sharply contracted at the shock. His concern was growing rapidly. It was beginning to look as though there were no logical steps to take here, no rational path forward. He knew he hadn't directly connected to Mentacron's mind yet, and he was quickly drawing to the conclusion that, not only could this experiment be an abject failure, but he could also be forever trapped in this nightmare firmament. The thought of it made him sick with unaccustomed fear.

In order to avoid panic, he tried desperately to ground himself in some way. His only option, he decided, was to think of something outside of this hallucinatory inner space. It was then he became aware of Cassandra's presence.

As with the previous entity, he could only discern a kind of aura, which gave him the mental picture of her. In a way, it was similar to viewing an infrared recording of an object. He perceived her floating horizontally before him, curled on her side as if she were asleep. Again, she could have been far away or nearby, dead or alive, all or none of the above at the same time.

In this wholly non-physical space, everything was in a perpetually hypothetical limbo. He thought her name, but she didn't respond. He sent out another psychic tendril, hoping he could make contact with her and give her some kind of substance, at least in his own mind. But, before the extremity made much progress, it came upon an odd barrier, a subliminal field he called it, which forced Cassandra away from him in degrees equal to the movement he put into trying to reach her.

With measured relief, he realized he had finally found some kind of probable physical law in this realm. Something which anchored his thinking, in a way. However, this realization brought with it the further understanding that this subliminal field would also prevent him from ever connecting with anything here, including Mentacron's essence. It abruptly became obvious to him that the disparities between their two minds were far too great and could never be bridged using the ambivalent enhancer approach which he had chosen.

The fact that he had made such a fatal mistake was a harsh blow to him. Before his despondency could truly take hold, though, it was quickly checked by a change in Cassandra. A green nimbus began to emanate from her. Shortly after, she began to move.

# CHAPTER XVII

Suddenly, the Doctor felt himself rapidly moving into total darkness again. And he instinctively knew he was traveling in reverse along the same path he had taken to get here.

Within a microsecond, he found himself back on the bridge of the *Cosmos*, perplexed and a bit unsteady, with Rollie directly in front of him, waving a hand, trying to bring him back to consciousness. He was mildly diverted by the subtle change he observed in Rollie's demeanor, his sojourn giving him fresh eyes with which to clearly see it. He could tell his companion had a different bearing from when he first met him; he was steadier now, more firm in purpose, less diffuse. The Doctor surprised himself by being pleased in a fatherly way; due to what was likely to come, he knew that Rollie would have to start relying on his own wits before long to keep himself alive going forward.

Rollie snapped his fingers directly in front of the Doctor's eyes. "Doctor, can you hear me?"

Realizing he was still lying flat on the gurney, the Doctor struggled a bit then, with Rollie's assistance, sat up and said hazily, "Yes, I think so." Running his hand through his hair, he assumed Rollie had removed the enhancer, because he was clearly no longer wearing it.

Picking up on the Doctor's concern, Rollie said, "You told me to take it off."

"I told you? When? I don't remember anything of the kind."

"Well, it wasn't necessarily you. It was your hologram, or I'm assuming that's what it was."

"Hologram!" The doctor wrinkled his forehead. "Whatever are you talking about?"

Rollie smiled lightly. "A hologram of you; it was similar to Mentacron's; it made an appearance, or actually, a couple of appearances. The last one, just a few seconds ago, told me to quickly remove the enhancer." He looked up as he searched his memory and recited precisely, "You said, 'Take the enhancer off – It's useless – I can't touch her.'" Then, Rollie went on as before. "You first appeared over near the console, looking up at the area where Mentacron usually takes his position, and the other time over there," he concluded with a somber tone, "and you were staring at the settee where we placed Cassandra before we moved her below."

The Doctor raised his eyebrows. "Really? Interesting. And this last one at the settee spoke to you?"

"Yes."

"Fascinating."

Rollie, exasperated now by the possibility of endless digressions brought on by the Doctor's current depleted state, pressed in bluntly. "Yes, it is. But did the melding work?"

The Doctor, while contemplating the mention of his hologram, and still being fazed by his experience, nonetheless became aware that the *Cosmos* was no longer under attack. The brainquakes which had started just before he had activated the enhancer were no longer present. Paying no heed to Rollie's frustration, he redirected the conversation by mentioning his surprise at this.

Disarmed by the Doctor's evasion of his question, Rollie replied offhandedly, "The quakes ended about ten minutes after you went under, but you've been unconscious for around two hours."

"Two hours! It felt as though I had only been there for mere seconds!"

Rollie again saw a chance to resume a more pertinent line of discourse. "Where? Where were you?"

The Doctor worked himself off the gurney. He wavered slightly and balanced himself against it as he answered. "In a place I can only describe as a liminal space. A region without physicality or any obvious logical coherence." He concluded distantly, "An infinite madhouse. A place of unspeakable terror."

Being sensitive to the Doctor's present condition, as well as the apparently nightmarish environment he had just escaped from, Rollie chose to probe more gently, and tease out the details, hoping they would eventually lead to a final clarification. "Did Mentacron speak to you?"

"In a way. If you can call crazed screams of horror speaking."

This numbed Rollie a bit, but he continued without hesitation. "Did you make any kind of contact at all with him?"

"Yes, I told you. The screams." The Doctor broke for a moment, then brought his hand up to cover his eyes. "It was grotesque." He proceeded to look up at Rollie with a deep sadness in his eyes. "Think of it. To devote yourself entirely to the pursuit of perfect reasoning and the accumulation of absolute scientific knowledge only to have it turn you into the very thing you were trying to conquer." He grabbed Rollie buy the shoulders now. "I couldn't truly accept it before, but it's just as he said! He's become a mad god of unimaginable destruction!"

Rollie's face fell. He slowly lowered the Doctor's arms and said defeatedly, "So, you didn't psychically merge with Mentacron."

The Doctor breathed deeply, coming to his senses. "No, no I did not." His eyebrows knitted as he tried to precisely describe what he had experienced. "I was able to enter his mind, yes, but I was still separated from it by some type of indeterminate field. There's a kind of sub-liminal barrier there, possibly quantum in origin, likely similar, in a way, to how the blood/brain barrier in the human body works. It seems to be utterly thin in nature, being that it exists within a non-physical space, but it's also impossible to pass through, which makes it an even more formidable boundary than the barrier in the human body. It's obvious, now, that our two brain capacities are far too divergent for this mechanical methodology to work." He lowered his head a bit and concluded bitterly, "I was foolish to think – to *hope* – it could."

Refusing to accept the Doctor's own misgivings, Rollie firmed up and became lost in contemplation as he considered the few options they had left. As he saw it, they could try the enhancer again and chance that the barrier the Doctor referred to was nothing more than a fickle anomaly and, thus, would be absent the next go round. Taking into account the Doctor's high scientific expertise and understanding of the situation, he recognized this speculation to be an extremely unlikely possibility.

Next, he hypothesized the existence of some chemical which could be injected into Mentacron's brain in order to break down the subliminal field and allow the Doctor's mind to directly connect, via the enhancer again, to Mentacron's.

This, he tossed aside as nothing more than wishful theorizing; if such a chemical did exist, the Doctor would have mentioned it in his previous explanation.

The penultimate angle he was able to muster up was to somehow find a way to link Mentacron's brain to the ship's own kirbyon-based computer systems and hope a solution could be formulated between the two that way.

He took this to be untenable, as well, being that a computer system would be far more divergent from Mentacron's mind than another mind derived from a living organism. No, the connection had to be between two biological, flesh-and-blood lifeforms if it were to work at all.

This brought him to his final plan which, in truth, was Mentacron's original brain absorption approach, but with a twist; he mulled the proposition over, taking into consideration all of the horrible ramifications of it, the pain, the loss, the grief, and even the distinct possibility of it not working, even after all of the damage that would simply come from the attempt. The fact that there was little doubt in his mind that it *would* work forced him to conclude it was the only viable route to take, just as Mentacron had said, no matter the unavoidable injury that would result from it.

The Doctor's own earlier anxieties echoed inside of Rollie's mind now: Failure to go through with the operation would most likely mean the end of the universe, and no personal sacrifice would be too great to keep that from happening.

Somewhere along this ridiculous journey they had been on, he had begun to think of the Doctor as a trustworthy, if unusual, father figure. The notion he had stated previously concerning the loss of the Doctor, along with Cassandra, became more palpable at this point due to the conclusive decision quickly taking shape in his mind.

After much deliberation, and with deep concern, he looked squarely at the Doctor, hesitated for just a moment, then said with a strained clarity, "*I* shall undergo the encephalopod procedure."

# CHAPTER XVIII

The Doctor fell into stunned silence. His face briefly tightened, becoming a mask of puzzlement, before softening into an understanding smile. "Surely, you're joking, Rollie." While the words themselves tended toward mockery, he made the strongest of efforts to temper them with a gentle inflection.

Understanding this, Rollie responded with matching grace. "I am not, Doctor."

Attempting to tease Rollie back from the precipice of a determined, yet unnecessary, self-destruction, the Doctor made a face and asked with as much openness as he could register, "But, why?"

With a feigned impartiality, Rollie said, "It makes perfect sense. After all, someone has to go through the process." His affected stoicism fractured just a touch as he concluded, "And I'm expendable, but you're not."

The Doctor was thrown off a bit by this last statement; his growing sense of familial attachment to Rollie was causing him to take a more protective stance than usual, one that went beyond the facts as he knew Rollie incorrectly presumed them to be. Because of this, he approached Rollie's comment emotionally at first by waving his hand with vigor, as if he were shooing away a fly, and bellowing, "Don't be ridiculous!"

Rollie explained his position further, absent equivocation, hoping the Doctor would accept it without making things more difficult. "I'm not, Doctor. Don't you see? In the end, my death means nothing, but if it can be of use in some way, at least that gives the rest of my life some kind of significance."

Until now, the Doctor hadn't quite realized just how drastic a change had overcome Rollie. He had appreciated and greatly admired the maturing transformation which had occurred up to this point, but he immediately recognized the present turn toward excessive gallantry as a mawkish step too far. It was obvious that Rollie, being new to the trappings of heroism, still hadn't quite got the hang of it. Like a novice, he was unconsciously acting out the duties he assumed came with the office. With time and discernment, the Doctor knew these tendencies would be moderated. Unable to accept Rollie's offer, he parried with, "Well, what about your wife, Melissa, and your son? Don't they need you?"

Rollie looked sheepishly at him. "There never was a Melissa. And, I don't have a son. I made them up. I was just using that as an excuse to get out of the insane situation I had found myself in at the time."

With this embarrassing confession,[9] the Doctor pulled back a bit in his manner and grinned sympathetically. "Interesting. I had my suspicions when I saw a touch of something growing between you and Cassandra." He sobered now. "It's a sad and maddening thing that happened to her. I am truly sorry for your loss."

After a self-conscious pause, Rollie said, "It's not your fault, Doctor. And, if truth be told, it's no one's fault. Mentacron doesn't want to be in the midst of this anymore than we do. I recognize that now." He hardened somewhat and concluded firmly, "But, if he were truly malevolent, if he had truly intended to kill her, it would be another story altogether."

---

[9] It is the opinion of the editors that Rollie was, in fact, lying when he claimed to have made up Melissa. But divorces in California are notoriously expensive, so...

The Doctor calmly considered all of this and touched Rollie's shoulder with a paternal hand. "Those are astute words, my son. Be that as it may, I still don't consider you expendable. Not in the least. And your disclosure puts your attempts at courageous martyrdom into a more illuminating light."

These last words shocked Rollie into an abrupt awareness. His myopic pursuit of selflessness was beginning to look quite silly now. He saw his own shallow attempt at heroism as the folly it was, almost a reversed miniature of Mentacron's own mad conceits. He was beginning to feel as though he had just been released from a mental fog. And, without knowing why, it made the loss of Cassandra a little bit easier for him.

The Doctor cupped his hands thoughtfully around the edges of his open coat and studied his companion closely as he spoke. "Granted, I do appreciate your desire to protect me from harm, but I refuse to let you make what would be a horrible mistake. No, I can't let you go through with it, Rollie. While your intentions are truly honorable, your reasoning is terribly flawed."

Rollie hung there, silent and amenable now to the Doctor's explanation.

"The whole purpose of the procedure is to meld the minds of two beings who thoroughly understand kirbyon mechanics. You understand nothing about the subject, so, what kind of help could you possibly be if you were to undergo the encephalopod process? None whatsoever. If it were just about data, and the relaying of it from one being to another, then Mentacron could have just as easily gotten the information he needed from a distance and wouldn't have required my immediate presence. It's really that simple. *I* have to undergo the procedure; at this stage, it would be pointless for anyone else to do so."

Rollie saw it clearly now, but still found it hard to accept. He said nothing, though, knowing the Doctor was correct.

The Doctor wrinkled his brow in a judicious manner. "I understand how this may be a bit rough for you, but I've been thinking." He continued with a view to easing at least some of Rollie's apprehension. "There may be a way I can go about this thing without perishing during the process."

With that declaration, Rollie's temperament switched from settled despondence to careful optimism. "And, how's that," he asked.

"I've been thinking, I might be able to get around this whole brain melting dilemma by injecting a diluted form of acid neutralizer into my system. This might prevent the encephalopod from digesting my brain while still allowing it to connect to my cerebrum. It won't be a one hundred percent mind meld, but it should be close enough."

The blunt logic of the plan gave Rollie a bit more hope, yet he still felt a certain trepidation. "Do you really think it will work?"

"There's only one way to find out." The Doctor waved Rollie over to him. He directed his attention to the large jar a few feet away which contained the squirming encephalopod.

A second later, the Doctor was distracted by an elusive flickering in the air. It could have easily been his imagination, the sudden radiance being so transient, but he was reluctant to take the chance. "Do you sense that? The energy build up? We must hurry; Mentacron will be breaking down again if we don't get to this soon."

With a mindful Rollie by his side, he studied the encephalopod through the jar. He found four small needle projections on the underside of the mollusk, two at the back and two at the front, bellow the eyestocks. "Yes, just as I thought. It's similar enough to the Eridani mollusk to make my theory plausible. Do you see these two barbs at the front?"

Rollie nodded.

"I believe those inject the digestive acid into the skull of the victim, while the back two barbs anchor the mollusk into the central nervous system and suck in the juices after the brain matter has been dissolved away. I'm guessing it's somewhere in those two anterior probes that the actual biological linkage and transmission starts, with the assistance of the cerebral acid, which will be neutralized in this case. Exactly how that's accomplished, I don't know yet. Regardless, the acid neutralizer should keep my brain tissue at a survivable pH balance for a while, counteracting the digesting process, yet still allow the mollusk to hook into my brain, and directly link my mind to Mentacron's. Or at least I hope it will."

The graphic description of the procedure, and the Doctor indirectly referring to himself as 'the victim', left Rollie feeling a shade tainted and insufficient for allowing the plan to go forward. While he desperately longed to be somewhere else at this juncture, anywhere else doing almost anything else, he also wished to avoid making the unpleasant task more burdensome than it already was; so, he collected himself and asked resolutely, "Are the odds good?"

The Doctor said breezily, "Not really."

Despite his misgivings, Rollie followed up with an ironic tone. "Alright, then. Since you're so positive about this thing working, I guess there's nothing left to do but do it."

"Exactly," the Doctor said energetically, hoping he could convince himself that everything would turn out well. Just before proceeding, the Doctor made sure to warn Rollie not to try removing the encephalopod before the process was finished; the shock of that would be the equivalent of short circuiting a computer, and would likely cause him severe brain damage, if not kill him outright. The only reasonably safe way to detach the thing was likely through the application of a mild shock of Gamma radiation, which they didn't have easy access to at the moment.

Rollie stated gravely that he understood, then lingered there awkwardly, waiting for the Doctor's next move, thinking the whole thing strange and uncompromisingly cruel.

After a fleeting moment of troubled hesitation, the Doctor moved to a nearby drawer and retrieved a hypodermic; he filled it up to a certain point with what Rollie correctly presumed was the acid neutralizer the Doctor had spoken of. He then set the hypodermic aside, removed his frock coat, and rolled up his sleeve. Before going further, he paused for a moment, as if he had remembered something. With some care, he removed a small object from his pocket. While holding it, he took both of Rollie's hands in his own and placed the item discreetly in his companion's palm.

Rollie felt something cold and metallic there, but couldn't look away from the Doctor's painfully aware face to see what it was.

The Doctor looked warmly back at him and said, "The key to the *Cosmos*, my boy. In case I don't make it. It opens all the doors, and locks them, and gives you complete control over the ship. It will help guide you home."

When the Doctor released his hands, Rollie looked at the item and saw a small, metallic object, rectangular in shape, and smooth on all sides. It was the baryonic key he had seen the Doctor use when he first came onto the *Cosmos*. He carefully put it in his own pocket and quietly wished this situation hadn't been necessary.

An ambivalent moment passed. Then, the Doctor exhaled decisively, nodded his head, and said, "Right. Let us proceed."

He took up the hypodermic and promptly injected the acid neutralizer into his arm. From there, he went onto the gurney again and adjusted himself in such a way that his head could hang just over the top of the matting in order to allow the mollusk's rear needles to access the back of his skull. He then instructed Rollie to use a pair of medical tongs, which he pointed out nearby, to get hold of the mollusk and remove it from the jar.

Once that was achieved, Rollie meticulously positioned the wiggling encephalopod at a precisely aligned point above the Doctor's head, as guided by the Doctor himself. A fraction of an inch off, in any direction, could prove to be fatal.

When the Doctor was satisfied, he closed his eyes and said, "Attach it. Now."

Rollie lowered the encephalopod until it was nearly touching the Doctor's scalp. At that point, he felt a terrific pulling force which apparently came from the encephalopod. It must have some kind of attracting autonomic impulse, he thought, which activated once it sensed the close proximity of cerebral matter.

For a moment, he was oddly fascinated by the idea, but that quickly vanished as the mollusk broke free of the tongs and shot directly toward the Doctor's head

.

# CHAPTER XIX

The encephalopod's needles bit brutally into the Doctor's skull, latching itself like an octopus onto his cranium.

While being horrified by the encephalopod's abrupt attack, Rollie was nonetheless glad to no longer feel the grotesque creature's muscular squirming through the medical tongs. For the brief time he had it within his grasp, he could unmistakably detect, through those repulsively jerky movements, the blindingly instinctual drive it had to do the one thing it was designed to do: digest the cerebral matter of other beings. The whole exercise sent a wave of nausea through him. He fought off the strong desire to rip the mollusk from the Doctor's skull, remembering the explanation of how the shock of such a thing could easily kill him.

He watched the Doctor's eyes suddenly shoot open. It was apparent that this action, and the encephalopod's current repellent undulations, were due to the injecting of digestive acid into the Doctor's cranium.

The Doctor let out a horrible scream as his head pulled to one side with small, spastic motions, exciting a great concern in Rollie. Not knowing what else to do, he called to the Doctor, hoping it would somehow bring him to and make the attack less difficult to handle.

That the spasms increased, and were now traveling rapidly throughout the Doctor's body, gave Rollie pause. There was nothing he could do about the convulsions, he now knew, and the best thing for it was to let it play out, as the Doctor had already said, regardless of how horrific it was. Going forward, whether the Doctor survived or not would be entirely up to his stamina and will to live.

The following hour severely frayed Rollie's nerves and left him spent. As the dreadful seizures played out, minute after appalling minute, he tried to distract himself by prepping the bridge for the Doctor's hopeful return to consciousness.

He moved items which had been scattered about by the previous brainquake to more secure locations; he checked gauges, to the best of his ability, to make sure the ship's systems were still running properly; he even tried cleaning the spots of dried blood left behind after Cassandra's collision with the wall. In a way, he was thankful for the opportunity to do so, since it was the only thing which did truly take his mind off of the Doctor's hideous ordeal, which was happening only a few feet away.

Throughout these attempts at diversion, he felt a slowly accumulating charge of static electricity in the air around him. The Doctor was correct; Mentacron was getting closer to having another brainquake. And, as the Doctor stated before, it may be the one which finally unleashes the full force of the Gamma Wave, setting in motion the complete destruction of the entire universe.

A memory flashed into Rollie's mind. He remembered the electrical pulse the Doctor had sent through the outer hull of the ship during one of the previous attacks by Mentacron's controlled creatures. Not only did it stop those creatures, it also seemed to have put Mentacron's uncontrolled brain activity back on its heels.

In anticipation of the coming final brainquake, he checked the gauges the Doctor had used to set off the earlier electrical pulses and confirmed the charge was active and ready for use again. He did recall the Doctor was reluctant to use any further pulses, fearing it may cause Mentacron to lose complete control of the Gamma Wave; but Rollie felt, at this point, a massive electrical burst may be the only option they had left to buy time for them to develop a better solution.

As he studied the gauges intently, he felt an uneasy presence approach from behind. He stiffened slightly and slowly turned.

Just before he caught view of the entity, he pivoted swiftly to take it in fully. His face contorted at what he saw. Expecting it to be Mentacron making another ominous appearance, he was even more terrified to see Doctor Omega standing before him, looking for all the world like an animated corpse, pale and vacant, yet seemingly filled with an inexhaustible anguish.

# CHAPTER XX

By itself, the presence of the Doctor in such condition would have been enough to cause Rollie great concern, but the realization that the Doctor's own eyes were sunken and closed, indicating that the snaking eyestalks of the encephalopod were providing his vision for him, made his appearance that much more unbearable.

Stunned, Rollie slowly backed away, his face drawn and his muscles taut, the tension of a fight-or-flight state growing within him. As he gradually moved from the control console toward the opposing wall, he noticed something else off to his side and slightly behind him. It was a glowing figure, but he could shortly tell it wasn't, as he had incorrectly presumed at first, Mentacron's hologram. He glanced to his side in order to see more clearly who, or what, it was.

To his astonishment, he saw that it was an iridescent image of the very same hideous insect creature, minus the claw he had removed from it, which they had first encountered at the beginning of their explorations outside of the ship. It came toward him methodically and with evident purpose, its one remaining claw reaching out to him and clicking with sharp, precise snaps, giving him the impression it could, with little effort, split his arm in half.

The Doctor and the insect humanoid approached Rollie in such a way as to leave him only one path for escape. He took it, bolting for the gravcap. Once there, the door automatically slid open; he rushed in and went to the back of the compartment.

To his surprise, when he turned around, he found the new, ghoulish form of the Doctor had entered right behind him. How this was possible, he didn't know, yet he was glad to see that, at least, the hologram insect creature hadn't joined them.

After the door closed, he was surprised by two things; the gravcap began to descend without him activating the indicator to do so, and the Doctor didn't move from his spot in front of the door, the disgusting eye-stalks worming about, taking in every inch of its surroundings with an unsettling awareness. This also gave Rollie the subtle impression that it was the encephalopod, or perhaps the Doctor somehow via the encephalopod, that sent the gravcap moving while not activating any of the controls in the conveyance itself.

In short time, the gravcap stopped, and the door opened onto the lowest floor. To Rollie's astonishment, the Doctor turned from him mechanically and left the gravcap, as if this whole situation were intended from the beginning.

Hesitantly, Rollie exited as well and followed the Doctor, not just because he was curious, but because he also felt as though this were expected of him for some reason, almost as if he were being guided toward a specific goal.

The pair made a half-circle around the gravcap and stopped at a precise spot on the other side of the conveyance's shaft, at an angle to the ship's entrance. Here, the Doctor gestured stiffly toward a sectioned part of the floor, directly in front of them.

Rollie looked at it, then back at the Doctor. He knew the Doctor was attempting to tell him something, but he wasn't sure what that was. He wavered slightly, trying to understand. "What? What is it?"

This time, the Doctor's arm slowly rose and stopped at a definite angle as he more exactly indicated a specific section in the floor.

Rollie examined the spot and realized the designated floor plate was slightly different than the others. This one had a small clasp evenly embedded into its surface, making it almost invisible to the unaccustomed eye. He knelt down and reached for it.

After a bit of difficulty trying to release the clasp, he was finally able to loosen it and pry it up. He then twisted it slightly, unfastening the mechanism, and lifted the plate. When he looked in, he saw nothing but darkness. He glanced back at the Doctor, who was still pointing to the same area. "What, you want me to go down there?"

With that, a soft, green glow began to emanate from the Doctor. Shortly, a ghostly replica of his body separated from him and took up a position off to his side.

Although astonished, Rollie clearly understood this to be the projected, holographic psyche of the Doctor himself, sans the encephalopod, just as he had witnessed during the previous mind-melding attempt with the cerebro-enhancer. Apparently, the Doctor was able to do this once he linked at some point to Mentacron's mind, which would naturally give him access to some of Mentacron's own abilities, as well.

The ghostly Doctor looked about for a moment, then said, "Ah, that's better!" Then, he looked at Rollie, directing his full attention to him. "Well, let's get going, my boy. The universe is about to come to an end!"

"But, Doctor, are you alright?" He looked back at the encephalopod on the Doctor's material form.

"If truth be told, not really. It's terribly uncomfortable in here right now. Or there." He pointed at his physical form. "Whatever the case may be, we must get down to work!"

Stuck for a moment, Rollie asked, "Here? Where is 'here'?"

The Doctor waved a spectral hand. "It's a bit hard to explain, Rollie, but it's a kind of liminal dimension, devoid of any physical presence. Not identical to the one I entered before, but similar. It's all a bit odd. However, I have been able to make direct contact with Mentacron's mind this time, and we seem to have come up with a solution to our dilemma. The answer is down there. I'll explain as we go."

"Now that you have a solution, can't we remove that slug thing?" Rollie gestured toward the encephalopod.

The phantom Doctor took a few wavering seconds, then said regrettably, "No. We've determined that will be impossible. I'm afraid I'm lost, Rollie. If I weren't so physically encumbered, I could stun it with my Martian aikido again or, if we had access to a Gamma Wave laser, it could be killed in a fashion which wouldn't affect me in a detrimental way, then it could be removed." He stopped here, seeing the fading light in Rollie's eyes. Determined to not allow Rollie's heartbreak to redirect his own necessary actions, he continued, but with a lighter inflection. "Either way, my recovery period would exceed the time we have left for dealing with Mentacron's issue. I can tell he's about to go again so, please Rollie, let's get to it!"

This final courtesy dislodged unwieldy things in Rollie's mind, allowing him to respond in the same durable way. He only hoped he could continue to do so after this was over and the Doctor was no longer with him.

He waved his hand over the aperture and said airily, "After you."

Pleased, the Doctor said, "Oh, no, after you."

"No, no, no, After you. I insist."

The Doctor grimaced with mock disapproval. "Fine. If I must." His apparition disappeared straight away, then reappeared down below, the faint glow from his phantom body producing a minor illumination in the darkness of the lower level.

Harrumphing in a stagy way, Rollie followed, lowering one leg down through the hatch; immediately, he noticed an electric light click on below, diluting the faint radiance coming from the Doctor's projected psyche. Apparently, the lighting system was motion-activated, which eased Rollie's concerns to a degree. *One less thing to worry about*, he thought.

When his foot touched what he assumed to be the top rung of a latter, he lowered his other leg and began to climb down. He stopped just before he lost sight of the lower deck and the Doctor's material form. While still gazing at the dire figure before him, he asked, "So, what do we do with it?"

"Do with what," the spectral Doctor asked from the cavity.

"Your body," Rollie said uncomfortably.

A forced conviviality tinted the Doctor's voice. "Oh, that old thing. Well, I would suggest leaving it there for the time being. When this is all over and done with, you can always send it out for a good pressing. It could use one, I think."

"Right," Rollie said ambiguously, wishing he had let the question go until later. Once at the bottom, which was about nine feet down, he turned and was shocked to see a cavernous enclosure far bigger in horizontal dimensions than the *Cosmos* could possibly contain. As far as he could tell, it was the equivalent of two city blocks in circumference. It was so large, he could barely see the end of the room; he also noticed the whole area was partitioned off into pathways and rooms of varying size due to the numerous layers of pipes and machinery. He reasoned that this must have been the heart of the ship, where the engines were housed. Not knowing what to do next, he looked at the Doctor for guidance.

Surprised to see the Doctor's phantom heading briskly down a narrow pathway, he darted after it.

"Quickly, Rollie! We haven't time to spare!"

"I understand that, but what are we doing?"

"We have to get to the kirbyon drive and reverse its polarity."

"And what will that do?"

"Produce anti-kirbyons, which will collide with kirbyons, creating a Gamma Wave energy vesicle."

Rollie was beginning to breathe heavily in his pursuit. "And what, exactly, is that?"

"The only thing capable of restraining the Gamma Wave."

Rollie caught his breath, then asked, "Restraining? I thought we were going to stop it."

They passed a small room and turned a corner before the Doctor answered. "Both Mentacron and I thought so, as well. But, during our lengthy conversation in the liminal space, the mathematics showed us, unequivocally and at every turn, that it's completely impossible to shut it off. There's nothing we can do to stop the Gamma Wave."

"Lengthy conversation? You were only in for about an hour before you left the gurney and came after me!"

"Yes, well, time is a bit different in liminal space, Rollie. I'm still partially there – or here – whichever the case may be! And I've been here – or there – for nearly a month now, in liminal time."

As satisfied as he could be with that answer, Rollie dispensed with it and went on to a more pertinent question. "So, how does this vesicle thing restrain the Gamma Wave?"

"By restraining Mentacron himself."

"Doctor, please, what does that mean?"

As they turned into another room, they arrived at the kirbyon drive, and the Doctor said, "Rollie, we haven't time! I'll explain it later."

He ushered Rollie over to the drive, which was little more than a v-shaped block, approximately eight feet long, four feet high, and two feet wide. It was smooth on all sides, except for a couple of embedded plates on top and neatly bundled wires running from it to a relay box in the wall. "I can't physically manipulate anything because of the intangibility of this form, so you'll need to handle the manual work here."

Rollie, his breath steadying, said, "Alright, fine. What do I do?"

The Doctor pointed to one of the small panels on top of the machine. "Remove that."

Rollie did so while also becoming aware of a modest rise in the Doctor's restlessness, an elusive change in his energy.

"Now, this is a delicate operation. You'll need to flip that yellow switch, which will redirect the power in this part of the unit." After that was accomplished, he continued, but with a rising stress in his voice. "Excellent. You see this green wire here? Disconnect it at this end."

Just as Rollie acted upon the Doctor's instructions, the ship began to shudder slightly. He stopped and looked at the Doctor uneasily. "Did I cause that?"

The Doctor abruptly touched his temples and winced, closing his eyes in a fit of sudden pain. "STOP!"

Rollie threw his hands up and backed away from the kirbyon drive, shocked by the Doctor's response, worried he may have done some kind of irreparable damage to the ship. "Alright, I'm not touching it!"

After a moment, the Doctor regained his composure and said with some difficulty, "Not you, Rollie. Mentacron. He's losing control again. It was the beginnings of another tremor you felt."

"Ah, I see. Should we continue?"

With care, the Doctor said, "Yes, we must."

He paused for a moment, the signs of stress building in his face. He continued with a bit of effort, pointing to another section on top of the kirbyon drive. "This panel, remove it."

Rollie did as he was instructed and waited for more direction, which didn't come. He looked aside and saw the Doctor twisted in agony.

The ship began to shake even more, reacting to the intensifying tremors which nudged Rollie a bit to one side.

Embracing the bulk of the kirbyon drive, Rollie tried to moor himself to the spot. For a moment, he thought he should attempt to make his way back up to the actual physical form of the Doctor, but he quickly realized the foolishness of that, remembering he could do nothing for him in the present situation.

In order to alleviate the feeling of helplessness, he endeavored to forge ahead and access the second plate, as he had just been instructed to do.

Before he could make a move, though, the startling presence of Mentacron appeared before him.

# CHAPTER XXI

Thrown off, Rollie lost his grip on the kirbyon drive. The strengthening tremors sent him stumbling back into the pipe-trimmed wall behind him. While the impact was jarring, it simply rattled his nerves without adding injury.

Upon regaining his footing, he watched the Doctor's agonized convulsions as his hologram shimmered for a moment, then vanished without a trace.

The fiery presence of Mentacron drew Rollie's attention away from the Doctor's shocking disappearance. It was apparent that Mentacron was wholly different now, sparked with a seemingly untamed energy disconcertingly aimed directly at Rollie.

Disoriented by Mentacron's emerging madness, and at a loss as to what to do next, Rollie realized his only choice was to flee; he rushed out of the room, turned, and went down one of the adjoining pipe-lined passageways. As the quakes became more severe, damaged pipes began releasing jets of steam, and equipment began dislodging from holding compartments, falling into his path, forcing him to work around the obstructions.

The compounding vibrations sent him slamming into a line of machines as he was taking a sharp turn. The impact dazed him somewhat, but as he regained his senses, he saw standing in the path he had been intending to take a glowing vision of the insect creature he had previously encountered on the bridge.

Its one remaining claw clicked menacingly at him, and it discharged a steady, intense flood of malevolent emotion toward him. He turned, and rapidly headed the other way. He passed a few other arteries before coming to a wall which forced him to go right. There, he halted.

Just a few feet ahead stood another glowing hologram, this one of the barrel-shaped monster, with its writhing tentacles, which they had encountered inside the last cavernous region of Mentacron's brain. This, too, sent a surge of loathsome malice through him. Each attack was leaving him weaker and more confused. It was becoming difficult for him to keep his bearings as well as his composure now. These things must have been summoned up by Mentacron's subconscious, he reasoned, inflamed as it was by the accelerating progression of the Gamma Wave.

Panicked, he reversed course and sped back to one of the other arteries he had passed, the shaking of the *Cosmos* inadvertently causing him to career back and forth against the piping as he went. Considering his waning stamina, he chose the first artery he came to. This one seemed narrower than the others, causing him to feel hemmed in and trapped. He did his best to ignore this and dash on, ducking and dodging overly stressed pipes shooting forth arms of brutally hot steam.

After a bit of dismayed running, he suddenly found himself in a moderately expanded area, one which was more like a small open-ended room, reminiscent of an arterial swelling, rather than a section of the pathway he had been on. He stopped for a moment to catch his breath. But, before he could achieve much relief, the holograms of the two creatures appeared near him again, on his left. And off to his right, the hologram of a savage, unrestrained Mentacron caught his eye as it materialized. With the giant's arrival came a wave of malice so extreme, it left Rollie feeling as though he would certainly die if he didn't take action now.

In a quandary as to what to do next, he wiped his sweating brow and tried to concentrate. His eyes desperately searched the area and suddenly caught sight of another figure coming into being on the other side of the small room, at exactly where the narrow pathway continued beyond.

Shortly, he was elated to discover it was the Doctor's projected psyche emerging from the ether again. Once truly in focus, Rollie eyed the Doctor and observed, in the few frenzied seconds available to him, that he appeared to be under terrific strain. "Doctor," he yelled, but he received only stormy exclamations in reply, which indicated the Doctor was in the midst of a titanic mental struggle of some sort, undoubtedly with Mentacron.

It was safe to assume, Rollie reflected, that the Doctor was attempting to gain a tenuous control over Mentacron's mind in order to dampen the progression of the Gamma Wave in some way.

As the fierce confrontation continued, the apparent upper hand switched repeatedly, at one point causing Rollie to fear the terrifying victory of Mentacron as he watched the Doctor nearly go to his knees before unexpectedly regaining his strength and reentering the battle.

Finally, after much difficulty and loss of strength, the Doctor regained a hairline degree of dominance and frantically gestured for Rollie, telling him to join him on the other side of the room before he completely lost his grip on the situation again.

Heeding the call, Rollie darted over, just dodging the sinister, yet reeling, presence of Mentacron.

From there, the Doctor ushered his companion down the confined passage, passed steaming pipes and protruding mechanisms. As they hurried along, he said,

"Out of that lot, only Mentacron's potent psychokinesis can affect matter. The other holograms were only sent by him to frighten you." Pushing through his punishing mental exertions, the Doctor concluded, "Our real enemy at the moment is time itself, and Mentacron's nearly exhausted endurance; once he goes, we all go!"

Moments later, the Doctor steered a frustrated Rollie around a corner which brought them back to the kirbyon drive, to Rollie's surprise.

Upon arrival, a seismic shock greater than they had experienced previously rocked the *Cosmos*, knocking Rollie aside and into the wall of pipes again. The Doctor swayed a bit, due to his mental battle with Mentacron, but stayed in place otherwise. The fact that he was, at present, nothing more than a hologram stripped him of his slavery to the gravitational laws of the material world. Still, he was beginning to lose what little potency he had left for such cerebral combat.

The violent reverberations forced Rollie to his knees. Grabbing the pipes, he used them to brace himself as he struggled back to his feet. The noise from the jolts and vibrations was becoming intolerable, causing Rollie to cover his ears. Even so, he struggled through these difficulties to get back to the drive.

The Doctor's projected psyche, still standing next to it, made a gesture and shouted above the cacophony, "The plate, remove the plate!"

With immense labor, Rollie was finally able to loosen the plate and set it aside. What he saw stopped him. It was nothing more than a small, rectangular space, smooth and devoid of any detail save a flat, glass lens in its center.

He was at a total loss as to what to do next; just as he attempted to work his way through the problem, the constant vibrations of the ship erupted into a savage battering.

He fell back again and stumbled into the nearby wall. Amidst the chaos, he arduously regained his balance and lunged back to the drive, neglecting his own safety. He looked to the Doctor for direction, but saw that he was once again wholly occupied by his battle to fend off Mentacron's reflexive attempts at preservation. It was apparent that Mentacron was now only moments away from succumbing to the unrelenting force of the Gamma Wave.

As the merciless vibrations continued, Rollie frantically thought through his options until he realized the rectangular slot reminded him of something. The baryonic key the Doctor had given him. It was the exact same size and shape, and just as oddly smooth.

Trying to ignore the Doctor's horrible struggles near him, he took the device from his pocket, and considered it. Yes, it was the same size. It should fit perfectly. Just as he was about to try it in the slot, the violent quakes escalated, causing him to lose his grip and drop the key to the floor. A slight, convulsive tip of the ship sent it sliding under the wall of pipes behind him. Seeing this, he allowed the unnatural tilt of the ship to carry him to the pipes. He dropped to the floor and visually located the device. Reaching through a gap between pipes, he attempted to secure it, but it was just out of range. Frustrated, he stretched further, his fingers negligibly brushing its edge. He pulled back a touch, then thrust his arm through again, just as the ship righted itself, sliding the key into his hand.

He frantically grasped it and brought it out. He struggled to his feet and rushed to the kirbyon drive where, without hesitation, he rammed the device into the slot, desperately hoping he was correct in his assumptions.

He brushed a finger along its smooth surface, trusting it would activate like it had previously; instantly, the drive sounded an alarm, and the vibrations began to ebb.

Everything seemed to be calming now; even the Doctor's own mental projection, while still clearly distressed, appeared to be easing its own mimicked breathing. As he gathered himself, he said to the Doctor, "I think it's working!"

Between simulated gasps for breath, the Doctor said, "It appears so, my boy. But we're still not safe. We must leave the surface of Mentacron's brain before the Tartarus Sphere closes!"

Rollie was shocked at this new turn. "Tartarus Sphere? What's that?"

"Once it's formed and sealed, it will be Mentacron's eternal prison. The containment vesicle I spoke of. Now, hurry! We must get to the bridge!" He told Rollie to brush the baryonic key again, which would deactivate it, and place it back into his pocket.

Doing so, he saw out of the corner of his eye the Doctor vanishing. When he turned to go to the ladder leading to the floor above, he saw the projected psyche of the Doctor already standing there waiting for him, as if to make sure he made it the ladder safely.

By the time he had gotten to the ladder, the Doctor's image had already vanished again. Anxiously, he rushed up the ladder.

Once his eyes got above floor level, he saw the Doctor's actual physical body still standing in the same hideous, deathly repose he had left it in. The Doctor's projected hologram, however, wasn't there and had evidently withdrawn back into his mind. The main thing

Rollie observed, though, was Cassandra, who was closely encompassed by a green aura; she had a blank stare in
her eyes, and her arm was reaching out menacingly as
she slowly and methodically approached the Doctor's
defenseless, immobile body.

# CHAPTER XXII

Rollie yelled out, "Cassandra," with a combination of shock and joy. He rushed up the rest of the ladder just as her hand, with fingers forming a terrible claw, reached out and vigorously clamped onto the encephalopod. The green aura instantly enveloped the parasite, searing its slimy flesh.

The mollusk squirmed, then slowly withered away as if it were being sucked dry of all of its fluids. Still in her trance, her eyes devoid of life, Cassandra pulled the creature, with its needles now contracted, from the Doctor's head, and crushed it in an iron grip.

The Doctor, finally free of the brain-absorbing creature, as well as Mentacron's mental hold, fell to the floor.

Rollie observed the aura quickly fade from Cassandra, then saw her release the encephalopod. He rushed over to her, catching her just as her knees gave, and held her tightly in his arms. "Cassandra!" He moved her over near the wall and eased her down, brushing her hair away from her face. "Cassandra. Is this real? Is it you?"

She said through a haze, "Of course it's me," then she drifted away again. Rollie cradled her devotedly as he watched the Doctor regain consciousness.

In short order, the Doctor was unsteadily balancing himself on an elbow while taking stock of his surroundings in a disoriented fashion. He said, while rubbing his aching head, "Well, it appears we're all back together. I wasn't expecting that."

After a bit, he recovered somewhat, then he awkwardly scrambled to his feet, and saw that Cassandra was coming to again, as well.

When he had regained some composure, he addressed them both. "While I'm profoundly happy to have Cassandra back, and equally surprised that she is, I'm afraid we haven't time to celebrate. We must get to the bridge immediately and get the *Cosmos* a good distance from the surface."

Having gotten his stability back, he went around and helped Rollie lift Cassandra up. From there, they made their way, as best they could, over to the gravcap.

Back on the bridge, they guided Cassandra over to the settee in order to let her recuperate, with Rollie cheerfully saying something about returning from the dead being tough business. Leaving her there to rest, the other two went over to the control console where the Doctor quickly ran through multiple displays.

With renewed energy, he said, "Just as I suspected! The Tartarus Sphere is forming. We must launch the ship before it closes on us!"

Rollie watched the Doctor's hands move swiftly over the panels without fully understanding what he was doing. "Tartarus Sphere? You said that before, and I still don't know what it is!"

As his fingers frantically worked, the Doctor said automatically, "A Tartarus Sphere is a sub-quantum prison, in a way." He paused his explanation and reached past Rollie to flip a set of switches lining the edge of the console.

"A sub-quantum prison?"

Frustrated, and still not entirely recovered, the Doctor stopped working the console long enough to attempt the best explanation he could, given the circumstances.

"Yes. Think of it as a kind of impenetrable force field prison, seemingly infinite in its spatial qualities. Epsilon particles are created by the collision of kirbyons and anti-kirbyons; in this case, the relay system I set up earlier within Mentacron's cerebral cortex for communication purposes acted as an accelerator, thus forming Epsilon particles along Mentacron's cerebral cortex, thereby anchoring the field along its surface and creating an empty pocket universe over it. It's forming right now around what's left of Mentacron's physical form, and will soon close him off from this universe entirely. Satisfied?"

Rollie nodded.

The Doctor went back to activating certain panels until he felt the ship begin to take off. "Steady yourselves!"

The *Cosmos* launched and, within moments, they had reached an orbit satisfactory to the Doctor. "I think we did it."

Shortly after, a familiar voice came to them out of the ether. It was that of Mentacron, yet it lacked the grandeur and authority that it once had. It was small, now, and distant, and somehow content. "You are safe now," he said. Just before they observed the pocket universe permanently shut, Mentacron said with a fading, yet grateful, voice, "Thank you."

With that, the field completely enveloped him, and the last vestiges of Mentacron's form disappeared forever from this universe.

With mixed emotions, Doctor Omega pressed a button on the console, sending what he called a Cerberus Device out to orbit the area as a surveillance apparatus. It was, he said with a touch of sadness in his voice, a signaling system which would notify him if the pocket universe should ever happen to be breached.

With that done, he sighed wistfully and guided Rollie back over to a reclining Cassandra. "Well, it seems that's over. A bitter sweet ending, if you ask me."

Rollie said thoughtfully, "That it is." He hesitated, then asked, "But, what about Cassandra?" He put his arm around her shoulders as she moved in close to him.

The Doctor touched his chin thoughtfully. "Yes, her resurrection is quite, shall we say, astounding?"

Cassandra, looking bewildered, then exclaimed, "I'll say! I still don't know what happened, and I'm the one who went through it!"

The Doctor chuckled. "True. True." Then, he addressed Rollie. "I think I may have the solution to that. Do you recall the moment Mentacron stunned you with the green plasma ray?"

"Yes."

"My hunch is that was a low-dose Gamma beam. You said before that you realized Mentacron hadn't meant to hurt Cassandra."

Rollie silently nodded.

The Doctor went on carefully. "I believe he was acutely aware of the feelings between you two, as he was of all of our emotions. Also, he guessed that, more than likely, Cassandra was simply on the precipice of death rather than actually being dead. Shooting you with a minuscule amount of the plasma halted you, while also giving you the power to resuscitate *her*. He suspected you were likely to give Cassandra one last kiss and, thus, pass the radiation on to her, bringing her back to you. Almost like Snow White, don't you think?" The Doctor smiled serenely, then continued. "It also stands to reason that, after her resuscitation, he could use what negligible radiation she had left to remove the encephalopod. I believe repairing the recent damage done was his one last attempt to prove to himself that he wasn't a monster after all."

In thoughtful silence, they looked at the holovid and grimly considered the void Mentacron's planet had recently occupied, taking into account the things both gained and lost in the aftermath. But, before they could give themselves over fully to a hard-won sense of security and measured triumph, an alarm began to sound.

The Doctor noticed one of the console panels blinking red. He went over to it and tensed slightly.

"What is it, Doctor," Cassandra asked.

He turned to them and said vividly, "It appears there's been an unusual energy emission in the Vega system!" He began to energetically program into the console a hyperspace jaunting sequence which would immediately take them to the source of the emission.

Rollie and Cassandra gave each other a judicious glance and said in unison, "Oh, no, not again," just as the *Cosmos* vanished, leaving only a diminishing whiff of tachyon particles behind.

*Professor Helvetius*

# DOCTOR OMEGA: THE TERROR FROM BEYOND TIME

At first, no one really took notice of the fog. Which is reasonable, considering it was an unusually moist week in Ealdwine, and the fog, itself, seemed to be keeping to the deciduous forest on the outskirts of the North Yorkshire village, for now.

The forest was only rarely visited these days, regardless of the village cemetery being there, due to the average age of the community balancing precariously between the excessively mature, who found it increasingly difficult to gambol about, and everyone else, who tended to find nature a poor competitor with modern technologies. This is why, when someone did finally take notice of the fog, it was too late.

The first indication there was something wrong in the village was when the bird flew through Mrs. Whittingham's open kitchen window while she was doing the dishes. It wasn't that the bird flew in so much, which was odd enough, but that it did so in such an awkward way.

Later, she told authorities it sort of tumbled through, reminding her of a plane which had lost a wing and spiraled to the ground. She repeated, it tumbled through clumsily, which wasn't at all what she was used to from birds, and it hit the opposite wall with a thud before falling to the floor and bouncing a few times, then rolling to a stop, like a rotting rubber ball.

She was slightly embarrassed to admit, this last bit about bouncing and rolling made her laugh somewhat.

She wasn't so amused when she went to remove the poor thing's little body and saw that it was horribly deformed by some kind of mold, and parts of it seemed to be on the outside instead of on the inside, where they belonged, as if it had exploded.

The second indication there was something wrong in the village was when Mr. Tolliver showed up at his own door late one evening, no more than a day after Mrs. Whittingham's bird incident. It was well past dinner, and Mrs. Tolliver was a touch annoyed that someone would be knocking at her door at such a late hour. To make the situation more bothersome, the knocking was ploddingly repetitive and dull, like the sound made by a heavy blanket flapping slowly in the wind.

That annoyance changed to horror when she opened the door to find Mr. Tolliver, who had died several months previously, standing dumbly at the step, as if he weren't sure he had the right address. It took Mrs. Tolliver a moment to recognize her husband, since his face and figure were, for the most part, covered in some kind of lumpy, dank fungus mottled with green, red, and purplish colors, twisting his body and head into grotesquely bent shapes. Eventually his animated corpse did, indeed, confirm Mrs. Whittingham's conjecture about the bird by exploding as well. Naturally, Mrs. Tolliver was never quite right after the *unpleasantness*, as the village gossips came to refer to the incident.

Considering this was an affair well beyond the scope of local authorities, it was then that Professor Helvetius, Director of the Center for Scientific Research, was called in to investigate.

Professor Helvetius was an elderly gentleman, bordering on chubby and relatively short, with impressively thick salt-and-pepper hair and beard, both tending more toward salt than pepper, with large and seemingly un-blinking eyes made comically owlish behind his thick, gold-rimmed glasses.

It was that fluffy, abstract stare which gave one the impression his personality lacked certain rough edges; this was true, to some extent, and always had been, as Dr. Ewan Tremayne, the immediate subordinate of Hel-vetius within the Center hierarchy had found out. Only a year before, Tremayne had been appointed to the position by Helvetius, based mostly upon what some referred to as his "spooky genius" in the field of mathematical physics.

From the beginning, Tremayne thought it interest-ing that the musty, unfashionable office which the Pro-fessor occupied here at Cambridge, under the auspices of the CSR, validated his opinion concerning the lack of rough edges while simultaneously masking it. He learned early on that the double-layered, smoothed-over masking was a prominent feature, possibly *the* promi-nent feature, of the cherubic Professor's persona.

Tremayne, with a touch of certitude, dropped the file on the desk, directly in front of a startled Helvetius, and said, "You'll want to read this."

The Professor had been closely examining a previ-ously unknown flower which one of his investigators had discovered while exploring a recently exposed cave in the wilds of Indonesia. He looked absently over the top of his glasses at Tremayne. "What is this?"

"The report you requested about North Yorkshire."

The Professor gave one of his rare blinks. "North Yorkshire? Undoubtedly a beautiful place, but I don't recall making any plans to visit."

Tremayne reluctantly accommodated the Professor's game and repeated, "North Yorkshire." He stopped to quickly reference the odd village name in the file again before returning it to its position in front of his superior. "Ealdwine. The fungus outbreak." He waited for the Professor to reply, and when he didn't, he finished with a mild show of irritation. "The persistent fog and the dead coming back to life, does that ring a bell? It sounds preposterous, I know, but someone felt it was serious enough to hand it off to us. At worst, it's probably the result of some sort of mass hallucination. Something the national health department could easily handle."

"Ah, yes, that is a curious situation! And what have we learned about it, other than your dismissive conjecture?"

Tremayne nodded toward the file. "All of the preparatory details are there. But you know them already, don't you? I suspect you'll want us to head out as soon as possible. I've directed members of the staff to begin packing things up for the trip."

Goaded by Tremayne's candor, Helvetius gave the file a perfunctory once-over, then set it aside and stared at him with those large, strigine eyes again. "You've made the right choice. But I'll be going along this time."

Tremayne was stunned. Professor Helvetius rarely left the offices of the CSR for any reason whatsoever. There must be something in this one to get him to take such drastic steps. Then it struck him, along with a touch of resentment; Helvetius was going along to keep an eye on him.

On the previous investigation Tremayne had led, one of the subordinate investigators suffered an injury serious enough to almost cause her death, and this was due to a deficiency of proper oversight on his part, or so it was implied by some of the accompanying staff. He said vaguely, "As you please. We'll get your equipment ready." Then, he turned and went off out of the room.

Arcadia, as the name implied, was an enchanted garden of a planet. Undoubtedly, this was one of the reasons why Rollie DuBay and Cassandra Troy, the Doctor's current companions, had chosen it for their wedding ceremony. Although neither, up to this point, had shown signs leaning toward any particular theology, they picked an especially devout priest from the planet's governing entity, the El Deus Omnipotens Synodal Cloister, to perform the ceremony.

Doctor Omega rightly presumed this was the second reason they had chosen this planet, along with the third reason, its proximity at the time, and was most likely due to the order's close similarity to the milieu within which Rollie had grown up. The relationship between the two companions had tightened considerably since its first blossoming during their encounter with Mentacron a while back and had naturally turned toward the desire for a more official bonding.

Even though the ceremony had been held months ago, the three had stayed on for an extended period for the honeymoon, an uncommon thing for the Doctor to oblige, since he was well-known as a stingy customer when it came to frittering away his time in ways he considered unproductive.

Still, he beamed approvingly at his companions whenever he saw them, as if he were their true paternal grandparent. And he did make serious efforts to not spoil their happiness. Regardless, he often distracted himself by dealing with minor mechanical issues aboard the *Cosmos*, working through various astrophysical problems, and charting courses to planets they could visit once the honeymoon was over. It was while working on one such chart that the couple, all smiles, made a welcome appearance on the bridge.

Doctor Omega turned from the control console, cocking his eyebrows. "Well, you two look keen as mustard about something."

Rollie smiled self-consciously at Cassandra, then back at the Doctor. "That we are, Doctor."

After a moment, the Doctor said jovially, "Spit it out, my boy. What's got you stirred up?"

Finally, Rollie said, "We're having a baby."

Delighted, the Doctor threw up his hands and aggressively waved them over. He gave them a huge hug, then said, "I couldn't be happier! Such wonderful news!" Remembering they were still on Arcadia, he said, "You know, we must plan a celebration. I assumed we'd be leaving soon, but I don't see the point, considering we're on the perfect planet for such an occasion."

Both Rollie and Cassandra happily agreed and held each other tighter.

Rollie watched the Doctor's thoughtful expression turn into a slight grimace. He waited for a moment, just to see if it was due to concentration, but realized quickly that it was, instead, due to some twinge of pain. "Are you alright?"

The Doctor drifted back against the console. Under duress, he got out, "Something wrong." He collapsed back into his chair, placing a hand across his chest. "Terribly wrong."

The Doctor's companions came over to him. Rollie asked, "What's wrong? What can we do for you?"

Sucking in air, the Doctor said, "I don't think there's anything you can do." Then, he quivered with shock and said with wide eyes. "Helvetius!"

Gathering his strength, he turned to the console and struggled to tap in coordinates. After a bit, he began to recover enough to explain what had happened. "I felt something had happened to a close acquaintance of mine – Professor Helvetius. You see, he's one of my, er, people, and everyone who's a part of it is connected through synchrosomes, a type of molecular machine at the cellular level, if you will, which connects one to another. Those who are in the same kinship group are the most closely connected. Helvetius and I share a group. And I sense something terrible has just happened to him."

To the surprise of his companions, the Doctor recovered rather quickly, but he was left feeling as though something were missing.

As the *Cosmos* landed at a secluded location in North Yorkshire, behind an abandoned barn within the village of Ealdwine, a small, red light on the console began slowly shifting in and out of vibrancy.

The Doctor noticed and said, "Strange."

Cassandra asked, "What is?"

"This indicator. It's an error light, but it's only supposed to flash when there's a problem with the coordinate programming."

Cassandra smiled, "Did you put in the wrong coordinates?"

The Doctor said flatly, "Hardly."

Rollie said disapprovingly to Cassandra, "Don't antagonize him. Let's not spoil things."

Cassandra nodded sheepishly.

Looking sideways at Cassandra for a moment, the Doctor followed through. "It couldn't be the wrong co-ordinates, because I simply instructed the *Cosmos* to take us to Helvetius's current location." He concluded introspectively. "It does appear to be England, at least according to these readings. And last I heard, he had taken up permanent residence at Cambridge."

Rollie piped in. "So, is he here or not?"

"It seems the indicator is saying 'yes' and 'no'." The Doctor shrugged. "The best way to find out what's what is to go investigate."

Rollie waved his hand toward the gravcap, an antigravity elevator which provided travel between floors of the *Cosmos*, and said, "After you."

The Doctor gestured and said, "Oh no, by all means, after you."

"I insist, after you."

The Doctor said, a little more sternly, "After you."

Smiling, Rollie yielded and led them all to the gravcap.

Once outside, the Doctor took in their surroundings, casually noticing a large barn several feet directly in front of them and a clump of mist-shrouded trees to their rear at around a thousand feet away and sectioned off by a prominent fence. "Well, it does most definitely look like England."

Cassandra said, "It does, but isn't this a bit rustic for Cambridge? I thought it was in a reasonably developed area."

Puzzled, the Doctor concurred. "That it is." After glancing about, he said, "Our best option, I think, is to find out what's on the other side of this barn."

Agreeing, they moved off in a body. Before taking more than a few steps, a large Land Rover Special Operations Vehicle came barreling around the barn; it was occupied by numerous people in hazmat suits and topped with a large weapon.

Without notice, one of the people aimed the weapon – a flamethrower, as it turned out – at something a hundred yards behind the Doctor and his companions, in the direction of the forest, and fired.

The three dropped to the ground as a massive stream of flame shot out and engulfed what at first appeared to be a man. But after a brief glimpse of the figure before it was entirely inundated, the Doctor wasn't entirely sure anymore.

In the midst of strangely artificial wails and an awkward writhing reminiscent of a stringed marionette, sparks began to fly from the man-shaped blaze, then it quickly crumpled to the ground as little more than a twitching, burning pile of ash and sludge, accompanied by the occasional electrical pop.

As the three got back to their feet, the people in hazmat suits could be heard calling in a clean-up crew.

One of the hazmat people left the truck and came up to them, a military rifle in one hand, swinging by his side. This, the SOV, and the hazmat suits were clear indicators to the Doctor that they were dealing with some sort of military special forces unit concentrating on toxic containment. And the toxicity of whatever they were trying to contain was extreme enough to grant them the authority to kill on sight anyone they suspected of infection.

While they could barely make out a face through the hazmat visor, they could tell by the subtle shift of the persons shoulders that he was cursorily taking in the oddness of the *Cosmos* as he approached.

Once upon them, the soldier asked firmly, "Where did you come from?"

Startled by the casual extermination they had just witnessed, the Doctor pushed back. "From Arcadia. What's going on here?"

"That's none of your concern."

Troubled, the Doctor pressed further. "This won't do. We have an appointment."

"Not in Ealdwine, you don't."

The soldier suddenly felt as though he had said something he shouldn't have. This started him into an authoritarian loop he instinctively knew he couldn't escape from now without exacting a certain amount of force.

Following the prescribed narrative, he gripped the rifle with both hands and held it against his torso, readying it for action if needed. He called to another soldier for support. He came over and took up the same stance as his associate.

Just as he arrived, the Doctor asked severely, "Really, what's this about? You're just murdering people, are you? Are we next?"

The soldier said stiffly, "Never you mind. You'll have to come with us."

The Doctor became stern. "And go where? As I said before, I have an appointment."

The soldier saw a potential way out. "With who?"

"Professor Helvetius."

The soldier started. After a moment, he said, "Wait here."

He left the other soldier to guard them while he made his way back to the SOV and began animatedly conversing with the driver.

The Doctor saw him pick up a radio and begin talking conspicuously with someone on the other end, presumably his superior officer.

Several minutes went by, along with various interactions, until the soldier Doctor Omega had been speaking with waved them over to him and said, "In the truck."

They skittishly got in, then the truck took off. As they went, they saw another group of soldiers pass them on the road, all wearing hazmat suits. They were going in the direction of the burning man.

The truck took them a little further into the village, passing along the way a sign reading "Ealdwine Market," then stopped.

The Doctor and his companions found a rather precise and orderly military set up. Shortly, before leaving the truck via a side panel, they were passed through what the Doctor presumed to be a sanitizing process involving sprays and mild radiation.

After this, and back outside again, a relatively young man greeted them abruptly, almost as if to bar them from going further. The first thing that came to the Doctor's attention was that the young man's right hand was bandaged and, judging from the brief glances the Doctor had of it, he could tell the ring finger was missing. He also picked up a faint odor identical to the sanitizing spray they had gone through moments before and thought it odd this man would still be carrying the odor with him, considering he had probably not gone through the sanitizing process any too soon before their arrival.

Beyond those two things, he saw that the man was tall and lean, square-jawed, and oozing a comfortable authority, perhaps too much so, the Doctor thought. Although, he did entirely lack the expected military bearing and accouterments that would normally come with such a demeanor.

Their guiding soldier whispered something to this seeming authority, then was instructed by this same person to head back to his post. The tall man looked the three over squarely and tried to make the necessarily blunt questioning as unobtrusive as possible.

"Who are you, and where did you come from? You're not from the village?"

The Doctor mimicked the serious tone. "I've already told your man, no, we are not from the village, and I have an appointment with someone. And who might you be?"

"Tremayne. Dr. Ewan Tremayne. How did you get past the barricades?"

"Easily."

Realizing this was an unfruitful line of questioning at the moment, Tremayne took another route. "The sergeant tells me you told him you have an appointment to see Professor Helvetius?"

"In a way, yes I do. I believe he may need my assistance."

"Really. What makes you think that? Did he contact you?"

"In a sense. Listen, Dr. Tremayne…"

"Just Tremayne. Or Ewan. I don't stand on pretense."

"As you wish, Ewan. I received a kind of message from Professor Helvetius indicating his need for assistance."

"A kind of message?"

Exasperated, the Doctor blurted, "My dear young man, Helvetius and I have known each other for longer than you've been alive! In a sense, we're even related!"

Tremayne stood back for a moment with an inquisitive look on his face. "What did you say your name was?"

"I didn't. But, if it helps, my name is Omega. Doctor Omega."

Tremayne showed a slight twinge of recognition at that. After studying the Doctor for a moment, he said precisely, "Come with me."

He then turned and made his way toward a nearby building without waiting for them to follow, because he knew they had no other choice but to do so.

The Doctor found the interior of the building quite fascinating. In its original capacity, it obviously served as the local pub and, most likely, the gathering place where official village business took place. Now, every conceivable nook was occupied by scientific apparatuses, some of which were quite exotic, as well as numerous scientists, surprisingly ragged in their appearance.

Tremayne offered them one of the few tables still available for general occupancy, and joined them at the end, in a separate chair. He let go one of the two soldiers who had followed them in; the other he kept guard at the door, just in case anything went sideways. "So, you're related to the Professor, and he sent you a message."

"In a way. How much do you know of him?"

"Quite a bit. I've been his second at the Center for Scientific Research for a year now, but I've been there for several. I'm surprised he hasn't mentioned me to you."

Ignoring this, the Doctor said, "Judging from your response outside, it appears he's mentioned *me* to *you*."

Tremayne smiled. "That he has, assuming you are who you say you are."

Rollie stepped in. "Oh, he's definitely who he says he is."

Tremayne looked sharply at him. "And you are?"

"Rollie DuBay. Trusted sidekick. And, this is my wife, Cassandra, also a trusted sidekick."

"Professor Helvetius never mentioned you two," Tremayne said suspiciously.

The Doctor interjected. "He wouldn't have. He never met them. Now, if we could stop with this foolishness, I'd like to see my old friend."

Weighing the situation and finding it reasonably plausible, considering the Professor's inclination toward keeping most of his past a secret and being profoundly eccentric at the same time, he mellowed slightly and said, "You don't want to see him."

"And, why's that?"

Tremayne hesitated. "He's not the same man you once knew."

"Oh, do please stop with these silly melodramatics. Take me to Helvetius, at once!"

Tremayne finally gave in. He rose from the table and took them out of the pub; a few doors down, he entered another building, this one much larger, yet equally filled with scientific instruments, but this one was extensively guarded, both inside and out, by many more soldiers.

They passed through the crowded laboratory and came to a door at the back of the large room. The door had a bulk identical to that of walk-in freezer entrance, with the heavy-duty latch which normally came with that. Humorless soldiers stood resolutely erect on either side of the door.

Before entering, Tremayne turned to his guests. He was hesitant. "As I said earlier, he's not the man he once was."

Judging from the hefty freezer door, the Doctor assumed Tremayne was being circuitous about Helvetius's death, which didn't seem quite right, since he hadn't felt a total cessation of the Professor's life, but only the sense that a piece of him had somehow gone missing, which really didn't make much sense to him, either. He put these thoughts aside, and quietly wished Tremayne would just get to it rather than act so affectedly.

Finally, Tremayne unlatched the heavy handle, swung the ponderous door open, and escorted them in. Inside were more statuesque soldiers, again on each side of the door, but this time both were wrapped in parkas due to the chill in the air. It wasn't freezing in there, but the temperature was low enough to cause discomfort. Presumably, the room was kept this way in order to prevent the massive amount of electrical equipment from overheating.

Beyond all of this gadgetry, the Doctor noticed, at the other end of the room and through a tangle of apparatus and tubing, a row of what looked to be chambers, each the size of a full-grown adult human, and in the shape of upright boilers. Unlike typical boilers, these had thick glass windows bolted into them, near the top, but facing forward, almost like observation windows. The thought startled him. He gestured toward them while addressing Tremayne. "What are those?"

"In a way, life support." He took them over to the objects, and to one in particular. "This one here is Professor Helvetius."

Shocked, the Doctor stepped up to the glass plate and looked in. What he saw was a hideously deformed hominid shape, but without identifying, distinctive features. It was entirely covered in some type of fungus, he realized, delineating its form in such a way as to make it unidentifiable as anything other than a fermenting, man-shaped mold. It twitched slightly but didn't seem to be able to move beyond that.

Tremayne said coldly, "There's not much he can do in there. It's heavily pressurized to prevent most movement and any further biological disintegration."

The Doctor stepped back and stared harshly at him. "You can't be serious! That can't possibly be Helvetius! That's nothing more than an abomination!"

"It is, but I assure you, that's Helvetius. At the beginning of our investigation here, he became infected." Tremayne displayed his bandaged right hand. "It happened just after *this* and before we better understood what was going on; near the forest, I had placed my hand on a large rock in order to steady myself but didn't realize it hosted a patch of the fungus. That same day, Professor Helvetius had to amputate the finger. I'm assuming that's how he became infected. He was fine one day, then the next, he was like this. We found him in his quarters on the second day. The infection must have already done considerable damage to his central nervous system, because it was apparent he was trying to get out of his room but had forgotten how to use a door, or even a window. It was if he were in a totally new environment he had never encountered before."

"This is extraordinary." The Doctor glanced questioningly at the five other pressure chambers lining the wall.

Tremayne said, "Yes, all occupied, some containing village residents, others containing my colleagues from the Center. We originally had the chambers on one of the trucks, but soon ran out of room and had to move them in here." He led them out of the cooler and back over to the pub-turned-headquarters.

Seated back at the table again, the Doctor asked incredulously, "What happened?"

"We're not entirely sure yet. Being that the CSR investigates scientific anomalies, we were notified relatively quickly about it. At first, it all sounded like rubbish to me, even after the preliminary report came in. Nonsense about the dead rising, a mysterious fog, this repulsive fungus. We've handled some real oddities before, but nothing this extreme. Still, Helvetius felt we should investigate anyway, so we packed up, and arrived soon after to find it was all true. We immediately brought in more equipment and specialists, cordoned off the entire village, and put another barricade up around the forest where this all seems to have started. We quarantined the infected, and we burned – I hate to say this – the living dead who had risen from their graves in the forest. The fog is slowly creeping out and getting closer to the village and our barricade. We haven't found a way to stop that yet. Not much else has come out of there since we've gotten here, other than the odd, deformed animal, and terrible sounds, a dull wailing like something out of Dante's *Inferno*."

"Have you made an expedition into the forest in order to find what started all of this?"

"No. We planned to once we got here and interviewed the villagers, but things quickly got out of hand."

"What are you doing to cure Helvetius."

"The only thing we can do at the moment. Keep him stabilized in the pressurized chamber until we find a remedy."

Doctor Omega said angrily, "Haven't you been looking for one? Other than containment, and burning men alive, is anyone doing anything around here?"

"Believe me, we're doing the best we can. And that was no man you saw them burn. It was a corpse."

"How is that possible?"

"I'm not sure, yet. The village cemetery is in the forest, and whatever this fungus is, it can reanimate the dead. Not for long, though, and not to its original capacity as a living human being. Not long after reanimation, the things simply explode, seemingly killing the fungi. The same happens with living forms of lower life, as well. Birds, insects, trees, grass. For some reason, in order to sustain itself for long periods of time, the fungus needs the higher neurological levels of living humans. Nevertheless, we burn the ones that burst apart anyway, just to be safe."

After a pause, he continued. "We only just arrived a week ago." He nodded in the direction of the building holding the pressure chambers. "It's taken almost all of that time just to try and find a way to contain this thing."

The Doctor cooled. "Yes, yes, I know. I apologize. I understand these things can be a bit, shall we say, exasperating."

"You sound as though you've had experience along these lines. With the Professor?"

"Both of us have had experiences with anomalies just as extravagant as this one, yet not identical to it. To say more may disrupt things and intrude upon Helvetius's private territory."

Tremayne nodded stoically.

The Doctor said, "Of course, I'm willing to stay and help out in any way I can, but, taking into consideration the possibility of infection, I think my companions should go back to the ship at once."

Tremayne squinted at the Doctor. "Ship?"

"Yes. Our conveyance, if you will." Then, he became agitated with Tremayne. "See here, young man, Cassandra is newly pregnant. The sooner we leave, the less likely she'll have complications." He softened a little. "I promise I'll return," he looked about, "with a bit more advanced equipment."

Cassandra protested, but the Doctor shut her down. "You will go back to the *Cosmos*, is that understood? I will not put that child in jeopardy. You know very well, if conditions were different, I would be of another mind."

Cassandra yielded to his grandfatherly concern.

"Better yet," Tremayne interjected, "why don't I escort you to this 'conveyance' of yours, to make sure nothing goes wrong and to help with bringing the equipment back." This was a statement, not a question.

Exasperated, the Doctor said, "Don't make this any more difficult than it has to be. You're needed here, and the ship will likely create more questions for you than necessary right now. Rollie can help bring back the equipment."

Tremayne repeated, "I'll escort you, and these soldiers will accompany us." Taking possession of the same SOV they had arrived in, the soldier doing the driving made quick time to the *Cosmos*.

Tremayne was incredulous. "This is your ship? A giant cannon shell?"

Perturbed, the Doctor said as they left the SOV and went to the *Cosmos*, "Yes, it is. Remember, my boy, looks can be deceiving." Once in the entry level of the ship, and past the Doctor's newly initiated sterilization process, the Doctor led them to the bridge.

Tremayne gave the area a cursory glance and was duly impressed.

The Doctor positioned Cassandra at the control console and instructed her on what to keep track of. He also pointed out the communication device required for them to stay in contact and relay information. He set it to pick up the radio signals which would be coming from the village base of operations. That done, he reminded Rollie to stay behind, and led Tremayne back down to the first floor and into a room near the ship entrance.

Upon entering, Tremayne was astonished. The room was much bigger than the ship could possibly encompass. At the entrance, there was a kind of dressing alcove with lockers and what appeared to be a row of atmosphere suits. Adjacent to the alcove was a large hangar containing a couple of tandem, two-seater tractor trailers, lined up in front of their assigned exit doors. Past this, after a good eight hundred feet further on, the Doctor turned right into one of the aisles and retrieved various bulky items from the shelving units, some of which he passed on to Tremayne to carry as they left the room.

Out of the room, they encountered Rollie as he came around from the gravcap. He said jovially, "I'm going back with you."

Astonished, the Doctor said, "You're supposed to stay here with Cassandra."

"That was *your* plan, not mine."

"Well, doesn't Cassandra want you to stay?"

"Yes she does. But, really, I'm of no use here."

"What about the baby?"

"You seem to have forgotten, Doctor, I'm not pregnant. Cassandra is."

"Funny, but you know what I mean."

"Of course I do, but I need to be doing something; besides, the people from CSR seem to have the infection relatively under control at the moment. If Cassandra stays secluded here, everything should be okay. The likelihood of anything happening to me is quite low, as long as nothing extraordinary happens. I mean, anything other than what's already happened."

"Point taken, my boy. And, if Cassandra agrees, then I shall, too! We shall make you useful right now!"

The Doctor handed Rollie some of the equipment he was carrying, then they left the ship. Outside, Tremayne, who was looking a bit fatigued now, gave instructions for some of the soldiers to remain behind as guards. The Doctor wasn't entirely sure if this was to protect Cassandra or to keep an eye on her.

The rest piled into the SOV and quickly drove back to the center of the village and parked near the pub/headquarters again. There, the Doctor was directed to the military's radio man who proceeded to connect him with Cassandra in order to insure he had set the ship's communication system to the proper frequency.

Tremayne and Rollie moved the equipment they had been carrying onto a military truck trailer, extended on both sides now in order to act as a highly sanitary and compartmentalized examination unit.

When he was satisfied Cassandra was in good order, the Doctor came to the back of the truck, joining Tremayne and Rollie, and began organizing items according to some secret knowledge he had of the devices and paraphernalia.

In brief time, he had everything aligned in a way which made sense to him; once together, the entire setup occupied a small part of an examination table.

Giving everything the once-over, Tremayne asked, "I've seen a lot of oddball lab gear before, quite a bit of it top secret, but this stuff's even got me. What's it all do?"

"Honestly, it's not that different from your typical laboratory hardware. It's designed to be more sensitive in its identifications and more expansive in what it identifies."

"Well, that's sufficiently vague enough," Tremayne laughed.

Smiling, Rollie said, "It seems to be his nature. I still don't know if it's intentional or not."

Tremayne shook his head and said knowingly, "Sounds a lot like my Helvetius."

This sobered the Doctor, who said, "Yes, back to it." He picked up a small box from the table, held it in his palm, and said, "I'll need a small fragment of the fungus for analysis."

Rollie, who felt he would be of better use quietly gathering information back at the pub, discreetly left the two scientists to their examinations.

Tremayne and the Doctor took the box and the Doctor's equipment to an even more secure compartment in the truck. Once there, Tremayne clarified, "We've not had much luck analyzing the fungus. Any penetrating examination sends off sparks for some odd reason, causing us to stop. Hopefully, you'll have better luck."

They donned hazmat suits and passed through another small sanitation area; then, on the other side, they entered a room where the Doctor set his equipment on another table. Other than the table, this room was empty;

opposite them was a double-thick window occupying almost an entire wall. Through this window, the Doctor could see an area no bigger than a closet. Seeing a small shelf on which sat rows of jars filled with samples, the Doctor instantly recognized it as a containment room, used to house and quarantine highly contagious biological agents. Also in the wall, just below the window, were two openings enclosed by robotic arms with which objects in the other room could be manipulated.

Tremayne pressed a button near the window. Bellow it, a square segment in the wall slid back to reveal a pre-sanitized drawer. He placed the box he had taken from the Doctor into the drawer and pressed the button again, sending it back into the wall. From there, Tremayne maneuvered one of the robotic arms over to the jars. He removed the lid from one and retrieved a mold specimen from the it, transferring it to the box, which had opened automatically to receive it, surprising Tremayne somewhat. The box closed, again automatically, and the drawer was dosed with a heavy anti-fungal foam, which evaporated once the drawer closed. Tremayne left the robotic arm and retrieved the box, handing it to the Doctor.

The Doctor placed the box in one of the pieces of equipment he had brought along and began the analysis.

"What is that?" Tremayne asked as he glanced over the apparatus.

Without looking up from the screen embedded in the device, the Doctor said, "A portable electron microscope."

"You're kidding. There's no such thing!"

"The fact I'm using one proves you wrong."

At that moment, the fungus began to pop off electrical sparks before completely vaporizing within the containment box. The Doctor instinctively jerked back. "Fascinating. The fungus just exploded before I could examine it."

"I told you."

"That you did, but I had to see for myself. Luckily, I brought along something I've been working on and may help us get around this issue." The Doctor removed the box and asked Tremayne to get another sample.

After doing so, Tremayne handed it back, saying, "It was taken from the rock on the edge of the mist."

Once back in his possession, the Doctor put the box into a smaller machine which was sitting near the first one.

"So, what's this thing do?"

"It's another type of microscope I've been working on; you might call it a neutrino force microscope."

"I might, if I knew how it worked."

"It picks up nanoscale imagery without interfering with the structure of the thing being scanned."

Tremayne leaned in, his fatigued eyes probing every inch of the device. "Remarkable."

The Doctor began the new analysis. After a moment, he straitened and said, "I think I've discovered why the fungus keeps sparking under those other conditions."

Tremayne asked excitedly, "Really, why?"

"Because, for one thing, it's permeated with polythiazyl, which is highly explosive, and secondly, it appears our little fungus isn't necessarily what we would normally call a living organism."

"It's not alive?"

"Oh, it's alive alright, but it's a living machine, a kind of nanobot organic substance. It's built up of trillions of organic nanosized forms which seem to mimic biological life, and are derived from a nanobot triple helix substructure instead of the typically known amino acid double helix. It sends off electrical sparks whenever these substructures are subjected to counter forces, and the polythiazyl simply exacerbates the reaction."

Tremayne was speechless, with a million calculations running through his mind.

The Doctor broke him from his spell. "I'd like to examine a specimen from Professor Helvetius, if you have one. You do have one, don't you?"

Tremayne regained focus. "Yes, yes I do. Right over here." He went back to the robotic arm and retrieved another sample, this one from a jar marked PH-1.

The Doctor put the sample into the neutrino microscope and watched the embedded screen as the machine began processing the imagery. After a moment, the Doctor said, "This makes no sense."

"What doesn't?"

The Doctor looked sharply at Tremayne. "You're sure this was taken from Helvetius?"

"Positive."

"Do you have any samples taken from one of the corpses or animals?"

"Yes." Tremayne took the box, returned the Helvetius sample to its jar and retrieved a sample from one of the corpses, then gave the box to Doctor Omega.

The Doctor watched the microscope screen intently and finally said, "Interesting." After another long moment, he suddenly said, "I think we're done here. Put the sample back, and let's return to the others. We must talk, immediately."

Once back at the pub, while Tremayne began pluckily calling his CSR colleagues to gather round, Rollie passed close by the Doctor in an unassuming way and whispered that he needed to speak to him after the meeting's end, then he casually took a position near the small window only a few feet behind the Doctor.

Tremayne got things going in his typically overbearing way. "I've called you all around," he glanced briefly at the Doctor, "because we've made an astonishing discovery." He gestured toward the Doctor, signaling him to take his place. "I think it's best that he explain our findings."

The Doctor, hiding well his displeasure with Tremayne's subtle encroachment, nodded in a measured fashion and exchanged positions with him.

The Doctor cupped the lapels of his coat and said as clearly and succinctly as he could, "I believe what we're facing here isn't some common biological outbreak. My analysis has shown, almost without question, that what we're experiencing is an alien invasion."

The room broke out into a low, confused chatter.

Rollie, still in his secluded nook, thought, for a fleeting moment, he saw Tremayne stiffen. He decided this was due either to the Doctor not telling him about his final hypothesis, or Tremayne knew something about this whole thing that no one else did, just as one of the investigators had suggested to him in an earlier private conversation while Tremayne and the Doctor were away analyzing the fungus.

The Doctor held up his hands, quieting the room. "I know, it's a shocking declaration, but I assure you, I'm not saying this lightly." He looked at Tremayne with a fine sharpness. "And I'm sure Ewan will corroborate."

Tremayne's bearing of authority returned. He scanned the room. "I agree with the Doctor entirely."

The room fell into low mumbling again, until one of the investigators spoke up, addressing the Doctor. "What makes you so sure?"

The Doctor explained. "The nanoscopic imaging I've just done clearly showed a triple helix configuration totally alien to our own DNA structure; a deeper scan also showed that that configuration is derived from infinitesimal nanobot mechanisms which, once built up, mimic what we call life. As you've already seen, the macro results of that instrumentation act as living, organic tissue; it grows, secretes, multiplies, and even seems to show some signs of trying to maintain its own existence by intertwining itself with earth-based organisms. Make no mistake: it's alive, it's growing, spreading, and it's incredibly alien."

A murmur filled the room until the Doctor tapped it down. "We have another issue, though. The whereabouts of Professor Helvetius."

The room was quiet, not understanding the statement, but Rollie observed a barely visible anticipation in Tremayne.

The Doctor addressed the confusion. "You're under the impression that Helvetius's infected body is in the pressure chamber in the other building. It is not."

There was a soft gasp from some in the audience.

"An analysis was done of three tissue samples. The first was taken from the surface of a rock and only showed signs of the triple helix nanorganic material. The second was supposedly from Helvetius; but it, too, only contained the nanobot triple helix material. The third was taken from one of the infected corpses which had made its way out of the village cemetery; it contained earth-based, human material mingled with the alien nanorganic substructure. Since the Helvetius sample contained no DNA at all, the conclusion has to be, the thing in that pressure chamber is *not* Professor Helvetius."

The audience was stunned.

The Doctor drove his point home. "Furthermore, if that's *not* Helvetius's body, which it isn't, then the rest of the bodies are, most likely, not infected villagers or your CSR colleagues, either. So the question now is: What's become of them?"

At that moment, a soldier rushed in from the outside, drawing everyone's attention. His eyes swept the room until they met Tremayne's, then he spoke in a sudden burst. "The fog, Sir, it's expanded its radius by twenty feet!"

Tremayne immediately took command. "Alright, everyone, I believe we've done all we can here. Go back to your work, and I'll have the relevant data for you shortly." Then, he addressed the soldier. "Right. Get out there and set up an extended barricade around the fog, and continue to monitor it. If anything changes, let me know."

The soldier nodded briskly and left the way he had come as the group dispersed.

Tremayne turned to the Doctor. "So, what do you think is really going on here?" The question didn't seem to match the moderate lack of concern his tone was approaching, which brought to life a subconscious ambivalence in the Doctor.

Over Tremayne's shoulder, the Doctor caught sight of Rollie approaching the two at a leisurely pace. He returned his attention to Tremayne and said slowly, "To be honest, I'm not sure yet."

Rollie arrived at their location, but the Doctor's focus was still on Tremayne. "One thing I do know, though, is that forest should be completely incinerated at once."

Tremayne said without reserve, "We can't do that. It's the center of this thing, and as such, it's too important scientifically. You said so yourself when you declared this situation an alien invasion."

Again, the Doctor noticed an odd lack of worry on Tremayne's part, but now he simply saw it as an excessive brand of scientific pigheadedness. "Maybe so. But I believe we have more than enough samples and data to cover the loss. After all, we are talking about a possible extinction-level event here."

"Out of the question. If we haven't worked this out by the time the fog reaches the village proper, then we'll burn it, and not a moment before."

"Well, that sounds definite. I can see we're going to get nowhere on this topic. So, I think it's best if I make contact with Cassandra, and let her know Rollie and I will be returning to the *Cosmos*, where we can perform more elaborate analysis."

Tremayne said coldly, "As you please," then he turned and went out of the building.

After watching Tremayne go, Rollie shifted his attention to the Doctor. "He wasn't all that cordial to begin with, but the end of this little soiree certainly turned him chilly."

"It seems that way." The Doctor knitted his brows and asked, "You wanted to speak with me after the meeting?"

"That I did." Rollie stepped closer to the Doctor and lowered his voice. "While you and Tremayne were working on the fungus, I had a confidential chat with one of the CSR investigators; she told me Tremayne's the only one that's been in that forest. After what happened to Helvetius and the rock incident," at this point, Rollie wagged the ring finger of his right hand in front of the Doctor, "Tremayne donned a hazmat suit and went all the way in, by himself. When he came back out, he had the whole thing blocked off from any access."

"Well, that does make sense, don't you think?"

"Yes, but what makes it suspicious is he refuses to say what he saw in there, other than to just say it's what would be expected. Now, what does that mean?"

"Most likely, exactly what he said."

"But, when we first met, didn't he say no one had been in the forest, period?"

The Doctor became thoughtful for a moment, then said, "He probably meant no one other than himself."

Mildly piqued, Rollie asked, "You don't find his behavior a bit odd?"

"To the contrary. I do find it quite odd. His behavior is beginning to seem like that of a logical absolutist, which tends to mark one as mentally unstable and weak in character. Look, despite what you may think, I'm in agreement with you. I'm just not willing to jump at anything, as of yet."

Letting it go, Rollie waved a thumb over his shoulder. "Are we really going back to the *Cosmos* because of the tension between you two?"

"Hardly. My excuse was entirely truthful. There's equipment in the ship I need to work with which is far too cumbersome to be brought here. And, you'll be glad to know, I would like to keep Tremayne in the dark about it, at least until I've gotten some other answers." Seeing that Rollie seemed to be pleased by this, he said, "First things first, though. The CSR unit has to have a medical doctor on hand; did your source happen to mention a name?"

"Yes, but here's more of that weirdness. Not long after Helvetius became incapacitated, Tremayne dismissed the doctor, saying his services were no longer needed. There seemed to be some kind of disagreement between the two."

"Interesting. I'll need you to quietly contact Cassandra and ask her to do two things for me. First, have her track down this doctor and find out why he was dismissed. And second, ask her to activate the chronolabe."

"What's a chronolabe?"

"I'll explain later. Please hurry, my boy. We don't have much time left. While you're doing that, I'll be gathering up my equipment so we can get back to the *Cosmos*."

After going through the sterilization process once again, the Doctor and Rollie brought the equipment back to the *Cosmos*, passed the guards without obstruction, and entered the ship, and went through their own sterilization process. They greeted Cassandra on the bridge, with Rollie giving her a warm embrace while the Doctor placed the equipment on a lab table. Allowing the two their moment, he finally inquired about her success with finding the medical doctor.

"I did contact him. He claimed he couldn't say much due to doctor-client confidentiality, but he didn't stick too closely to that, though, because he said Tremayne was using an isotope to mitigate the fungal infection, and that he was dismissed because of his objection to that."

The Doctor raised his eyebrows. "So, the infection wasn't stopped by the amputation. Interesting."

Rollie asked, "Doesn't that mean he could be infecting others?"

"Unfortunately, yes." The Doctor turned back to Cassandra. "Did you ask him if he had contacted higher authorities with his concerns?"

She smiled knowingly. "Yes. He said he hadn't – again because of doctor-client confidentiality."

Frustrated, the Doctor exclaimed, "Such silliness! Contact him again, and tell him to do so immediately. The authorities are more likely to listen to him than to us!" He didn't wait for her reply.

In a blur of motion, the Doctor headed for the chronolabe and confirmed it was active. The machine itself was about the same size as the ship control console and had similar inlaid control panels. Its main point of difference was in the large, holographic sphere projected above it from a lens on the smooth ridge located on its top. Satisfied, he went to the neutrino force microscope he had brought back and retrieved a small chip from its base.

He placed the chip into a slot on the chronolabe, worked some of the panels, and waited for results. In short time, a series of numbers began to appear, each greater than the last and in column form, on a large, in-laid display panel off to the side. After a moment, an expression of unease began to cross the Doctor's face, its tension matching each increase in the numbers. Finally, the numbers ceased, and a small, red dot began blinking in the center of the holographic globe.

The Doctor, now stunned, stood erect and said in a deadened tone, "It's true."

Rollie and Cassandra came to his side. Cassandra asked, "What is? What's wrong?"

"We must get to Tremayne and tell him. Perhaps with this, we can convince him to shut this whole thing down and turn himself in so he can be cured of the infection."

The Doctor rushed to the gravcap, bringing Rollie and Cassandra along almost by a gravitational pull of his own personality. In the gravcap, he attempted a compressed explanation. "The chronolabe calculates both spatial and temporal coordinates on a cosmic scale. It measures where a thing is and where it has been. When it just analyzed the so-called Helvetius fungus sample, it precisely pin-pointed its time of origin as being fourteen billion years ago; that's several hundred million years before the beginning of our universe, which makes its *place* of origin in an earlier universe."

The gravcap door opened. They headed to the ship exit. Before either of his companions could respond to this absurd news, the Doctor activated the exit door release, causing it to slide open. They were met not by the guards who had been stationed there previously, but by Tremayne, who was aiming a gun directly at the Doctor.

Tremayne wavered slightly as he slowly crept into the ship, forcing the Doctor and his companions back. A sinister grin curved his mouth as he spoke. "Going somewhere, Doctor?"

"Why, yes. We were coming to see you," the Doctor said smoothly. "We were worried you might not be feeling well."

Tremayne steadily moved forward, with gun leveled, as he taunted them. "Why wouldn't I be feeling well?"

"You've been looking a little under the weather, that's all. We thought you might have a bacterial infection from the…"

The Doctor gestured toward Tremayne's bandaged hand, which appeared to have swollen somewhat since their last encounter just a while ago.

"Go on, say it. The amputation?" He had them near the gravcap door now. He looked it over and said, "This goes to your control room, does it not?"

"The bridge, yes," the Doctor said, pretense dropping away.

Tremayne twitched the gun at the door. "Good. Get us there."

In the gravcap, the Doctor and Rollie subtly placed themselves between Tremayne and a pregnant Cassandra, quietly using every means at their disposal to distance her as much as possible from potential fungal contamination, as well as the gun.

Staring at Tremayne from beneath evened brows, the Doctor said flatly, "You know, don't you."

"Of course. I knew not long before you did. Remember, Doctor, I'm the world's foremost authority in mathematical physics. Some say I'm spooky that way."

"Just behind Professor Helvetius," the Doctor reminded him.

The gravcap door opened, and Tremayne waved them onto the bridge, using his gun.

Rollie asked, "Knew what?"

Tremayne, seeing the chronolabe with its holographic sphere, guided the Doctor over to it. "I take it this is your navigational system?"

"In a way. It simply provides the coordinates. The control panel back there does the actual navigating."

Tremayne finally acknowledged Rollie's question. "I realized two things, but only a hair's breadth shy of your brilliant Doctor, here. Within moments of his discovery of the triple helix, and the lack of human DNA in the sample from the rock, I began a series of mental gravitational and emissions calculations, at the end of which, I understood perfectly where Helvetius had gone and how."

The Doctor was startled. "You know *how* it happened?"

Tremayne laughed. "You really don't know? It's quite simple. The answer is quantum entanglement, Doctor. By infecting a human here with their nanorganic substructure, as you called it, the alien Fungoids created a quantum entanglement, stretching across billions of years, between one of their own kind and the infected human. At the critical mass of infection, the two automatically switch places. The Fungoid instantaneously transferred here with Helvetius doing the inverse. Don't worry, Doctor; with your brilliant mind, you would have come to the same conclusion soon enough. That's why I had to get to you first. I couldn't possibly let you go without me and deprive me of my destiny."

Rollie asked, "Go? Go where?"

"Didn't the Doctor tell you? The existence of the Fungoids proves the universe is infinitely cyclical, going through an endless series of deaths and rebirths, Big Crunches and Big Bangs. The Fungoids came from a universe immediately prior to our own. Helvetius is in that prior universe, and we're going there to rescue him. Isn't that correct, Doctor."

Rollie glared at him. "Listen, you may be right on all the scientific aspects, but it's clear to me, you need help. You've gone mad."

The Doctor could see in Tremayne's rheumy stare that he was subconsciously playing out some ill-conceived law of expositional determinism, the certainty of which was buried deep within his fevered mind and possibly made worse by the infection.

The disordered smile evaporated from Tremayne's face as he calmly pointed the gun in Rollie's direction. Both Rollie and the Doctor tensed up.

Tremayne, his gun-hand grimly firm, asked coolly, "What is she doing?"

Rollie briefly glanced over his shoulder and saw Cassandra stop midway through tapping various panels on the control console. She turned to them gingerly, as if she had been caught with her hand in the cookie jar.

Rollie said, "Nothing. She was just making sure the systems are working properly for our trip."

"Really. I don't believe you. But I do think that's a good idea." He pointed the gun at Omega. "So, this holographic globe is a star map of the universe, yes?"

"A good guess."

"Oh, Doctor, you know I don't guess. And the blinking red dot? That, I presume, is our doorway to the primordial universe."

"You presume correctly. It's the identifier for an aperture at the event horizon of the black hole centered in our universe."

"Good. Do what you need to do to get us there, now."

Not wishing any violence to come to anyone, and realizing he was unlikely to fool Tremayne, the Doctor read off the coordinates to Cassandra as she put them in. At the end, he said, "Set it for jaunt mode. Considering our situation, I think it best we get there as soon as possible."

Tremayne's face was pale now and slightly moist with fever; a wry expression spread across it, for some reason giving the Doctor the fleeting impression of mist moving along the surface of a body of water.

Tremayne asked, "Jaunting?" Then, he snapped the exposed fingers of his right hand mockingly. "Zero Point travel, I take it. Nearly instantaneous transit, from one location to another. Remarkable. Creating that process had to require real brain power. I applaud you."

"Thank you. We should arrive at the aperture shortly." The Doctor held the moment by asking a question. "By the way, once you knew what was going on, why didn't you just let the fungal infection reach critical mass and automatically transfer you?"

"Ah, because, by that time, I was worried about the radiation damage from the isotope, to myself and the fungus. I can tell by your lack of surprise, you know of the isotope. Anyway, who knows where I would have wound up during the transfer process because of that."

In the mere minutes it took for that back and forth exchange, the ship had reached its destination. The Doctor caught an ephemeral slip of Tremayne's nonchalant demeanor when Cassandra announced they had arrived.

Bringing the mask back up, Tremayne said, "Excellent. You provide outstanding service."

"So far, yes. The next step isn't as straightforward."

Tremayne thought for a moment, then said, "The Barnard Differential."

An enthused manner, typically only shared between intellectual equals, diffused the serious disposition the Doctor had been cultivating since Tremayne had come aboard. "You know of it?"

"When I was twelve, I wrote a paper on it, clarifying and proving the elements of the theory Barnard himself didn't quit understand, in particular in the area concerning tensor fluctuations in massive gravitational fields. It was that paper that brought me to the attention of Helvetius."

"And, rightly so."

Bothered by the inexplicable bonding between the Doctor and Tremayne, Rollie put in, "Excuse me, Doctor, but you do remember, we've been kidnapped."

Tremayne said breezily, "Think nothing of it, my boy. The Doctor's only trying to get me to lower my guard so you can take the gun away. I'd do the same thing in his situation."

Although he thought he had made some progress in softening up Tremayne, the Doctor, nonetheless, felt as if he had been thwarted by Rollie's intrusion. Forcing himself to let it go, the Doctor simply grimaced and said, "We might as well proceed. The gravitational pull is becoming too great for the *Cosmos*, anyway."

Tremayne kept his light tone while insinuating a warning. "I'm sure you're going to approach the aperture at the proper inflection angle to the event horizon, yes? I'm assuming you wouldn't want to try anything stupid and crush us into discordant atoms, would you?"

In a show of irritation, the Doctor's eyes became wide orbs. "No, I wouldn't want to do anything stupid. We'll get through safely, I assure you." Since it was such a delicate procedure, the Doctor chose to handle the angular approach himself. After tapping in the trajectory sequence, he watched the inlaid panel as it began its silent countdown.

There was no sudden change in the ship once the counter reached zero and the *Cosmos* had dropped into the primordial universe. No excessive cinematic special effects or pyrotechnics. Only a superficial, transitory ghosting of their surroundings, a short-lived muddling of vision, and an indistinct queasiness, similar to mild motion sickness. Although he didn't suffer much, Tremayne was the one who experienced the most discomfort as a twinge of pain shot from his wounded hand up through his shoulder. Other than that, it was all over so quickly, and with so little incident, most experienced a certain level of disappointment.

While they had clearly achieved something truly monumental by traveling over thirteen billion years into their own past, thanks to the Doctor's Zero Point space-time compression technology and the stellite sheets the ship was wrapped in, what they had actually done by crossing through the infinitely small aperture was to arrive at the bleak and horrifying end of this older universe's life. It would soon devolve into a Big Crunch, explode, and expand again, becoming the universe they had just left.

Knowing they would have only a split second to move backward in time, toward their goal, and away from this catastrophic event, the Doctor had already programmed in the emissions decay factor, which pinpointed precisely the alien invader's place and time of origin.

As the *Cosmos* took off again, the Doctor brought up the holovid, which blinked into existence just beyond the control console, so they could observe their temporal movement through this new, unexplored realm.

In truth, the Doctor didn't expect to see anything via the holovid, considering they were so close to the collapse, but he did expect to observe some form of matter or light the closer they came to Helvetius's location.

The time stamp was still well within the dead zone period of cosmological cessation, where most nuclear activity stops and an infinite coldness prevails, yet he reasoned, where Helvetius was now had to be capable of supporting life since that would be where the Fungoids had transported from.

While understanding Tremayne was still an actual danger, the Doctor now felt as though the whole villainous charade with him had thoroughly played itself out, partially due to Tremayne's waning health and partially due to the fact he was in the absurd situation of, essentially, being trapped in another universe and, therefore, at the Doctor's mercy. Being a bit tired of it all, he snapped at Tremayne. "Oh, do put that gun away! It's not like we're going to chuck you from the *Cosmos* at this point!"

The boldness startled Tremayne. Being a man of almost purely logical makeup, he didn't entirely understand why the dynamic between himself and the Doctor had suddenly shifted, but he knew it had somehow. So, as they arrived at their destination, Tremayne put the gun in his pocket, but was clearly still not entirely comfortable enough to relinquish it altogether.

Looking at the holovid, they saw nothing but blackness at first. After a moment, giving their eyes time to adjust, they began to pick out a large half-circle taking up the bottom of the frame. The awareness of it was only made possible by the gradual discernment of a diaphanous, dark-purple watercolor splashed across the deep recesses of space on the far side of the curved object.

It was obvious to the Doctor and Tremayne that the semicircle was, in fact, a fragmentary image of the planet they were seeking.

Even being millions of years removed, at present, from the final disintegration of the universe, the Doctor continued to maintain an urgency with regards to finding his old friend, Professor Helvetius. And as such, he rushed to land the *Cosmos* as quickly as possible.

Once on the surface of the planet, it was decided, with some contentious negotiations, that Rollie would stay behind to assist Cassandra, if need be, while the Doctor and Tremayne went on the search for Helvetius and the others who had fallen victim to the transporting procedure.

With that question out of the way, Rollie did accompany them down to the lower deck storage room, from where they had previously gotten the neutrino force microscope and other equipment, and helped them put on the ship's atmosphere suits.

They made short order of the process, but the Doctor found time during it to assure a wary Tremayne that the suits were quite safe and, essentially, capable of withstanding the greatest of degenerative effects. Of course, this was an exaggeration, but only to a degree. During the discourse, neither Rollie nor the Doctor noticed Tremayne discreetly placing his gun in an outer pocket of the suit.

For safety reasons, Rollie made his way back up to the bridge as the Doctor and Tremayne progressed through the sterilization process and exited the *Cosmos*. The door closed behind them, giving them the unsettling feeling of being cast adrift in an endless body of water.

Immediately, they saw that it was a world of appalling night. Although they knew this from the start, having clearly seen through the holovid that it was a desolate planet missing an illuminating star, and they had perfectly understood that it existed within a dying universe fading into uncompromising darkness, the real psychological truth of that situation was lost on them until they stepped from the ship and onto the planet's surface.

The next thing to catch their attention was a deep rumbling sound, heard through the external micro-receivers in the suit helmets, periodically reverberating in the distance. Undoubtedly, the thing making the noise was massive and slowly shambling toward them.

Finally, taking in the area directly in front of them was, as far as the eye could see in this almost totally caliginous murk, an otherwise even landscape blemished by what appeared to be a low, craggy stratum. A sluggish fog clung to the broken crust and drifted languidly between the flinty spurs. Strangely, there was also an opaque gel which covered everything and occasionally got lost in the fog due to sharing a similar coloration.

The Doctor, at first, concluded that it had some hitherto unknown type of consciousness, since it somehow sensed their presence and suddenly divided where their feet landed, exposing the planet's obsidian slag to their stride. He subsequently abandoned this conjecture, though, instead attributing the behavior to an autonomic reflex, at least until he could gather more data.

This brought Cassandra to mind, who was waiting in the ship to provide just such assistance. Before going further, he decided to ask her to give him the readings on the atmosphere and to send out the Chariot, along with one of the mid-sized wains, and a bundle of compact volant cots. The rig, along with the cots, would not only help them traverse the rugged landscape, but would also aid in bringing survivors, if there were any, back to the ship.

Cassandra replied efficiently. "Chariot's on the way. Rollie's heading down to prep it right now. As for the atmosphere, it's extremely interesting. It seems this universe is very similar to our own when it comes to fundamental atomic structures. Like Mercury, this planet has limited chemical composition, consisting mostly of helium, potassium, nitrogen, sulfur, some oxygen, and larger traces of polythiazyl, somehow dispersed as a gas throughout the atmosphere. That's where it differs from our standard."

"Interesting," the Doctor said thoughtfully, "and potentially quite dangerous. Gaseous polythiazyl should be impossible. Go on."

"Exactly my thoughts. Anyway, like Venus, the troposphere is extremely shallow, lying close to the surface. It looks to be about ankle-level."

"Yes, we've observed that."

"Something even stranger, though."

"What's that?"

"On the other side of the *Cosmos*, where the Chariot is currently exiting, I've picked up some kind of large structure approximately fifteen hundred yards from the ship."

"That is strange, considering everything within our limited vision projects only a few inches upward from the surface. Is that the thing making that brutal sound?"

"No. Whatever that is, it's incredibly large, and it is heading our way, but it's going so slowly, I doubt it'll reach us before we're done and gone." She broke for a moment, then continued. "You'll be glad to know, though, that I'm also picking up readings of human signatures, and they're coming from that stationary structure."

"Excellent work, my dear!" The Doctor asked with anticipation, "Are they alive?"

A long moment passed before Cassandra answered. "Yes."

"Excellent! We'll work our way around to the Chariot and head off immediately in the direction of the readings!"

Fearing visual loss of the *Cosmos*, Doctor Omega and Tremayne slid their hands along its face until they came to the Chariot on the other side. The Chariot had a forward-mounted light projecting a high beam which broke the darkness in front of it. Beyond that beam, however, all was lost in complete blackness.

The Chariot itself was a long, narrow craft sporting two seats, one in front of the other, and had in tow a rounded, atmospherically-sealed wagon capable of carrying numerous people, if need be. And, due to the Chariot's magnetic motors, it hovered over land rather than roll along it like conventional hauling vehicles.

Once aboard, the Doctor switched on the location sensors, identified the structure Cassandra spoke of, and started the Chariot speedily toward it.

Tremayne, who had taken up the rear seat, quietly observed undefined things off to the sides and just out of reach of the beam's residual glow. He was fascinated by them, in almost a familial way for some reason, yet he was also disgusted by their very existence.

The Doctor watched similar things, these more clearly, flop and twist madly through the vehicle's headlight as it sped along. Some things, with cracked and serrated tentacles, writhed grotesquely in the split second the light flashed across them, languidly trying to reach for the Chariot but were too slow to touch it. Once, something even slammed into the bottom of the vehicle, momentarily shocking both driver and passenger.

As they came up to the structure, and the light began to illuminate its facade, the Doctor felt some relief that the sinister pilgrimage was at an end. He was relieved he could feel, through the synchrosome, that Professor Helvetius was close by and still alive.

While this gave him comfort, the structure's surface countered that feeling. Compared to the surrounding landscape, it was tall, nearly twenty feet high, and rounded like a rough dome. Its exterior was entirely covered in chitinous sections, similar to that of an insect, with each section the size of an ancient military shield; and beneath that, loosely sticking the chitin in place, was a curved configuration of thick jelly, identical to the stuff they had encountered earlier covering the slag. This became visible when the structure expanded and contracted, as if it were a slowly beating heart.

The Doctor only noticed Tremayne had left the Chariot when he heard him struggling a few feet away. He removed a small, handheld light from a compartment and pointed it at the noise. Tremayne, facing toward the Doctor and with the gun in his left hand, was violently battling against the grip of one of the Fungoids.

Abruptly, the gun, which Tremayne had somehow precariously aimed at the creature, went off. In truth, the bullet did little damage, but the ignition of the bullet propellant did. This set alight the polythiazyl, which the creature was naturally saturated in, causing its nanobot substructures to detonate and blast the beast apart, knocking Tremayne unconscious.

Before the Doctor could move to help, another Fungoid emerged from a dilated section of the jellied structure and dragged Tremayne inside, with the opening rapidly closing behind them.

Hearing the commotion through the helmet micro-receivers, Cassandra burst out with, "What was that?"

The Doctor replied tensely, "Tremayne just destroyed one of the Fungoids and knocked himself out in the process. He's been dragged into their fortress!"

A moment later, another entrance took shape, like a moist worm dividing itself, squarely in front of him; standing in the gap were three more Fungoids. Without hesitation, the Doctor pushed a gear forward. The engine rapidly gathered power and shot the Chariot directly into the monstrosities, splattering them instantly across a large room.

Once the Chariot had completely entered the chamber, the orifice closed behind it, and an unsettling growling intonation began to sound off in regular intervals, giving the Doctor the impression of a deeply toned elephant call. The Doctor presumed this to be an alarm of sorts. He was also aware of the illumination in the chamber. Marginal though it was, it still provided enough light for getting about. It appeared the jellied edifice itself was somehow generating it.

Setting this aside, he said to Cassandra, "I'm in."

"Are you okay?"

"Yes, but I need to know where Tremayne has been taken and where Helvetius and the others are being kept. Can you help with that?"

"Scanning now." In a few moments, she said, "It looks like a human form is about a hundred feet away, down a tunnel to your left, and the other human lifeforms are all lined up, and immobile, in a cavity deeper in the structure, about three hundred and fifty feet away from you. It looks like you should be able to get there by using the tunnel that forks off from the other one a short distance in."

"Again, excellent work, Cassandra. I'm heading after Tremayne first."

"Doctor, I just wanted to let you know, Rollie added a laser welder to the Chariot kit, along with the cots you requested. Considering how the Fungoids pop off, he thought a welder would probably be useful in setting a match to them, if the need arises."

The Doctor paused and smiled. "Please tell Rollie, thank you, and he is correct. It will most likely come in very handy."

He leaped from the Chariot with surprising dexterity for one his age, reached into the supply compartment behind the rear seat, and retrieved the welder and the secured bundle of compact volant cots, which was small and lightweight enough to go under his arm. Then, he headed off to find Tremayne.

It wasn't long after entering the tunnel that he encountered more Fungoids, who were obviously responding to the alarm, which was still kicking up a fuss throughout the structure. Not wishing to backtrack, the Doctor decided now was as good a time as any to try out the welder. He aimed at the first of the two and fired. The laser hit its target with razor-sharp precision. He watched the vile creature fly into a thousand pieces and splatter across its companion. He instantly realized this method of elimination was far more well-tuned and quicker than the previous methods he had seen used.

He looked admiringly at the welder and said, "Let Rollie know, the laser worked magnificently." Then, understanding Rollie's appreciation for the reference, he added, "I'm beginning to know how Buck Rogers must have felt!"

Catching sight of the other Fungoid advancing briskly toward him, he leveled the gun again and fired, watching as the creature flew into numerous wet chunks before him.

He gingerly proceeded past the sloppy mess and moved deeper into the structure. Along the way, he began regularly calling for Tremayne, hoping he had regained consciousness by now, but he received no reply. He arrived at the fork Cassandra had spoken of and asked her to re-scan for Tremayne's whereabouts.

Straightaway, she said, "Just to let you know, Doctor, that large mass that was creeping toward us that I said shouldn't be able to reach us before we leave, it's seemed to have picked up speed and could very well reach us within a half an hour now."

"That's not good. I should be finished shortly, though, with any luck. Our only problem appears to be finding Tremayne. Have you got anything on him yet?"

She said, "That's weird. The signal on him is much weaker now. If that's him, he's moved on into the heart of the complex. Hold on a minute." After a pause, she continued. "He, or whomever is moving him, seems to be anticipating your actions and heading to the chamber where the other humans are being kept."

He called for Tremayne again and still got nothing. He returned his attention to Cassandra. "Strange. He's not responding. It must be a prison cell of sorts; the Fungoids must be taking him there."

The Doctor moved on, periodically calling for Tremayne but got no results, and dispatched several more Fungoids before reaching the chamber he was seeking. It was then he realized that the tunnel itself was essentially a large, semicircular junction, with many offshoots leading to the edges of the complex and into its upper chambers. If he kept going through the tunnel he was already in, it would simply take him back to the Chariot which, he decided, was a very good thing to know.

Turning his attention back to his goal, he could just barely make out, through the congealed wall, humanoid shapes contained within something in the room. There was no door to speak of, so he assumed it simply dilated an opening if a presence came close enough, in a similar fashion to how the outer wall and the surface gel behaved. He tried this, but nothing happened. Not having any time to waste, he used the laser again, melting a large section of the jelly away.

He stepped in and saw a line of what looked like man-sized capsules, or test tubes, but these were made of what appeared to be a thick, vaguely translucent substance, hardened to a degree, with some form of organic membrane at each end, attaching them to the throbbing, clotted wall. It gave the Doctor the sickening impression of an incubator. Since the humans inside were alive, as Cassandra stated, it was reasonable to conclude, the Fungoids were keeping them in suspended animation, either for experimentation or because they were needed to complete any future quantum entanglement transferences which may arise in the future, or perhaps they were preserving them for both.

Either way, the Doctor expanded the volant cots to their full capacity. When he finished, there were three floating next to him, each capable of carrying two of the five capsules. He then used the laser to detach each of them, inadvertently releasing a viscous liquid from each, and then maneuvered the cots in such a way that would allow the capsules to gently slide from their oily ledges and into place without much effort.

Relieved this was done, the Doctor began to depart with them, but he was stopped by someone he rightly assumed to be Tremayne, due to the person wearing an atmosphere suit from the *Cosmos*. He was standing in the shadows and blocking the exit.

Taken by surprise, the Doctor spoke falteringly. "Tremayne! I called for you. You seem to have survived the attack. Are you all right?"

Tremayne said nothing.

"Anyway, I've gotten everyone on the cots, but I could use your help fending off any Fungoids that come at us as we make our escape. That foul alarm won't shut off, as you can hear."

He got nothing but silence for a reply; then, he saw Tremayne raise the pistol and aim it at him. The Doctor said carefully, "I see you've retrieved your gun. Or did you ever really lose it?"

The Doctor heard an offensive slurping sound through his micro-receiver as Tremayne stepped out of the shadows and into the room.

While what the Doctor saw was horrifying, it wasn't entirely unexpected. The right side of Tremayne, from his hand up to, and including, his head was shockingly swollen, putting terrific pressure on his suit. It was causing his whole body to twist somewhat to the left.

The Doctor could see, through the nearly indestructible, transparent helmet, that half of Tremayne's head was caked beyond recognition with mottled fungus, and his right eye was so distended and marbled with red veins, it seemed as though it should have popped long ago from the stress.

Now, Tremayne spoke, but his words were coated in a sickeningly muculent enunciation. "Don't lie, Doctor. You were going to leave me behind again, weren't you?"

Rollie broke in cautiously over the micro-receiver. "Need help, Doctor?"

"No, Rollie. Stay on the ship," the Doctor said rigidly.

Tremayne laughed wetly. "Yes, Rollie. Stay on the ship. You can do no good here or there, really, because you're all going to die, anyway. In here, you can die by the festering hand of my fellow Fungoids, or you can die by being absorbed by that giant macrofungus that's crawling your way."

The Doctor stared at Tremayne. "Fellows? Is that how you see them, now?"

"Any truly intelligent person would. I was just joking about you leaving me behind, you know. Of course, you didn't understand the irony. When I found out what was happening, and how, I knew I had to get here, so I could learn from this superior race of beings. In hindsight, I realized your arrival was proof of my destiny to ascend. Your ship fell into my lap for a reason, Doctor."

"Superior race? *These* monsters?"

"Of course. Think of it, Doctor, think of what they had to do to start their invasion of earth. It's mindbogglingly ambitious!" Tremayne wheezed and coughed up a bit of dark green slime. Recovering, he continued. "They had already worked out that the universe was cyclical in nature and that their universe was nearing its end. Yes, it was several million years away, but that gave them the time needed to work through the bewildering mathematics of nearly incomprehensible probabilities."

As if trying to cut to the conclusion of a tired anecdote, the Doctor said, "I see. Like any sentient creature, they couldn't face their own extinction."

Tremayne winced in pain from the spreading infection, which had rapidly increased since stepping onto the surface of the planet. "And why should they? Genius of that magnitude should live on, *forever*!"

His breathing was becoming difficult now, his words coming out in a torrent, as if he were afraid he wouldn't be able to get them out in time. "Your technological achievements are, indeed, impressive, Doctor, but theirs are a tad bit more so, which puts you in second place, at best. Any species that can calculate the probability, down to trillions of decimal points, of a habitable planet existing fourteen billion years in the future, at an exact location at a particular time, and in a new universe existing immediately after their own, which then finds a way to send a shielded microscopic invading force through that cosmic breach at the end of time, and creating an entangling transference process, should rule *every* universe, don't you think?" The excitement caused bubbled air to froth from his mouth. "And I'm here to make sure that happens, *Doctor*!"

"But you killed one of them earlier with your pistol."

"That was an unfortunate accident. I was trying to kill *you*, but it misunderstood my actions and tried to stop me. Since I haven't fully transformed yet, I don't quite possess the telepathic qualities necessary to clearly communicate with them, but I was able to get my general intentions across after I regained consciousness inside the dome. All of that will soon change, though."

"You're sick, Tremayne. We can get you back to earth and cure you."

Tremayne's mouth oozed olive-green saliva as he laughed again. "I don't want to be cured, Doctor. I *want* to be one of them. I *am* one of them, now. I didn't understand any of this before the infection really took hold, but I do now. I hear them, Doctor. They speak to me. I hear the macrofungus, too. I'll stay here. I'll nurture them. I'll guide them. I'll *learn* from them, become one with them!"

The Doctor smirked. "What you really want is to rule over them and, subsequently, the entire sequence of universes to come, isn't it?"

The human part of Tremayne seemed genuinely puzzled by this. "Doctor, you're disappointing me. It's nothing so gauche. It's the only species I consider worthy of existence, really. That's the whole of it. Any other species, if they are to exist at all, should be treated like nothing more than the lab animals they are, then be disposed of when they've served their purpose. Truth be told, it's as simple and pure as that."

The Doctor grimaced. "I see. That's how you want it, eh?"

"It's not how I want it, it's how it *should* be."

"Alright, you stay, Tremayne, and we'll go in peace. Just let me pass with these people." He gestured toward the volant cots carrying the capsules.

"Don't be silly. You know I can't do that." The constriction from the suit was becoming unbearable and was showing on the human side of Tremayne's face. Sorting through the pain, he said. "If I let you go, you'll return to earth and stop the invasion. I can't have that. I've told you before, this is my destiny. I'll soon become one of them, and we'll use your ship to go to earth, as fully ripened Fungoids."

Cassandra anxiously interrupted. "Doctor, the macrofungus, as he called it, will be at the ship in fifteen minutes."

"I understand, my dear, but there doesn't seem to be much we can do about any of this. He's got us in a tight spot, which I don't think we can get out of."

"I'm glad you've come to your senses, Doctor. Care to join my Fungoid army, now?"

"Possibly, but only if I can be on equal footing with you. We'll have to discuss it at length." He went on hesitantly. "Until then, I can see you're having problems with the suit. You know, I don't think I have to tell you this but, the more the fungus spreads, the more it will expand. And, as I said before, these suits are indestructible. The way it looks, you'll be crushed by it soon, if you don't give the fungus room to breathe, so to speak."

A brown liquid, mixed with traces of blood, washed over Tremayne's lower lip. "You are correct. The time has finally come. I should be far enough along now to be able to live in their atmosphere. This is the big moment, Doctor, where I fully transform. Before I do, though, throw that welder over here."

The Doctor did so, but made a show of being a bad aim and landed it closer to the exit than Tremayne.

Annoyed, but still satisfied the Doctor couldn't reach it, Tremayne dropped his own gun and depressed the locks holding his helmet in place. With anticipation, he slowly removed it and let it fall to the ground, a look of triumph occupying what was left of the human side of his face.

After a moment of intense discomfort, areas on his infected side began to erupt in micro-explosions. The look of triumph vanished. Blood, purple-green pus, and diseased flesh began to splatter across the inside of the suit and out through where the helmet had been. His knees buckled, and he crashed to the ground, dying in quick, convulsive jerks. In one final act of liquidation, the entire right side of his head detonated, showering the chamber, as well as Doctor Omega, with sterilizing, radioactive slime.

Cassandra, who had heard some kind of unidentifiable commotion, frantically asked, "What happened?"

The Doctor said hurriedly, "I'll explain later. I'm on my way. Get the ship ready!"

He rushed forward with the cots, stopped long enough to pick up the welder, and moved as quickly as he could through the tunnel, passing the occasional Fungoid as it succumbed to the ravages of abrupt, and unexpected, physical decomposition. Others of a slightly sturdier nature he used the welder on, blasting them to bits as he moved swiftly toward the Chariot.

He got back to the ship just as the macrofungus was within a few hundred feet of it. It seemed to have slowed up a bit, and its vitality appeared to be rapidly waning, in comparable fashion to every other living monstrosity he had evaded along the way.

Working briskly, he and Rollie were able to secure the survivors' capsules and take off before the giant, dying fungus was able to reach them, returning to Earth in the same manner in which they had come.

Safely back in Ealdwine, the Doctor instructed the CSR crew to team with the military in order to destroy the Fungoids, along with the pressure chambers in which they were being contained, and to burn every inch of the forest and, just to be safe, an even wider area around that.

Although he had no real authority, his exactitude, expertise, and close association to Professor Helvetius caused everyone to willingly accept his orders. He also let them know that it would probably be a good idea to raze the whole place and salt it with sterilizing chemicals. But he would let the actual authorities make the decision on that once they turned up.

It was days later, and many hours of careful medical attention, before the people who had experienced quantum entanglement, and who had been transported to that hellish planet, were fully revived and given a complete bill of health. Mercifully, none of them had any memories of anything that happened once their infections bore fruit.

When the Doctor, Cassandra, and Rollie popped in at the hospital to greet Helvetius not long after he came to, the Doctor filled in the gaps at the Professor's request, explaining how they had tracked everyone down and rescued them, making a trip of fourteen billion years, both ways, in the process, and that he would be sending a substantial fuel bill to the Professor's Center for Scientific Research as a result.

They were all amused by this until Professor Helvetius asked about Tremayne. The Doctor told him everything at that point, including the details of Tremayne's excruciating death.

Helvetius said somberly, "Truly astonishing. All of it. And, truly sad about Tremayne. I did have my concerns about him. I came on this investigation to keep an eye on him, to save him if I could, and it seems as though I failed rather grandly at that, doesn't it?"

The Doctor touched his forearm warmly. "You had no idea. None of this was your fault."

Helvetius shook his head appreciatively. But then, he paused thoughtfully for a moment and asked, "How did you know?" Seeing the Doctor's questioning look, he elaborated. "How did Tremayne taking his helmet off kill all the Fungoids? How did you know that would happen?"

The Doctor's face opened into a knowing smile. "Ah, that. A little observation, a bit of deduction, a little induction, some guess work – and a lot of luck! Early on, I noticed Tremayne almost reeked of the pungent fungicide we were all being subjected to; this told me his body was somehow absorbing it. Therefore, it seemed odd that his fungal infection was worsening, which I observed in due course. At one point, Cassandra told me Tremayne had been using a radioactive isotope to mitigate the infection. This made things clearer; the only conclusion I could come to was that the isotope had mutated the alien fungus in such a way as to cause it to soak up the fungicide without dying immediately itself.

"It seemed, on their planet, these creatures had some kind of common biological link between one another through the autonomic gel that covered everything, and even made up the building you were housed in. I assumed, if the mutated fungus, saturated with fungicide and radiation, were to make contact with their atmosphere and this gel, it would poison all the other Fungoids. Where luck comes in, is the fact that the isotope also apparently mutated Tremayne's fungus in a manner which made its own home planet's polythiazyl-saturated atmosphere poisonous to *it*, causing it to explode on contact."

Again, Helvetius shook his head. Finally, he breathed deeply, staring off in the distance, and said, "The things we've seen." Then, he focused on the Doctor again. "Just like old times, don't you think?"

Doctor Omega smiled with sincere fondness. "Yes, it is, old friend. Yes, it is."

Disturbing this affectionate bonding over past lives, a rather efficient nurse entered the room carrying a tray. She unceremoniously nudged the others aside and positioned an overbed table in front of Helvetius, placing the tray on it. She removed the cover from a shallow plate of gray liquid, saying, "Eat up. You need your strength," and turned to leave.

Before she got far, Helvetius glared at the gray liquid and called after her. "What is it?"

Without slowing her departure from the room, she said, "Cream of mushroom soup. It's good for you."

With those large, owlish eyes, Professor Helvetius looked sickly at the plate as he slowly pushed it away.

*This semi-comedic story was originally penned for the program book of a U.S.-based* Doctor Who *convention, but ended up not being used. It draws its inspiration from memories of various Hollywood story conferences and pitch meetings we attended. Cassandra Troy, the Doctor's companion, is the heroine of a science fiction comics story drawn by the late Gerald Forton, published in* Tales of the Hexagonverse.[10]

## DOCTOR OMEGA AND THE PRODUCERS
*(by Jean-Marc & Randy Lofficier)*

"We appear to have landed, Doctor," remarked Cassandra Troy.

The elderly gentleman with a rebellious tuft of white hair looked around as if events were, for once, overtaking him.

"Landed? Ah, yes. That would have happened when I restored the ancillary power to the *Cosmos*. I flicked all the switches at random. Like flipping *I-ching* coins... Well, let's find out where we are, shall we?"

A brief look at the scanner told the Doctor and Cassandra that the *Cosmos* had taken them back to Earth.

"What a surprise," sighed the Doctor. "The Mother of All Cosmic Catastrophes!"

"But, Doctor, we're in America. California. The 1980s. I did a paper on California once!" said Cassandra.

The door of the *Cosmos* slid open and they stepped outside. The *Cosmos* had rematerialized in what, at first glance, appeared to be a grungy industrial park. There

---

[10] Hexagon Comics, ISBN 978-1-64932-088-9.

were blank, anonymous-looking warehouses, separated by dull, tar-covered alleys.

Suddenly, the towering figure of an Electroman rose to confront them…

"Boy, it's hot inside that suit!" said the Electroman.

Cassandra had never seen the Doctor so completely taken by surprise before. He looked genuinely confused as the lumbering silver giant took off his head to reveal the jovial, if sweaty, face of an ordinary mortal beneath.

"You're here for the movie, aren't you?" asked the ex-Electroman, unaware of the effect he had just had on the Doctor.

"What?"

The word triggered something in Cassandra's memory. Suddenly, she knew where they were.

"A movie, Doctor," she exclaimed. "We're in Hollywood!"

Roland DuBay—Rollie to his friends—was a professional movie extra, a bona fide, dues-paying member of SAG and half-a-dozen other unions. He had been a U.S. cavalry officer in *Geronimo II* (shot in the third scene), a drug-crazed terrorist in *Die Hard V* (blown to smithereens in the middle of act 2) and even one of the Wicked Witch's child-stealing monkeys in Woody Allen's remake of *The Wizard of Oz*. But what he hated the most were sci-fi pictures, because it was always so damned hot inside the suits.

*Still,* he thought, *bills gotta be paid, Melissa has to be kept in the Valley lifestyle she's grown accustomed to, and the kid's gonna be going to college one day. Not to mention that the electric Ocelot needs new plugs.*

Meaning that Rollie DuBay needed the job badly, and if this was what it took to get it, he was prepared to be the best Electrogoon ever to lumber across a Hollywood set.

Not one to let an opportunity pass—he had gotten the job of the Flying Monkey in the *Oz* picture by reading Mia Farrow's best-seller beforehand—Rollie realized at once, with the unique feeding instinct that only actors and predators share, that the funny-looking elderly stranger in the black frock coat might be his ticket into the picture.

"*Doctor?*" he said. "I'd heard they wanted to cast a big-name star. Someone like Robin Williams or Danny DeVito. But I can see why they went with you. Neat threads. It always helps to dress the part. That's why I borrowed this suit from Props. But they're so darn hot. Too much insulation."

Now that he had a firm grasp on the situation, the Doctor was back to being his unflappable self.

"Well, you look the part, and I do have some experience in the matter," he said firmly.

"Thanks," Rollie replied. "But do you think you could put in a good word for me with Mr. Bialystock? I'd really like to be in this picture."

"Mr. Bialystock?"

"You know, the producer."

"Yes, of course. Silly of me. I don't see why not," said Doctor Omega. "Take us to your, er, producer."

"Glad to. Follow me."

Rollie DuBay put his electro-helmet back, thanking the muses for bringing him together with the two strangers. While lumbering forward, he thought, *The little guy must be one of these Famous Foreign Actors from one of these foreign films Tom and Annie like to watch on* Bravo... Tom and Annie were his neighbors, a university professor and a high school teacher. Rollie, himself, preferred the Moron Channel and hated anything that sounded even remotely foreign. *The bird must be his entourage. Hey, she's kinda cute in that leather outfit.*

Unaware of Rollie's mercenary thoughts, Doctor Omega and Cassandra Troy followed the extra along the studio's alleys, crossing paths with a variety of people dressed in diverse costumes and uniforms. No one paid any attention to them.

"They must be making a movie about you, Doctor," said Cassandra.

"Oh, dear. Then it is a good idea to take a little look around. I was here once before. Can't say that I cared much for it. I mostly remember a lot of running around. A sense of great chaos and disorder..."

"A sense of great chaos and disorder" was precisely the state of mind of Janice, the blonde receptionist who was desperately trying to make sense of the messages left for her boss, Mr. Bialystock, taken during her lunch break by an intern.

Suddenly, she saw a lumbering metal giant walking into the bungalow, followed by an old man and a tall red-head girl in a skimpy leather outfit. She sighed. No, definitely, today wasn't her day...

"Jhani Ista Bialustin?" said Rollie.

Actually, what he had said was, *Janice, is Mister Bialystock in?* but the electro-helmet had not been designed for speaking parts.

Janice started to reach towards the can of mace she kept under her desk just in case. The week before, an extra from *Dances with Werewolves* had bitten a receptionist, and she was not going to take any chances.

Rollie fathomed at once what was going on and removed his helmet. He had learned early on his career to ingratiate himself with the studio Cerberuses that secretaries and receptionists were.

"It's me, Rollie," he said. "These folks are friends of Mr. Bialystock."

Janice, who had been hired only two weeks earlier, had no idea who was a friend of the producer or not. The authoritative manner in which the small stranger (*Obviously a famous Foreign Actor,* she thought) was studying the framed posters of Bialystock's previous pictures, *Springtime for Hitler, Honey I've Shrunk My Tits* and *Beverly Hills Robonuns II*, convinced her that he was indeed *someone*, instead of being merely *anyone*.

"Mr. Bialystock isn't here yet, but I'm expecting him any minute. Why don't you wait for him in the conference room with the other foreign gentleman," she said, pointing towards an open door.

"We'll be happy to," said Doctor Omega with a courteous nod of the head. Followed by Cassandra and Rollie, who wasn't going to let his meal ticket out of sight if he could avoid it, they walked into the room.

"Doctor! You! Here!"

The person who had been waiting in the room was a small, blond man, with a deceptively angelic face, who looked a lot younger than he really was. Although he was dressed in a nattily-tailored blue suit, something about his bearing suggested a military man.

"Lieutenant Langelot!"

"Captain, now, I'm afraid."

The two men shook hands, obviously and genuinely happy to see each other. The Doctor introduced Langelot to Roland ("Please call me Rollie") DuBay and Cassandra, who came from the Year 586 of the Terran Hegemony, far in the future.

"This is quite a surprise, Doctor," said the Captain from the Service National d'Information Fonctionelle (SNIF for short), one of France's top military intelligence service. "You're just about the last person on Earth I'd expected to see at this hearing."

"Hearing? I'm not sure what you're referring to, Captain. I thought this was a movie. Please tell me more."

"You're not here for the hearing? But then how?... Ah, I should know better than to ask. You've always had the knack of showing up whenever you're needed the most. Although, to be frank, this is not quite in the same league as the threats we used to fight."

"Isn't it, Captain?" replied the Doctor. "And what is the threat this time? Vampires? Electromen? Mr. T?"

"Worse, Doctor. Lawyers. Hollywood lawyers."

"Ouch," grimaced Doctor Omega, amused by his friend's gloomy face.

"It's not a joke, Doctor. SNIF's reputation is at stake. Yours, too."

"How can that be?"

"The people who run this studio, Miracle Pictures it's called, are making a picture about SNIF's glory days. They're calling it *Is Paris Boring?* The producer is a madman! Anyway, even though the Élysée eventually decided to cooperate with the project—it was either that, or let him do a hatchet job on us—my direct superiors felt that Mr. Bialystock was approaching the project in, shall we say, a very cavalier fashion. So they requested, as a condition for their cooperation, that SNIF be allowed to have a consultant on the set, with the right of script approval. Needless to say, Bialystock fought tooth and nail against the idea, but he was out-voted by the Studio brass who felt it was too good an opportunity to let pass. And that, Doctor, is how I came to be in this wretched place."

"Come now, Captain, surely a trip down memory lane can't be that painful?"

"If only that were the case, Doctor," sighed Langelot, "but ever since I arrived, it's been one row after another with Bialystock. The man is impossible. He decided to have some crazy Belgian play me—Jean-Claude Van Dumb or something like that. A great Q rating he said—as if a Q rating had ever defeated an Hormovar! And, as if that weren't enough, now there's this damn lawsuit. The BIDI has objected to the way it is depicted in the film. They feel that they're being portrayed as a bunch of ruthless villains led by a power-hungry madwoman."

"So?"

"They say it's damaging their reputation."

"But that's exactly who they were."

"If I've learned one thing here, Doctor, it's that truth has nothing to do with motion pictures. The BIDI is a big defense contractor now. Their president is Madame Schasch's own son, Anton, and a hearing has been set to resolve the issue. That's what I assumed you were here for, you being there at this time..."

"No, this is the first I've heard about any of it, but I'll be glad to give SNIF a hand, Captain. For the sake of the truth, of course."

Most of the Doctor's and the French Captain's conversation had flown over Rollie's head, but the actor had

279

managed to grasp an important fact or two, such as, *If the small fella isn't an actor, but the real thing, then he must have some kind of creative approval deal. If I stick with him, I'm a shoo-in.*

This current of speculative thought was interrupted by Janice

"Max, er, Mr. Bialystock's back. He'll see you now," she said.

"Come, Doctor," said Langelot. "Let me take you to meet my arch-enemy."

"??"

"The producer, of course."


A few minutes later, the Doctor and his growing entourage walked into a plush office.

Such is the power of entourage that the word had begun to spread around Miracle Studios that a FFA (Famous Foreign Actor) was taking a meeting with Max Bialystock. Worried producers were making discrete inquiries to nervous agents, while deal memos for a remake of *Gigi* were being unearthed from the drawers of legal departments and dusted off. Fortunately, the Doctor remained blissfully unaware of this flurry of activity on his behalf.

Bialystock himself was a portly man with a strange haircut and a hyper kinetic attitude. He was presently on the telephone but gestured to everyone to sit down. Finally, he hung up and addressed Langelot.

"Great news, kid, I've got my extra $3 mil. We can blow up the Eiffel Tower!"

"But we didn't blow up the Eiffel Tower," said Langelot with genuine frustration.

"I know, but you need a big pay-off. This is a big budget picture, kid. The audience wants to see big things. We can't just end the show with half-a-dozen electroguys being discombobulated in a warehouse."

"But that's the way it happened."

"So what? I'm giving them the way it should have happened. Why should you care, anyway? It means a bigger part for Jean-Claude and the little fellow..." Suddenly, the producer's eyes noticed the Doctor at last and lit up. "You must be Doctor Omega!"

The Doctor nodded enthusiastically while smiling from ear to ear. Bialystock got up and began pumping Omega's hand.

"I'm thrilled to meet you. I've been pushing for Robin to play you from day one, but the Studio won't come up to his percentage of the gross. Now that I've seen you, I know my instinct was right. It's got to be Robin."

*Maybe I can get a speaking part this time*, thought Rollie. *I'll need to change agents then.*

Bialystock rushed back to his desk and pushed a button on the intercom.

"Janice. Send a memo to the Studio head! I've gotta have Robin. It doesn't matter what it costs." Then, without a break, he asked the Doctor, "What do you think of my idea for the ending? Do you agree with the kid?"

"No, I don't agree with the kid," grinned Doctor Omega. "I wish we could have blown up the Eiffel Tower too. I never liked what Gustave did."

"Oh no, not you too, Doctor," sighed Langelot, raising his eyes. *This is it*, thought the Captain. *He's gone Hollywood.*

At that moment, Janice walked into the room.

"The hearing is scheduled to start in half-an-hour, Mr. Bialystock. The lawyers are waiting for you in Conference Room 4."

"Guess we should get a move on, then," said Bialystock. He suddenly noticed Cassandra and Rollie's lumbering figure. "Who are all these people?" he inquired.

"Friends of mine," said the Doctor.

The producer cast a puzzled look towards Rollie, who grinned.

"Ah. Well. Oh, fine. Come on, all of you," he said, waving them along.


A few minutes later, Bialystock, Langelot, Doctor Omega and his still-growing entourage walked into a plush conference room. In its center was a long black marble table. A dozen lawyers in business suits sat around it, representing the marshaled forces of Miracle Studios' legal department. Langelot introduced Doctor Omega as "SNIF's then-scientific advisor," accompanied by his assistants. No one thought of questioning the Doctor, Cassandra or Rollie's strange attires. Being lawyers, they merely assumed that everyone who was not a lawyer was a kook.

"I assume you're here to corroborate what the Captain has already told us?" asked a well-tanned, middle-aged man named Rosenberg, the head of Miracle's legal team.

"Essentially, yes," said Doctor Omega.

"Terrific. We can use an extra witness. The other party has been very aggressively claiming that we're defaming the character of their late chairwoman and founder..."

Before Rosenberg could continue, a secretary opened the door and let in another half-dozen participants: the BIDI lawyers, who went to sit down at the opposite end of the black table. A grey-faced man named Wharton, obviously the senior attorney, began speaking.

"The Bureau International de Documentation Industrielle, or BIDI, is an important and respected organization, with an impeccable record. We have no intention of allowing the name of our late chairwoman and founder, Madame Angelique Schasch, to be slandered. The woman was a humanitarian, and no one will say otherwise. This 'Electromen' business is nonsense. We have files in our archives that will clearly establish that SNIF fabricated the entire thing for its own, political reasons. To sum up, I'm afraid that the script, as it stands now, is totally inacceptable. Unless all mention of the BIDI and Madame Schasch are deleted in their entirety, we shall have no option but to continue with our lawsuit."

"See you in court then, you stiff-necked, sheepschtupping, Nazi-sucking shyster!" erupted Bialystock, who had quickly reached his boiling point.

"Now, now, Mr. Bialystock, please calm down," said Rosenberg. "Those words are uncalled for. Especially that bit about the sheep." He then turned towards Wharton, and continued smoothly. "We have commissioned a revised screenplay—at considerable expense to Miracle Studios, I might add. We're confident that it more than adequately deals with your objections by removing several possibly questionable scenes..."

At that point, there was a loud *harrumph* noise from Bialystock, who raised his eyes to the ceiling and shook his head, but Rosenberg pointedly ignored the producer's glaring disapproval.

"We at Miracle," Rosenberg continued, "feel that the film now presents a balanced version of the events in question, and does not in any way defame the management of your company."

One of Rosenberg's assistants handed several copies of the revised script to the BIDI attorneys, who began studying it as one.

"SNIF just wants to make themselves look as if they were doing something other than sitting on their duffs, sucking up the French taxpayers' money," remarked a younger BIDI attorney, with a face which the Doctor thought bore an appropriate resemblance to that of a weasel.

"How dare you!" shouted Langelot, slamming his fist on the table. "Your vaunted Madame Schasch was a dangerous, power-hungry maniac, and if we're all sitting here in this room today, it is only because SNIF was able to stop her! Several brave and decent men died during that mission, and you have no right to sully their memory with your lies!"

"More likely, they shot themselves during one of your ill-conceived training exercises. We should add civilian endangerment to our charges," snickered the weasely lawyer.

This time, the Captain stood up, almost sending his chair reeling backward. But Rosenberg, grabbed him by the arm before he could vent his wrath upon the arrogant lawyer. "Captain, please. I'm sure we can straighten this whole thing out to everyone's satisfaction. Sit down. Have a glass of Perrier."

He snapped his fingers and one of his assistants ran out of the room, quickly returning with a glass of sparkling water.

*Please, God, don't blow my chances now*, begged Rollie silently.

There was a long, painful silence while the BIDI attorneys reviewed the revised script. Finally, Wharton raised his eyes.

"Pending a more detailed review, this would indeed appear to be adequate," he said.

There was an audible sigh on the Miracle side of the table.

"Of course," the attorney continued, "it must be made more obvious to the casual viewer that this character... this 'Doctor Omega'... is the real villain of the piece. He is the one who clearly entrapped Madame Schasch and besmirched the good name of the BIDI..."

"*What?!*"

This time, it was the Doctor's turn to jump to his feet. His face was red, and if looks could kill, Wharton would have been reduced to a small pile of ashes on his chair.

"May the Vahks feed on your bones, you Phtooz-infested maggot. I'll bring the Curse of Kheoba on you and your Hobbal-brained lawfirm..."

"Shut up, Doctor, or I'll personally see to it that you never work in this town again!" shouted Rosenberg, finally losing his composure. Then, turning towards Wharton, the attorney added with a tired smile, "I believe we have a deal..."

Rollie DuBay smiled.

Things were going to be all right after all.

*Cassandra Troy – Page 1*
*Art by Gerald Forton*